T0007194

PENGUIN BOOKS

Malibu Summer

Libby Gill grew up on two continents before starting her career at Norman Lear's Embassy Communications, eventually becoming head of communications and public relations for Sony, Universal, and Turner Broadcasting's television divisions. She is the founder of Libby Gill & Company, a leadership consulting and executive coaching firm, and is the author of six nonfiction books. She lives in Oregon.

Malibu Summer

Libby Gill

Penguin
Books

PENGUIN BOOKS
An imprint of Penguin Random House LLC
penguinrandomhouse.com

LIBRARY OF CONGRESS CATALOGING-IN-PUBLICATION DATA
Names: Gill, Libby, author.
Title: Malibu summer / Libby Gill.
Description: [New York City]: Penguin Books, 2024.
Identifiers: LCCN 2023048184 (print) |
LCCN 2023048185 (ebook) |
ISBN 9780143137924 (trade paperback) | ISBN 9780593512012 (ebook)
Subjects: LCGFT: Romance fiction. | Novels.
Classification: LCC PS3607.I43563 M35 2024 (print) |
LCC PS3607.I43563 (ebook) | DDC 813/.6—dc23/eng/20231101
LC record available at https://lccn.loc.gov/2023048184
LC ebook record available at https://lccn.loc.gov/2023048185

Printed in the United States of America
1   3   5   7   9   10   8   6   4   2

Set in ITC Berkeley Oldstyle Pro Book
Designed by Sabrina Bowers

To David

Give sorrow words; the grief that does not speak
Whispers the o'erfraught heart, and bids it break.

—WILLIAM SHAKESPEARE

You said move on, where do I go?

—KATY PERRY

Malibu Summer

Summer

1

*I*vy stared at the printed outline of her presentation—compelling original hypothesis with supporting alphanumeric data points beneath—but was having trouble focusing. All she could think about was how angry she was at Will.

She flipped the page and frowned when she saw the note her investor, Alexandra Varsha, had scribbled in the margin, *add humor here*. Humor wasn't exactly Ivy's strong suit, especially when it came to her research. But Alexandra had practically beaten it into her that if Ivy wanted the backing to continue testing HydraHold, the irrigation product she'd invented, she'd better dazzle the agrigeeks from UC Davis. It hadn't been easy to get a Silicon Valley venture capital firm interested, especially in a product created by a female scientist, but Alexandra had seen how innovative—and potentially profitable—HydraHold was.

Ivy looked out across the long worktable that ran through the center of the greenhouse research lab, ringed by raised wooden planting beds. She pulled at a nervous curl that she could never seem to corral. Will loved to tease her by stretching it long and then letting it boing-yoing back into its natural ringlet.

Will, she thought, gritting her teeth. She'd never been so pissed off at him before. And there were times she'd been plenty pissed. When they'd first started dating, Ivy was shocked to discover that opposites really could be attracted to one other. Where she was reserved and analytical, he was sloppy, sweet, and inexhaustibly exuberant about life and literature. No wonder everyone loved him.

She was used to his running late, of course, but to be a no-show for their doctor's appointment, especially this one, was unthinkable. Ivy picked up her cell to call him again. *You've reached Dr. William Richardson. Literary quote of the day: Most men and women will grow up to love their servitude and never dream of revolution. If you know who said it, or even if you don't—*

She hung up before the beep, annoyed as always at how long his greeting was. No one had ever accused Will of brevity. He was probably schmoozing with his department chair or one of his students right now, their appointment completely forgotten.

But what really made her mad was that Will was the one who wanted to start a family in the first place, and he'd sworn he'd be at her side for every step of this whole gut-churning fertility process. She'd suggested they put off having a family for at least a couple of years since her work was at such a critical stage. Wrapping up her PhD, launching her environmental product, *and* beginning her career as a research scientist required her full-time focus. But Will had convinced her that they should start a family while they were still young.

Ivy stood up slowly. Five foot three in her beat-up Crocs with chestnut hair, gray-green eyes, and wire-rimmed glasses, she'd never felt as old as she did today. She was only thirty-one, but apparently her eggs had already given up the ghost, while Will's sperm were raring to go.

She started toward the kitchen to brew a cup of chamomile tea, but stopped midstride to square up a pile of books so that they were all parallel to the table edge.

"Thought you could use this."

Ivy's lab assistant, Marlena, plopped a mug of tea onto the table.

"You're reading my mind," Ivy said with a grateful sigh as she sat back down, picked up the tea in one hand and her outline in the other.

"Nervous?" Marlena asked.

"Yeah, but not about . . . Never mind, I don't need to bore you with my personal drama."

There was a banging at the front door, and Marlena excused herself to answer it. Ivy shoved her glasses up the bridge of her nose and tried to focus on the outline once again.

"Dr. Bauer?"

She looked up. Ivy's first thought was that she had forbidden her lab assistants and students from calling her *Dr. Bauer*. She still had to defend her dissertation and had adopted the admittedly unscientific view that calling her *doctor* prematurely would somehow jinx her chances of getting her PhD.

But these weren't students. They were police officers. Serious-looking, uniformed police officers. Like the ones on the TV shows her grandmother had adored. With sidearms and stern faces. The two officers looked so out of place standing amid the planting beds and grow lights, Ivy wondered whether she was dreaming.

"Is there somewhere we can speak privately?" one of the officers asked.

"I'll leave," Marlena offered, turning away.

"No. Stay," Ivy said, grabbing for Marlena's arm as she slowly pushed herself up from the table. Whatever this was, there was no way out. She could tell from the determined look in their eyes, the squaring of their shoulders, the harsh curve of their jawlines. Ivy steeled herself and walked a few steps toward the officers, Marlena behind her. She suddenly had the sense of being closed in, cornered, like the lab mice she'd caged so often she'd nearly ceased to think of them as sentient beings.

"What . . . why?" she finally managed to ask, the words feeling thick as clay in her mouth.

"We're sorry to have to tell you this, but your husband has been in an accident."

"Oh, Ivy," Marlena gasped.

"He was hit riding his bicycle." The police officer hesitated a moment. "Pronounced dead at the scene."

"We're very sorry for your loss, ma'am."

Ivy stared at the officers, refusing to believe them, but knowing it was true. She felt bile electrify inside her gut, a jolt that started in her intestines and wended its way up to her throat. She thought she might throw up, but some rogue part of her brain imagined vomit splashing the scientific texts and journals on the table, which she knew would be too expensive to replace on the lab's lean budget. Suddenly, her vision went black, and she clutched blindly for the table edge. The officers caught her underneath her armpits just before she hit the tile floor. She wasn't sure how long she was in their arms in this half slump—it could have been a minute or an hour—but she thought she heard a voice from somewhere telling her to stand up straight if she wanted to be taken seriously. Ivy shook off the hands that were holding her, the officers' and Marlena's, and leaned against the wall for support.

"How?" Her voice came out in a whisper, nothing like the confident classroom delivery she'd worked so hard to develop.

"He was hit broadside in the intersection at Main and Northbrook."

"He ran the red, ma'am. Looked like he was going somewhere in a hurry."

Ivy tried to breathe but it felt like her nasal passages had swollen shut. Her body suddenly turned on her, her spine and muscles giving way until they could no longer support her weight. She staggered forward and clamped on to the edge of a planting bed so hard she could feel the splinters beneath her fingernails.

It was all her fault. She'd told Will just that morning that if he was going to be even one minute late to their appointment, he shouldn't bother coming at all. *You want a kid, you better start acting like an adult.* Those were the last words she'd said to her husband, the lover of words. They were the words she'd have to live with the rest of her life.

2

Will would have hated this, Ivy thought, as she watched the postfuneral crowd milling around her parents' dining-room table, which was piled with enough food to feed the entire Bay Area. He'd have been happy with a tray of brownies and a poetry recitation. But no, as usual, Elaine and Howard had taken over the preparations, putting their stamp on everything. Just like they'd done with her wedding. Just like they'd tried to do with her education, calling soil science "dreary." Only this time, she was grateful. There was no way she'd have been able to wrap her head around funeral arrangements—or anything else—in her current state.

"Thank you for coming," Ivy said, as she hugged her friends Charlotte and Randy, who'd known Will from their days in academia. Charlotte had been Ivy's undergrad botany professor and had not only opened her eyes to the wonders of horticulture, but also to the possibilities of a career in science. And not just as an academic, something Ivy had never aspired to or felt suited for— that was Will's gift—but as a research scientist who could make a positive impact on the planet.

"Of course, sweetheart. And you call us anytime, I mean twenty-four seven, okay?" Charlotte said, dabbing at her eyes with a handkerchief as she and her husband turned to leave.

Exhausted, Ivy escaped to the adjoining den, where she watched her mom and dad finish the hosting duties—shaking hands, returning hugs, and thanking people for their kind regards and thoughtful casseroles. Ivy knew she should go back and join them, but she couldn't seem to get her feet to move. Instead, she collapsed onto the couch and observed the guests from a safe distance. Her head was throbbing, and she leaned over and put it between her knees, not caring a bit that her black knit dress was creeping up her thighs. She began to breathe deeply and slowly.

Why don't they all just leave? There's nothing anyone can say or do to help.

Ivy felt the nubby cool of a washcloth on the back of her neck.

She didn't need to turn her head to know that it was Mak. Makayla Gabriella Suarez, her best friend since their undergrad days at Berkeley. Will had always said she was the smartest teaching assistant he'd ever had, even though she'd deserted him for Hollywood.

"I know this day sucks, babe. More than any other day in your entire life. But I promise you, somehow we are going to get through this."

Ivy sat up and wiped the cloth across her forehead.

"I'm in freefall, Mak. I don't know where my life goes from here. Will was the one who held it all together, who held me together."

"You can start by eating this," Mak said firmly, handing her a plate. Ivy flared her nostrils at the pair of pretentious little cucumber sandwiches with tiny sprigs of dill on top, but dutifully ate.

"Good girl. Now drink this." Mak handed her a brandy snifter with a small shot of brown liquid.

"To old friends," Mak said, clinking her glass against Ivy's.

"Old friends," Ivy murmured, tentatively sipping the brandy. "Thank you for coming up. I know you're in production on a TV pilot or . . . something."

"You didn't think I was going to leave you alone with Elaine and Howard, did you? I love your parents, but if I weren't here to keep them in check, they'd have you working the room like a whore in a fish camp."

Ivy smiled vaguely in spite of herself. Mak could do that to people. As she frequently told Ivy and anyone else who would listen, she was blessed with an abundance of charm.

"Incoming. Eleven o'clock," Mak warned as a youngish man and woman in slightly grungy head-to-toe black approached. "Want to escape outside?"

"No, they're my lab assistants."

Ivy started to stand, but Mak smiled at her, placing a hand on her forearm, as if to say, *You don't have to be polite today.*

"Ed, Marlena, this is my friend Mak." They all nodded grimly.

"Ivy, if there's anything, anything at all that I can . . ." Marlena's voice trailed off.

"We'll take care of the lab, of course. I mean, that goes without saying. But I wanted to say it. So don't worry. I mean, don't worry about the lab," Ed added awkwardly.

Ivy looked up at them nodding, aware she was staring. She could see the microscopic gold flecks around Ed's pupils. And Marlena's acne scars looked like lunar craters on the surface of her ruddy cheeks. They spoke to her for a few more minutes, but all Ivy heard was a wah-wah sound like the teacher in the Peanuts cartoons. The next thing she knew, she was looking at their backs as they walked away.

"One more," Mak whispered. "It's the Dragon Lady."

Alexandra, ever fashionable in her navy suit and Louboutin heels, leaned down to give Ivy an air kiss just as Ivy stood up to shake her hand, resulting in a clumsy midair collision.

"Thank you for coming, Alex," Ivy blurted out.

"Of course, my darling. And you take all the time you need before you get back into the lab. We will carry on, you just heal," Alexandra said with a magnanimity that almost sounded sincere.

"Thank you for coming," Ivy repeated, then flopped back down on the couch. Mak put an arm around her in solidarity, while Alexandra strode off.

"I can't do this anymore," Ivy said, burying her head on Mak's shoulder.

"It's okay, doll, they're just about all gone now. You'll get through this, one day at a time."

"That's for drunks," Ivy said. "I'm a widow."

Ivy bolted straight upright and looked at Mak in shock. "Oh god, Mak. I'm a *widow.*"

"I know, sweetie," Mak said gently. "But you're not one of those widows. You're a smart, successful, beautiful young widow."

"I'm thirty-one, Mak. Too young to give up, too old to start over."

They turned back to watch the last of the mourners depart. Ivy felt the tears that wouldn't come all day beginning to well up behind her eyelids. *Emotional tears, higher in prolactin, adrenocorticotropic hormone, and leucine enkephalin than reflex tears*, she couldn't help thinking as they began to spill over and roll unchecked down her cheeks.

3

onrad Reed, handsome at forty-four in his uniform of black Armani T-shirt and fitted jeans, sat on the orange leather couch across from a trio of network television executives. With his Brad Pitt looks, he'd often been mistaken for an actor and always pretended to be flattered, even though that was the last thing he'd ever wanted to be in this crazy business.

A tight smile on his face and a zippered leather binder embossed with a *CR* monogram in his lap, he'd dreaded the awkward formalities he knew they'd have to dispense with before he could get on with his pitch for the new TV series he hoped to sell.

"We were so sorry to hear about your wife."

"She would have been such a huge star."

"The next Meryl Streep."

Conrad's heartbreaking loss was the last thing he wanted to discuss in a business meeting, but he could hardly jump into his series idea without letting them acknowledge the death of his wife, so he'd nodded and mumbled an awkward thank you. He'd been asking his agent, Billy Greene, to set up a pitch meeting at the network, any network, for months. But no luck. He knew

Billy was too kind to tell him the truth: that after his last television series—the one that was supposed to be a megahit—crashed and burned, no one was in a hurry to meet with him.

That is, until Dawn died two weeks ago. And what do you know? His old network decided they wanted to schedule a meeting after all. He didn't care if it was a pity pitch. He needed this shot. Billy had urged him to take a couple of months off before he got back on the horse, but Conrad was running out of time. It wasn't just his dwindling ego at stake, either—he needed a deal to keep his career, his mortgage, and his four-year-old stepson afloat.

Pitch completed, the trio of execs exchanged unreadable glances. Based on the lukewarm reception, it was clear to Conrad that sympathy only got him into the room.

"Okay, I think we got the gist," said Adam, the development team leader, as he fiddled with the iPhone that was glued to his hand like an extra appendage. "Anthology series, stand-alone episodes, different slice of LA police life each season."

"Sort of a SoCal cops-and-robbers melting pot," added Sara, the team's female executive.

"*Law and Order* meets *American Horror Story*," said Lonnie, the young development guy with the hip tortoiseshell glasses.

"Not exactly how I'd put it—" Conrad started to say, until he was cut off by Adam.

"I feel you, but it sounds a little . . . hmmm . . . disjointed. I think we need something more accessible. Ongoing storylines, recurring characters, maybe a little glitz along with the grit. You know, like *LA Law* or *NYPD Blue* back in the day," Adam said.

"*LA Law*?" Lonnie asked curiously.

"Prime-time soap set in a LA law firm. Fabulous," Sara gushed. "Before my time, of course, but I caught it on Hulu."

Conrad thought for a moment, trying not to boil over with

frustration. "Look, I get that my last series was too, ah, experimental for the network. Of course, the audience only got to see three episodes before you canceled it, so it's up for debate if they would have embraced it with a little more time."

"Hold on, Conrad," Adam interjected, getting a little hot under the collar. "It wasn't that *A House Divided* was too 'experimental' for our viewers. It was that the audience clearly did not want to peek behind the curtain of American politics. Period."

"They were already living it. And, honestly, politics isn't really your métier," Sara said.

"Granted, it was a miscalculation on *all* our parts. But we're happy to move forward with something more . . . traditional," Adam said.

"And you're so amazing with police procedurals," Sara added.

Conrad put his hands up in a *you win* gesture. "Okay, I hear you. You want good guys and bad guys and long, soapy storylines with glamorous yet accessible recurring characters."

"Oh, and skew it young. Our research department is always begging for that," Lonnie added, glancing at Adam and Sara for approval.

"Tell you what. Come back with a new pitch and a sizzle reel. Three minutes max. Sharon, can you schedule a follow-up meeting for Mr. Reed?" Adam said, opening his office door, iPhone still in hand, and shuttling Conrad off to an assistant with bangs and braces, who looked like she belonged in a high school marching band instead of a global media conglomerate.

Barreling down the carpeted corridor lined with cast shots from the networks' current crop of series, capped-tooth smiles gleaming, Conrad burst out of the building as though it were on fire. He blew past a uniformed security guard without acknowledging the well-meant *Have a nice day*, and chucked the entire pitch packet into the first garbage can he passed.

Damn those spoiled Ivy League twits, Conrad thought as he slammed the car into gear. Six Emmys and they still had to bring up his big flop. But this was his best shot, maybe his only shot, and he needed a deal. His time and money, in what entertainment people so preciously called "the business," were both running out. God, it made him laugh when *Variety* referred to someone's spouse—whether a senator or a neurosurgeon—as a "non-pro." Who did these ridiculously entitled people think they were, and why did he so desperately want to get back in their good graces? Well, he knew why, and it was all waiting for him back in Malibu.

Conrad gunned the Mercedes and caught the light on Sunset just before it turned red. He drove aimlessly for a few miles, then turned north onto Beverly Glen like some kind of force field was pulling him there. Without even thinking about where he was headed, he wound his way up to the top of Mulholland Drive, then pulled the car over to the shoulder and shut off the motor. He'd visited this site, which seemed to have materialized out of thin air, every day since Dawn died. Fourteen days, fourteen visits, and he still couldn't decide if he found it more comforting or agonizing. One thing he knew for sure—he couldn't seem to stay away.

DAWN'S DESCANSO, the little handmade sign read. *Dawn's Resting Place*. The eerie practice of erecting folk art–style roadside shrines where loved ones died had migrated up from Mexico and spread across the country, just like the freeway off-ramp vendors selling fruit and flowers. It wasn't actually a gravesite, of course, but a visual reminder of a fallen loved one. Kids hit by drunk drivers, exhausted workers who'd fallen asleep at the wheel, even your run-of-the-mill head-on collisions were memorialized by the curbside tributes. It was illegal, but who the hell was going to stop it?

Dawn Delaney's shrine had been built by her devoted fans—at least, that's what the tabloids had reported, noting that her favorite color was yellow. The day after her death, she had already become something of a legend—a female James Dean who died well before she hit her artistic stride—and there were plenty of yellow roses, yellow teddy bears, and yellow candles at the site where her car had swerved and plunged down the hillside, smashing into a tree below.

Conrad hadn't bothered to roll down the car window, and he scarcely noticed the sun beating down so hard that it was making droplets of sweat pool on his forehead and trickle down the front of his shirt. He was staring at the descanso sign with the now-famous photo of his deceased wife, the love of his life, staring right back at him. That face with its slightly mismatched features—piercing green eyes, delicate pointed chin, sensuous pout, and the long sweep of honey-blond hair cascading over one shoulder—slayed him every time he looked at it.

"What do I do now, Dawn?" he asked aloud, hating how pathetic he sounded. "How am I supposed to live without you?"

He'd always suspected that the marriage was doomed right from the start, yet there'd been no way he could help himself. She was young and wild and so fucking beautiful, and her career was already starting to take off. Conrad was all too aware that it probably wouldn't be long before she'd have so many work opportunities and romantic prospects that she'd cease to need him. But he'd wanted to be with her as long as she'd have him, even with her kid as part of the bargain. And he was willing to live with the pain he knew would swallow him whole in the wake of her departure. He just hadn't expected her to depart like this.

"I know exactly what you'd say," Conrad continued, his eyes still transfixed by the photo of Dawn. *Just sell the show, Connie. And keep it light. That's what people want from you.*

A rivulet of sweat streaming down his forehead finally roused him from his trance, and he started the engine, a Freon-tinged blast hitting him full in the face as he headed home to Malibu.

4

*I*vy stood in her little walk-in closet with her face pressed into one of Will's flannel shirts, just as she'd done every morning since he died two months earlier. If she inhaled deeply, she could almost smell the lingering fragrance of his sandalwood aftershave, earthen and woodsy. *I know it's an olfactory hallucination*, she told herself, *a phantom odor that no longer exists.* But she didn't care; it was as real as it got.

When she'd cleaned out Will's office in the humanities building, ignoring offers of help from his former colleagues, she'd packed up every single one of the hardback books Will had collected since he was a boy. *Paperbacks and e-readers are for sissies. Where's the commitment in that?* she could hear him say in the big booming voice he used for lectures. She'd find room for them somewhere, maybe even dive into some of the classics that Will forever suggested she read. *There's more to life than microscopes, you know.*

Ivy threw on yesterday's jeans and a fraying sweatshirt, yanked her hair into a greasy bun, and plodded down the staircase into the pocket-size kitchen they'd restored just three years before. For the first few weeks after Will's death, it had taken all her strength just to get out of bed in the morning. She'd wander around the house in her pajamas, attempting to read or watch TV until it was time for her daily Zoom check-in with the lab to see how the agriculture testing was going. Some days she couldn't even do that, and she'd give her excuses and crawl back into bed, wrapped in Will's bathrobe.

Every light fixture, every doorknob, every tile reminded her of that year, so precious now, that they'd spent happily entrenched in domestic improvements, building the foundation of their marriage as they built their rickety little house into a home. They'd done a total gut job on the kitchen, their favorite room, adding hardwood floors, a quartz counter, and stainless steel appliances they couldn't afford. It was here they began their days, swapping sections of the newspaper over toast and coffee, and ended their days with a simple dinner and catch-up conversation. Will did the cooking, Ivy did the cleanup, and they both cherished the quiet intimacy of daily life.

Ivy sat down at the kitchen counter, powered up her laptop, and opened a Zoom screen, a cup of tea and notebook in front of her. She heard a double ding, and her laboratory aides, Ed and Marlena, popped up on the screen.

"Hey," Ivy said halfheartedly. "How's it going?"

"Not much to report since yesterday," Marlena replied. "We're still waiting for the guys from Davis to send over the test results."

"We should get the report sometime this afternoon," added Ed.

"Has Alexandra been by?" Ivy asked, concerned that her sole investor might, at any moment, change her mind about the generous bereavement leave she'd granted and insist that Ivy report back to the lab in person full time. But so far, that hadn't happened, and uncharacteristically, Ivy hadn't felt the need to push herself. Grief had kicked her ass, and she had finally learned there were times she'd simply have to succumb to the soul-crushing weariness that accompanied it.

Zoom call completed, Ivy stood at the microwave nuking a mug of canned tomato soup for lunch, thinking about the repeated calls from her parents asking if she was eating enough and if she wouldn't rather come home and stay with them for a while. They meant well, but the truth was, it had barely felt like her home even when she lived there. They were always at their gallery or traveling to art shows. Ivy's Grandma Rose had raised her almost single-handedly, until she died when Ivy was nineteen. Ivy thought she knew what heartbreak felt like then, but it wasn't even close to the crushing sense of loss she felt now. Like one of those horrible carnival rides where you're spinning around and suddenly the floor drops out from beneath your feet. Only this ride wouldn't stop.

She grabbed her soup and took it downstairs to the den, flipping on the television to some mindless courtroom show then switching to a drippy soap opera. Daytime television. *Who knew all this crap even existed?* No matter, anything was better than wandering the house, half expecting to see Will around every corner—Will napping on the couch, Will in the kitchen making his famous stir-fry, Will reading next to her in bed.

Days were difficult enough, but nights were unbearable. Ivy would toss and turn, the pain so stifling that she couldn't breathe, until she finally got up to pop a sleeping pill. But nothing—not booze or Ambien, not even the fitful sleep she'd finally fall into—could keep the last thing she'd said to Will from replaying in her head in an agonizingly endless loop. *You want a kid, you better start acting like an adult.*

· · · · ·

*I*vy was still in the den, soup mug and a long-cold cup of tea on the table in front of her, when she heard the doorbell. She listened for a moment, waiting for the salesperson or well-meaning neighbor to go away. *Leave me alone, whoever you are.*

The bell rang again. Ivy groaned but couldn't find the strength to stand up.

Then her cell phone rang from somewhere upstairs.

Next, the ding of a text message.

Now she heard someone pounding, the doorbell clanging, and her phone ringing all at once. Defeated, Ivy dragged herself up off the couch and headed toward the front door.

"Ives, open up. It's me."

Ivy opened the door a crack, blinking at the unexpected sunlight.

"Girlfriend, I've been ringing the bell for ages."

Without a word, Ivy fell into Mak's arms right on the front stoop, her chest heaving with big, gooey sobs.

Twenty minutes later, Ivy came down the stairs in clean jeans and T-shirt, a towel wrapped around her freshly washed hair. Mak had set the dining-room table, and as Ivy sat down, she began to pull sandwiches, chips, and fruit out of her giant Mary Poppins tote bag.

Mak produced a Sara Lee lemon pound cake from the bag and cut Ivy a big slice. "Remember when we used to eat these for breakfast?" Mak asked.

"I'd come back to the dorm after swim practice and I could eat the entire cake myself."

"Except I'd already eaten half."

Ivy stared at her plate for a long while, then looked up at Mak. "What am I going to do now, Mak?"

"You're going to get through this however you can. And I'm going to help."

"Did my parents send you?"

"Are you kidding? If they knew what I had in mind, they'd kill me."

"What do you mean?"

"I think it's time you had a change of scenery. You're going to come down to Southern California with me," Mak said firmly.

Ivy frowned. "To do what? Get a studio apartment in the Valley"—she put air quotes around *Valley*—"and start waiting tables?"

"Hardly, girl genius. You'll extend your leave of absence, keep managing your lab remotely—"

"I can't just—" Ivy started to protest.

Mak made a *talk to the hand* gesture and cut her off. "Yes, you can. I've found you a job. And a house. With a swimming pool."

Ivy considered Mak's plan. "I guess I could work virtually a little while longer, go up to SF once a week or so, maybe rent out my house temporarily."

"Now you're talking!"

"Honestly, I just want to drop out and be invisible."

"Perfect. So you'll come to LA with the beaches and sunshine and all the beautiful, self-centered, materialistic people. No one will even notice you."

5

urry up!" Conrad yelled impatiently as he dragged Rory, Dawn's yellow Labrador, along the foothill path above his Malibu estate. He wasn't too crazy about taking the big dumb Lab on his morning hikes, but Dawn had loved the slobbering beast, so what else could he do? Besides, it helped him to imagine Dawn walking beside them on the trail, sparkling with energy, her long legs outpacing them both.

Conrad zipped his sweatshirt against the morning chill as the wind whipped through the canyon. The grass along the path was almost entirely brown, with only a few scraggly patches of pepperweed sprouting here and there, the drought dragging on as though it might never stop.

He tried to shift his focus back to his work as he walked, Rory loping along behind. The uphill climb and ocean view usually chilled him out completely, especially when the serotonin kicked in, abating the pain and worry that ran through him like an underground stream, trickling at times, raging at others. Today he couldn't seem to shake off his anxiety. No wonder. He had his return pitch meeting later that week with the same shit-for-brains who had nixed his anthology series about the LA policing community.

It was kind of funny, but no one in the entertainment industry ever used the word *selling*, it was always *pitching*, though selling was what it was. You started by selling yourself. Where you grew up, where you went to school, who you married, how you got started in the business. Only after selling yourself—and a chunk of your soul—could you move on to selling your creative idea or your business proposition.

In the end, Conrad knew he had to cave. If he wanted a sale, he knew he had to come up with yet another flashy cop show that would be an audience pleaser and a network moneymaker. A show that could easily be cast with an attractive newcomer or two, maybe a recognizable star in a supporting role, and plotlines that were enjoyable but not too challenging. As much as he wanted to explore stories with depth and gravitas, he had prepped a little sippy cup of a show that anyone—including a network executive—could wrap his or her pea brain around.

When he was a boy growing up in Fairlawn, New Jersey, where his second-generation Polish dad had owned a small kosher butcher shop, everyone thought he was nuts to be thinking about a career in the movies. But by the time he was twelve, Conrad had a vision. He was going to Hollywood, and he was going to be a writer. Where this idea came from, no one knew, least of all his parents. But while the other neighborhood kids were playing video games, Conrad was sitting in a darkened theater watching movies like *Boyz n the Hood*, *Silence of the Lambs,* and *What About Bob?*

He couldn't believe his good fortune when, while still in high school, he won a short fiction contest and had his very first story published in a literary magazine. It didn't land him the agent or studio job he'd hoped for, but it was enough to convince him that he had the talent to try his luck in Hollywood. His parents wouldn't let him go until he graduated from high school, but the day after school let out, his mom took him to Newark Airport, crying her eyes out as she kissed him goodbye and gave him three hundred dollars from the household account.

"Make something of yourself," she'd said, then pulled away from the curb and drove off without once looking back.

Now, as Conrad headed toward the fork in the path, the usual turnaround point for his hike, he thought about how he'd gotten his first studio job as a page at Paramount, thanks to a tip from a patron where he was tending bar. He'd shifted over to television after discovering how difficult it was to break into film as a screenwriter unless you possessed that one precious gift— an uncle in the business.

But TV was fun, fast-paced and more open to kids without connections, so he'd been happy to start over in the less rarified air of the small screen. And he'd done well. Well enough to get some shows on the air. And well enough to land Dawn, a film actress who'd made a name for herself in a small but splashy role playing a medical student who gets addicted to painkillers. Now, two months after Dawn's death, grief and solo stepparenting had nearly edged him out of the game altogether.

But Conrad wasn't giving up. He needed a win, and fast. What else did he have? A finicky four-year-old and a great big empty house that was meant for a family. Dawn had fallen in love with the place at first sight, and as soon as she referred to it as their "forever home," giving him a look that was a cross between a little girl determined to get her own way and a femme fatale who could wrap any man around her finger, there was no way he could resist buying it for her.

Funny how forever had changed.

It wasn't just being saddled with a pricey estate that Dawn

had envisioned as their showplace that kept Conrad up at night. After her unexpected death, the tabloids had jumped in with their version of her accident. "Former foster child turned film star dies in suspicious car crash, leaving behind toddler son." The rags had made it sound downright Dickensian, as if Dawn were the latest member of the 27 Club—the ghoulish moniker referencing the age when Kurt Cobain, Amy Winehouse, and Jim Morrison had all died—a glamorous actress leaving behind her poor orphan child with no one but a washed-up producer to look after him.

What am I, Conrad had thought, *chopped liver? And Hudson was almost five, hardly a toddler.* Conrad was so pissed off at the time. As if he couldn't provide for Hudson. As if he wouldn't cherish the boy almost as much as Dawn herself had. But Conrad had since discovered how difficult it was raising a child alone, especially one like Hudson, with all his quirks and fears. But whenever he wondered whether the kid might be better off with someone else—even though there was no one else—he heard Dawn's throaty voice in his head.

Snap out of it, Connie. You're all he's got. And just so you know, nobody—and I mean nobody—feels sorry for a white guy living in Malibu. She was right, of course. He had always worried about money, a product of his upbringing, no doubt. But still, he knew his younger self would have been blown away if he'd gotten even a glimpse of the life ahead of him.

"You're right, Dawn," he said aloud, pulling Rory to heel.

Newly energized, thanks to Dawn or some infinitely wise unknowable source, Conrad started to jog back down the trail toward home, Rory huffing behind, dry leaves and brush crunching underneath their feet. When the house came into view just below the tree line, Conrad stopped as he always did to gaze down at it. The realtor had laid it on thick, citing the semifamous architect who'd built the house in the style of a European villa. Seven bedrooms, eight bathrooms, ten acres of land, tennis court, swimming pool, and ocean view. Distant, but a view nonetheless. As soon as Dawn had seen the round turret that soared above the roofline, she was hooked.

When they were first married, he liked to look down and admire the house and think about the life he'd have with Dawn and Hudson. Now all he saw was a crazy high mortgage, a kid he could never make happy, and a ten-acre garden he'd let go to hell.

Garden. Shit!

Conrad picked up his pace, wondering why on earth he'd agreed to let Mak's friend move into the gardener's cottage. What was he thinking? Especially right now. It was nice that Mak's pal would fix up the yard, but the last thing he wanted was someone else he'd have to worry about.

But how could he say no to Mak? She'd saved his ass when they worked together on that torturous lawyer show with the story arc about a middle school principal. All those child actors and their harpy stage mothers and uptight social workers and restrictive labor laws. It would have been a total nightmare without Mak as his production manager to keep them all in check. And in all the years they'd worked together, she'd never once asked for a personal favor. No screenplay to read or cousin to hire. Putting up her buddy for a while was the least he could do. And even though he didn't want to displace Hudson, if he ended up putting the house on the market, at least the yard would be a selling point.

Just then, a couple in spiffy athleisure wear with a spotted pit bull mix approached them on the trail. Rory gave a tentative sniff, ready to make friends, but the pit snapped, straining its leash to get at her. *Dog eat dog, just like Hollywood*, Conrad thought as he yanked Rory's leash tight and they continued their descent.

Fall

6

Hey! Want to give me a hand here?" Mak yelled, as she began removing boxes from the trunk of Ivy's Prius and loading them onto a handcart.

Ivy stood rooted to a spot in the driveway alongside the Malibu mansion, transfixed by the massive house—from its steeply pitched slate roof and rounded turret to the expansive grounds below.

"Look at this place," Ivy murmured, more to herself than to Mak.

"Beautiful, right? Conrad told me the architect was famous for his country luxe–style houses." Mak put a snooty Downton Abbey accent on "country luxe." Sure, Mak came from a working-class family in East LA and was proud of it, but after nearly a decade working in the entertainment industry, she was hardly a stranger to the upper crust.

Ivy ignored her comment, her mouth turning into a frown.

"Can you imagine what it costs to cool it? Not to mention electricity and water."

"Okay, maybe a tiny bit excessive, but you should see some of the other homes around here." Mak grabbed the cart and headed down the driveway. "Come on, let's go check out your new pad. I've been dying to see it."

"Wait! You dragged me all the way down here and you've never even seen the place?"

"Nah. It was a caretaker's cottage until Dawn claimed it as her office. I got the sense it was sort of her sanctuary, but Conrad assures me it's clean and furnished."

"At least it's compact," Ivy said, as the little cottage came into view. "I could never live in that energy guzzler of his."

They continued down the path to the cottage, which was wood-framed with modest lines and vines arching above the doorway, giving it a kind of storybook feel.

"These are pretty," Mak said, nodding at the bright-blue flowers spilling down beside the front door.

"Morning glory, invasive species," Ivy said glumly, as she jiggled the key in the lock, keenly aware that the next phase of her life awaited her on the other side of that door. As the door swung open, a swell of fresh grief washed over her. *What am I doing here? Is this really my home? My life?*

"Oh my god," Ivy exclaimed as she stepped over the threshold.

"Cool. It's like a ten-year-old girl's fantasy house. Maybe the childhood home she never had?"

Ivy and Mak looked around the tiny house with its cozy lemon-yellow couch and floral chintz side chair, gauzy scarves draped over table lamps, beaded curtain hanging in the kitchen alcove, and a spindly antique birdcage, thankfully vacant, hovering in the corner.

"Is this rickrack?" Mak said, fingering the trim on the dotted swiss curtains. "I thought it died in the fifties."

"Wow!" Ivy said as she spotted the massive oil painting hanging over the fireplace. She moved closer to inspect the portrait of the young woman with long blond hair swept over her shoulder, a sensual smirk playing on her lips. "Is that his wife?"

She would have been around my age, Ivy thought. *I wonder if we'd have been friends or hated each other's guts.*

"Yep, meet Dawn. Her headshot got so much play after she broke out as a film star, Conrad had it reproduced as an oil painting for her wedding present. Shades of *Rebecca*, right? You've even got your very own Mrs. Danvers up at the big house."

Ivy glanced at Mak, not grasping the reference, then turned and gave the painting a tentative touch with her forefinger. "Nice to meet you."

"It used to be in the living room of the main house, but when she died that photo was everywhere—TV news, talk shows, tabloids, you name it. Conrad told me he just couldn't look at it anymore. I'm sure you can move it if it freaks you out."

"I don't believe in ghosts," Ivy scoffed. "What was she like?"

"Beautiful, obviously. Ballsy, but also surprisingly sweet. She had this way of being totally sexy and completely down-to-earth at the same time. Of course, she was only twenty-four when they got married, so she hadn't had time to become as jaded as the rest of us," Mak replied, laughing.

"Did you know her well?"

"Not really. I saw her with Conrad at a few industry events. And I went to their wedding at the Four Seasons. So gorgeous. Her dress was covered with tiny seed pearls and there were these humongous flower arrangements everywhere. That was kind of her thing—flowers."

"She was a gardener?"

"Nah, I don't think so. But she grew up in the foster care system, and I always got the impression that she aspired to some kind of genteel existence."

"The opposite of what she had?"

"I guess so. I think that's why Conrad wanted that big-ass garden in the first place—for her. But she started working so much, she never got a chance to do anything with it. And I don't think Conrad has even turned the sprinklers on since she died."

"That's a shame," Ivy sighed, thinking of the house she'd loved but couldn't fathom living in without Will. She was grateful that her friends Randy and Charlotte had rented her home while they hunted for a downsize place now that they were both retired. Ivy wondered if Will would think she was a sellout, working on an estate that was the furthest thing from energy efficient. No, he'd probably tell her to give it the eco-Ivy treatment and turn it into an environmental showplace.

"When Conrad mentioned that he was thinking of fixing up the grounds, I told him I knew just the person."

"You're a giver, Mak."

"True that. But it really is perfect for you, right? No reminders of home, no annoying people trying to make you feel better. Just sun, sea air, and communion with the dirt."

"Communion with the *soil*. There's a difference, you know, organic versus inorganic. Never mind," Ivy said, pushing aside the funky beads as she went to check out the kitchen.

"I bet Conrad hasn't been back there in years."

"Wrong," Ivy yelled. She returned to the living room, a bottle of wine in one hand and a little deckle-edged notecard in the other.

"Welcome, signed Conrad," Ivy read, showing Mak the otherwise blank card.

"You've got to hand it to him for succinctness. Come on, time for me to introduce you to the boss."

As they headed up the brick path back toward the main house, Ivy stopped to take in the giant deck overlooking the pool and spa in the backyard. "It looks like a Russian oligarch's dacha."

"No helicopter pad," Mak quipped, opening the back door and ushering Ivy inside. "When you and Conrad are finished hammering out a design plan for the garden, I'll introduce you to the real boss."

"Wait a minute. There's another boss?"

"The live-in housekeeper, Fernanda. She runs the show."

"Oh my gosh, he has staff?" Ivy paused as a new realization hit her. "Wait a minute, *I'm* staff!"

"Welcome to Malibu, Dorothy."

· · · · ·

A few minutes later, Ivy sat stiffly in an antique fiddleback chair, wondering why exactly she'd agreed to move onto the estate of a total stranger. A Hollywood television producer no less. Conrad's study was a picture-perfect Ralph Lauren–inspired male bastion with a mix of dark-green plaids, gory hunting prints, floor-to-ceiling bookshelves, and a giant partners desk, which might have dominated the room had Conrad himself not done that.

He'd given her a *just a second* gesture, apparently needing to finish a thought before he could start their conversation. Ivy watched as his eyes shifted back and forth from a huge computer monitor to a yellow notepad that was tucked inside a leather binder, surprised to discover how handsome he was. Even sitting at his desk, she could tell that he was tall and lean, with blue eyes that were startling in his Malibu-tanned face. For some reason, she'd assumed that only on-screen personalities qualified as LA's beautiful people, and that everyone who worked behind the camera would be more or less ordinary looking. She suddenly felt underdressed in her work uniform of jeans and denim shirt.

Conrad made a final notation on the notepad, closed the binder, and peered across the desk at Ivy with his hypnotic blue eyes. Their intensity made Ivy feel like she'd just been called into the principal's office, and she started to twist a curl around her finger.

"Sorry to keep you waiting," Conrad said. "If I don't grab my thoughts out of the ether and put them into writing immediately, they tend to evaporate on me. So you're Mak's friend."

"Right. We went to college together. Before she moved down here to work in television. Obviously."

"Obviously," Conrad said, with a hint of a smile.

There was a not-quite-awkward pause, then Conrad said, "Mak told me about your husband. I'm very sorry for your loss."

He sighed, shaking his head as though something had thoroughly annoyed him.

Ivy stared at him blankly, wondering what had gone wrong.

"Sorry for your loss," Conrad repeated in a self-mocking tone.

"You're not sorry for my loss?" she asked, confused.

"No, I am, of course. But it's such a cliché. I've heard it so many times myself, I can't believe I just said it to you. If anyone in my writers' room had submitted that as dialogue, I'd have taken their head off."

"In that case, I'm glad I didn't say first. You'd have had me packing the Prius and heading back home," Ivy said.

Conrad started to laugh, and after a moment, Ivy joined in, as if the absurd coincidence of their bleakly similar situations had just occurred to them both.

After their laughter subsided, Conrad asked, "So what do you want to do with the place?"

Ivy twisted a curl as she thought. "Well . . . I'd need to do a little research. Soil sample, pH test, see what the land wants. Is there anything special you'd like?"

Conrad's lips turned up in an easy grin. "Yeah. An overall deal and a Dehler 38 sailboat."

"I meant in the garden," she replied. "I guess Mak told you that I'm an edaphologist. That is, a soil scientist. Well, *gardener* to you."

"Right. The gardener with the PhD." He drew out the phrase, making it sound almost lascivious, and Ivy could feel herself starting to blush. "Surprise me, Dr. Bauer."

"I haven't finished my doctorate yet," Ivy said. "So it's Ms. Bauer, or Ivy is fine."

"Okay, Ivy," he said, rolling her name around in his mouth. "Pretty much anything you want to do with the yard is fine with me. Flowers, vegetables, a giant bocce court. I just want to enhance the market value in case I decide to put this behemoth of a house up for sale."

"I see. So I'm just adding a little curb appeal?"

"I guess you could say that, but it's also a kind of homage to my late wife," he said, sinking into his own private thoughts.

Ivy waited for Conrad to continue, but he didn't say anything more. Not sure whether to stay, go, or interrupt his musings, she stood awkwardly. He didn't seem to notice, so assuming she'd been dismissed, she started for the door.

"Ivy," Conrad said, calling her back. "Dawn had some kind of garden schematic drawn up. It's probably in the cottage somewhere. If you find it and it makes any kind of sense, feel free to use it."

Their eyes locked for a moment, and Ivy was surprised to feel her heart begin to race. She took a deep breath, turned, and walked out of the room before he could see her cheeks begin to color.

7

*I*s he always so, so . . . ?" Ivy asked as she rejoined Mak.

"Drop-dead gorgeous? Yup, pretty much," Mak replied.

"How long have you known him again?"

"Forever. I've been his UPM—sorry, unit production manager—on two series and three pilots. So about eight, nine years," Mak said.

Ivy frowned. "I guess this is a good time to admit that I've never really understood what you do."

"That's okay. No one does unless they're in the biz," Mak said, laughing as she led Ivy through the house. "Basically, I manage all the operations and logistics for his television series. Locations, camera equipment, actor call times. Sort of a TV concierge. The first show I did with Conrad had a gaggle of child actors, and I somehow managed to keep all those damn kids happy. He's loved me ever since. Fortunately for Conrad, the show got canceled after two seasons. He hates kids."

"So how does that work now that he's got one of his own?"

"Yeah, his stepson, Hudson. Poor guy. He's sweet, but he's a little odd until you get to know him. Then he's really odd," Mak said, leading Ivy down the hall and into the living room.

To Ivy's surprise the house managed to be both stately and cozy, that is, if an eight-thousand-square-foot house could ever be considered cozy. She stopped at the grand piano, topped with family photos of Hudson, Dawn, and Conrad in every configuration and location imaginable. Disneyland. Dodger Stadium. Dolby Theater red carpet.

"Check this out," Mak said, calling Ivy's attention to a collection of gleaming awards displayed on the mantel of a massive flagstone fireplace.

"Are those . . . ?"

"Oscars? No. But they're Emmys, next best thing."

"Impressive," Ivy said, unimpressed. "Do you know what they're for?"

"Of course. Two Emmys for *Tricked Out*, one for *No Notice*, and three for *Past Laurels*."

"I think my grandma watched *Past Laurels*."

"Everybody did, doll," Mak said.

They walked through the chef's kitchen, spotless and as gleaming as a nuclear sub.

"Come check out my favorite room," Mak said as she led Ivy down the back kitchen stairs and into the cavernous wine cellar, shelves stocked high with bottles.

"Oh my god," Ivy exclaimed as she looked around the museum-like surroundings, with display cabinets and pin lights highlighting Conrad's massive wine collection. "What possesses a man to buy so much wine? He couldn't possibly drink all this."

"I don't know, but it sure beats my dad's beer fridge," said Mak, pulling her sweater tight against the chill of the temperature-controlled room. "Conrad said to tell you you're welcome to grab a bottle or two from the 'everyday shelf' once in a while."

Ivy wandered through the labyrinth of wine racks. "I wonder

how Dawn felt. A kid from the foster system marrying into all this?"

"Some people think *all this* is why she married him in the first place. Ocean-view mansion, state-of-the-art kitchen, household staff."

"Didn't she have money?"

"She had money. Santa Monica money. But he had Malibu money."

"You think she loved him?"

"No doubt about it. And he loved her. He barely even dated until he met Dawn, then they were practically inseparable, they were so crazy about each other," Mak said. "Though I should probably give you a little backstory."

Ivy took a deep breath, fortifying herself. "She died in a car accident, right?"

"Right. Dawn was coming home from a shoot in the Valley. Only that day, she wasn't driving. Her costar on the film—do you know who Fletcher Lawson is?"

"That hot British actor?"

"Yup. Fletcher was driving Dawn's Porsche over the hill on Mulholland. Most people assumed he was texting and that's what caused the accident. But the rag mags claimed that the two of them were an item and that she was—hmm, how do I put this in scientific terms for you?—giving him a blowie, which caused him to veer over the line just as an SUV came around the blind curve. The driver of the SUV reported seeing only one person in the car, which turned out to be Fletcher, who swerved to avoid hitting them, thank God, because it was a mom driving a car pool of kids."

"That's horrible."

"Fletcher lost control, and the car went over the side of the hill. If they hadn't hit a tree, they might have survived, but Dawn was killed on impact, and Fletcher died in the hospital three days later without regaining consciousness. They ran some pretty gruesome footage of the crash scene on local news. Tons of blood, twisted metal . . ."

"The media can get their hands on all that?"

"This is Hollywood. They've got spies everywhere feeding them—or selling them—photos, videos, you name it. No one believed it, about Dawn having an affair, but the story was already out there."

"It must have been awful for Conrad. I never heard about any of that," Ivy said.

Mak switched off the cellar lights and started up the kitchen stairs, Ivy following.

"No kidding. Somehow I don't see you and your lab assistants gathered around *Access Hollywood* every afternoon while you catalogue soil samples. Besides, it all came out around the time that Will . . ."

Mak broke off, then switched gears. "The studio released a statement saying that Dawn was sick and Fletcher had driven her home that day, which was why she was lying down on the front seat of the Porsche and the other driver never saw her. But people love to gossip about the older guy-younger gal thing."

"It is pretty hard to see a wealthy older man and a younger woman without thinking gold digger," Ivy remarked as they stepped back into the kitchen.

And there, just on the other side of the door, was a pretty, plumpish Latina woman in her midforties wearing neat black slacks with a white blouse and apron. Ivy and Mak stopped dead in their tracks. *Shit*, Ivy thought, *there's no way she didn't hear that.* Ivy's cheeks began to color as Mak tried to salvage the situation.

"Fernanda, this is my friend, Ivy Bauer. Ivy, this is Fernanda Ortiz, Conrad's majordomo. She runs the place."

"Pleased to meet you, Ms. Ortiz," Ivy said, grabbing at a stray curl and giving it a nervous twist. She extended her hand, but the housekeeper turned to open a cupboard.

"You must call me Fernanda. And I will call you Ivy. After all, we are both employees of Mr. Reed," the housekeeper said coolly. Fernanda began pouring dog food into a bowl, the sound of the dry chunks clanging against the sides of the metal dish.

"Rory, come," Fernanda called, and the big yellow Lab came careening through the swinging door, her tale swishing wildly in anticipation. Without so much as another glance at the women, Fernanda placed the bowl on the floor and commanded "wait" to Rory, who was prancing in place as though the brown nuggets were a three-star Michelin meal.

"Take it," Fernanda said sharply after a few beats. On command, Rory began devouring her food, and Fernanda returned her gaze to the women, smiling politely as her eyes blazed with unspoken fury. "She is a good dog, very loyal."

8

*I*n a city where crime never sleeps, two police officers have forged an unbreakable bond that goes beyond the badge," the deep bass voice-of-God announcer blared over the skittering images on the office flat-screen TV.

Conrad, back at the network, was seated on the guest couch viewing the sizzle reel for his new series pitch with the trio of development executives he privately referred to as the Three Stooges. But today, he reminded himself that playing nicely in the sandbox was part of getting his show sold. After his last debacle, when the group pissed all over his multilayered anthology series idea, he'd come back with a straightforward cop show. But who cared? He needed this deal.

The development team had settled in for his pitch, talking over the video as though they'd seen it a hundred times before. Conrad prayed they'd shut up and pay attention.

"Hmm . . . cop show?"

"Looks like."

"Big twist, I hope."

On the screen, a black-and-white patrol car burned rubber, skidding to a stop. Two gorgeous female police officers clad in street-cop uniforms leapt from the cruiser—Jones, a Black woman with braids and an athlete's build, and Pulaski, a tallish white woman with platinum-blond waves. They drew their weapons on an unseen assailant.

"Freeze! Hands where we can see 'em, punks," yelled Jones, dreadlocks flowing and skyline in the distance like one of Annie Leibovitz's famous images of LA.

"Down on the ground. NOW!" commanded Pulaski, planting her feet wide in a power stance.

Conrad thought the development gal, Sara, was about to crack a smile, but her poker face held tight as she continued to watch the video. The angle widened, revealing that the cop car had ground to a precarious halt and was teetering on the edge of a gangplank leading up to a sleek Navetta yacht. The lady cops had cornered a group of badasses who were loading suspicious-looking cargo onto the boat.

"Ready to rumble?" Jones asked.

"Born ready," Pulaski responded.

A dozen police cars with sirens blasting and lights flashing careened onto the scene. A group of backup officers joined the melee, as the women shoved the perps into the back of a paddy wagon and slammed the door.

Pulaski remarked nonchalantly, "And that's how it's done."

To which the Jones replied, "Let's bounce, partner."

The women gave a tandem head nod directly to the camera, jumped into their squad car, reversed, and peeled out as the image dissolved to an end title card and voice-over announcing: "*They're bad ass. They're best friends. They're . . . PULASKI AND JONES.*" The title jump-cut with abrupt finality to Conrad's company logo, an animated rotating image of Pan's pipes overlaid with the name ReedWorks.

Conrad opened his mouth to do the closing sell if they liked it, or damage control if they hated it, but before he could say a word, the three execs started giving one another subtle head nods and eyebrow raises. Conrad watched their tics and twitches to see if he could discern a reaction in there somewhere.

Finally, lead guy Adam turned to Conrad and smiled drolly. "We like it, we like it a lot."

What do you know? The little bastards ate it up.

"We've been looking for something with this sensibility," Lonnie added.

"Oh my gosh. It's got everything viewers want," Sara waxed rhapsodically. "It's got that woman in a man's world thing combined with the classic female buddy style like in *Thelma and Louise.*"

"Plus the retro appeal of *Charlie's Angels*," said Adam.

"Movie or series?" Sara asked.

"There was a series?" Lonnie asked, his brow wrinkling.

"It has to be smart," Conrad interrupted, insistence in his tone. "It's fine if the women are beautiful, but they also have to be brainy and believable."

"Totally," agreed Sara, with just a hint of the Valley Girl she used to be in her tone.

"I think we've got a potential hit on our hands. And I want to thank you for taking our notes to heart," Adam said. "That doesn't always happen with writers."

"Well, you guys really know your stuff," Conrad said, managing to sound sincere as he suppressed his gag reflex. "I just wanted to give you something you can be proud of."

"Let us take it upstairs to the chief and we'll get back to you. Give us twenty-four hours. Deal?" Adam asked Conrad.

Conrad paused, savoring the moment.

"Deal," Conrad agreed, making sure he conveyed a hint of

reticence. "I'll wait to hear back from you tomorrow, but no longer than that. There are a couple of streaming services that would kill for a crack at this show."

Guffaws, handshakes, and air kisses all around, then Conrad hurried down the hallway lined with the smiling star headshots, picturing the cast photo for *Pulaski & Jones* that would soon be joining the network's gallery wall. He exited the building, giving the security guard a friendly wave as he sank into the driver's seat of his Mercedes.

He couldn't hold it in any longer. In a gesture borrowed from Hudson, Conrad balled his fist, thrust his arm back elbow-first, and yelled "YES!" To the network, to the television gods, to Dawn, he wasn't really sure. And it didn't really matter. He was back.

9

*D*ressed in denim overalls and floppy straw hat, and carrying her gardening kit, Ivy walked past the pool and tennis court. The pool itself was beautiful, and the grounds around it were in decent shape, but as the brick path gave way to gravel farther away from the house, she saw that the yard was shriveling under the Southern California sun.

Although working outside with her hands in the soil usually lifted Ivy's mood, today she couldn't seem to shake off the dark cloud of despair. She felt so lost in this city that wasn't her own, working in a garden she had no connection to, that she'd considered calling it quits and returning to her real life nearly since the moment she'd arrived.

But what is my real life without Will?

Will had been her champion, the person who encouraged her to take risks, to change the world. Biased though he was, Will had always regarded his wife as a scientific genius, and he'd been the biggest champion of her irrigation product, HydraHold, through multiple iterations. He'd been a longtime observer as Ivy's male colleagues discriminated against her and other female scientists, and he couldn't wait for her to beat them at their own game.

Everyone else, including her own professors, assumed she'd become an academic. But for Ivy, teaching was only a means to an end. She'd fulfill her commitment as a teaching assistant when she resumed work on her PhD, but her heart wasn't in it. Will, on the other hand, loved pouring his passion for literature into his students, making an author's words come alive, arguing about a passage of poetry. But Ivy felt a sense of rapture only when she peered into a microscope or charted the growth of her plants in the stillness of the lab. She had no desire to become an adjunct professor, then an associate professor, then a full professor, publishing papers and praying for tenure. She was determined to become a leading research scientist—which meant HydraHold had to succeed.

Returning to the task at hand, Ivy gazed across the ten-acre spread, where she saw about twenty untrimmed fruit trees, mostly lemon and orange with long, leggy branches and yellowing leaves; a forlorn little herb garden; and dozens of scraggly rosebushes. *Yuck*, she thought, *why does everyone insist on planting roses? Yeah, they're pretty. They're also notorious water hogs that people load up with chemicals to force the blooms year-round.* Ivy vowed on the spot to replace as many of them as she could with drought-tolerant native grasses that were indigenous to the area. *Why was that so hard for people to figure out?*

Kneeling on the ground, she opened up her tool caddy with its array of Fiskars trowels and short- and long-handed shears, and began to hack away at the dead canes. It wasn't an ideal time; she'd have much preferred to prune in early spring. But the plants had been ignored for so long, she needed to whittle back the deadwood to encourage new growth and get rid of any lingering rot.

She clipped aggressively for more than an hour, grateful to

immerse herself in sun and wind and physical labor as she tried
to keep the dark thoughts at bay. *Come on, Ives, enjoy it. This is the
perfect temp job for you until you get back to the lab full time*, she
could almost hear Will saying to her. Will, who could turn even
the most stressful situation into a party.

"Why are you chopping down my mom's bushes?"

Ivy was startled out of her thought bubble when she heard a
disembodied little voice somewhere close at hand. There, half
concealed behind a tree on the periphery of the hedgerow, she
saw a skinny, blue-eyed, blond boy.

Dawn's kid.

The boy wandered a bit closer, eyeing her tools in fascination. "Those look sharp. Are you being *extra* careful?"

"They're very sharp. Maybe you shouldn't get too close," Ivy
said. She was surprised how much her tone smacked of rebuke.
She sighed, wondering if her sharpness was an unconscious reflection of discovering that she might not be able to have children. Grief compounded by more grief. *Though without Will*, she
thought, *I wouldn't want them anyway. Would I?*

The boy took another step closer. "What's your name?"

Ivy turned away from him and back to the rosebush, not sure
she was ready to engage.

"Ivy," she said.

"No, those are roses. I know because that's my mom's favorite
flower," the boy said emphatically in his croaky little voice.

Ivy abruptly stopped clipping the rose canes and gave the
boy another look. He took a couple of steps closer, wary, like a
deer ready to bolt at the first sign of danger. She began to clean
her shears on a rag, giving him a surreptitious sideways glance,
trying to dissect what gave him such a strange air, all pinched
and fussy. Maybe it was his hair, slicked, parted, and combed to

the side. Or his Lacoste polo shirt, pressed shorts, and pristine white sneakers that made him look like a tiny adult ready to tee off at the country club. *Don't kids wear SpongeBob or Star Wars shirts nowadays?*

"No, my *name*. My name is Ivy."

"So you're named for a plant."

"I guess I am," Ivy said. *Maybe Dawn had taught him something about flowers, just like my Grandma Rose taught me.*

"Why are you living in my mom's office?" he blurted out, hostility hanging in the air like a bad smell.

"I'm helping your . . . Conrad . . . with the garden," she explained, surprised to be put on the spot by a child. "What's your name?"

"Hudson," he said.

"So you're named for a river."

"Hey, how'd you know that?" Hudson asked, as though no one else had ever made the connection.

"I've heard of the Hudson River."

"It's in New York," he said, proud of his vast knowledge.

"What do you know? So I'm a plant and you're a river."

"I could water you," Hudson responded, laughing at his own joke.

"I guess you could. Well . . . nice meeting you," Ivy said, ready to return to her own thoughts. Once she got past her black mood, she'd planned on using the time outside to think through the study she'd read on using chrysanthemum extracts as a natural pesticide.

Hudson didn't budge. They fell silent, and Ivy went back to her pruning, cutting back only the deadwood now that she knew these were Dawn's favorite flowers. The boy followed along at a safe distance, his little frame casting a shadow on the ground beside her as she continued chopping. As she pruned each bush, she moved down the line to the next one, Hudson moving along behind her in a clip, scoot, repeat rhythm until Rory came bounding into sight. She had the energy of a pup but the heft of a full-grown canine, with an enormous head and feet to match. Like most Labs, she was all cuddles and kisses, and after an exploratory sniff or two, she leaned in to give Ivy a big, sloppy slurp, leaving a trail of dog spit across her face.

"Look, she likes you," Hudson said.

"Oh joy," Ivy replied, as she shied away from the dog's ebullient slobbering. "What's her name?"

"Well, she's got a regular name and she's got an AKC name. Do you know what the AKC is?"

"American Kennel Club," Ivy said.

"That is correct. Her official AKC name is Princess Santa Monica Aurora Borealis, but we just call her Rory."

"That's quite a name," Ivy said.

"Do you know what the Aurora Borealis is?"

"Waves of light in the sky." *Quite the smarty-pants*, Ivy thought, wondering if that's how she came across when she was a kid.

"Yes, you can see them in the northern hem-o-sphere," Hudson said. "We have to go now. Bye."

Ivy watched as Hudson turned and ran back toward the house, Rory at his heels. She watched them go, noticing how quiet it suddenly seemed.

10

*I*vy felt her shoulders tighten as she scrolled through the directory of the Culver City industrial park, silently cursing herself for promising her parents she'd find a grief support group when she moved to Malibu. Somewhere among the sound studios and postproduction facilities was her destination.

She wasn't sure what to expect once inside but had a vague notion of popcorn ceilings, metal folding chairs, and bad coffee in paper cups. To her surprise, Healing Haven, with its hardwood floors and mellow lighting, looked more a yoga studio or meditation class than a grief group. Not that she actually knew what a meditation class, much less a grief group, was supposed to look like. The people seemed normal enough as they helped themselves to green tea and assembled on a sea of cushions on the floor.

Ivy hovered in the doorway, thinking she might bolt before anyone saw her, when a giant hand-painted mural on one wall caught her eye. She pushed her glasses up on the bridge of her nose and read the message: GRIEF IS THE PRICE WE PAY FOR LOVE. She assumed the colorful mural, depicting a giant tree with branches shooting across the wall and onto the ceiling, was meant to be comforting, but she found it oddly disturbing. Maybe it was the general tackiness, the overbright colors, or the unscientific rendering of roots, trunk, and branches. She looked more closely and saw that attached to each branch were construction paper leaves with names, dates, and in some cases, photographs. In the spiky grass at the base of the tree trunk a jaunty sign invited you to "Add your grief leaf," as if giving your grief to the tree might somehow magically lighten your load.

"Welcome to Healing Haven, everyone. I'm Toby, your bereavement counselor. Please have a seat and let's get started," said a tall, thin woman with a slight Eastern European accent and a chestful of exotic jewelry. "I see that we have a couple of newcomers. Could you take a seat and introduce yourselves, using only your first name, please?"

Trapped like a rat in a maze, Ivy thought, echoing a phrase one of her chemistry profs used to say whenever a student was up against a thorny problem. She grabbed a cushion and joined the outer perimeter of the circle. Heads swiveled, not unkindly, toward her and a youngish Latino man a few cushions over as they settled on the floor.

"I'm Ricardo. I go by Rick," said the man, with a little self-conscious wave. A murmur of welcome, soft as a cashmere blanket, came from the group. Ivy glanced over at Rick, glad he'd gone first, and wondered if he'd lost a wife, child, maybe a lover. The room grew still and she realized everyone was waiting for her.

"Oh, sorry. I'm Ivy Bauer. Oops, just Ivy."

Ivy received the same gentle welcome. *Hey, I'm just here on a trial basis*, Ivy thought, *I'm not so sure this is going to work for me.*

"We're glad you're here," Toby said encouragingly to Rick and Ivy, then turned to face the entire group. "Grief is a very personal journey, and we all move through it at our own pace. So let's join hands and close our eyes and take a moment to go inward and be aware of whatever it is that you're feeling right now. There's no right or wrong, no judgment, just feel your feelings."

A middle-aged man sitting near Ivy made room so she could scoot her cushion into the circle proper. She flinched when the man took her hand and gave it a little squeeze, but forced herself to leave her hand in his rather than make a scene. Around the circle, hands intertwined, heads bowed, and eyes closed.

After a few minutes, Toby lilted, "Take your time . . . and when you're ready, let your eyes flutter open, and come back to the present moment."

Slowly, everyone opened their eyes, some rimmed with tears. "Now, let's go around the circle and share your high and low points of the past week or anything else you care to talk about. Who wants to go first?"

"Okay if I start?" asked a young ginger-haired man whose name tag identified him as Calvin. He recapped a bit of his grief journey, as Toby referred to it, mostly for Ivy's and Rick's sake, sharing that he'd lost his wife, the mother of his little girl, recently. At age twenty-five, he'd been robbed of the opportunity to raise his child as part of a couple, to argue about sleep patterns or cloth diapers versus disposable.

Calvin pointed out his grief leaf, and Ivy turned to see a wedding picture with Megan in mid-lift as the couple danced their first and last dance as husband and wife. She felt her cheeks blaze with shame for all the times she'd thought about how grateful she was that she hadn't gotten pregnant.

After some head nods and gentle smiles, Ray, the oldest person in the group, added, "I don't know what's worse, to lose your loved one just as you're settling down to enjoy your golden years or to lose them right at the beginning of your life together."

"Either way, it sucks," a chubby woman, who'd introduced herself as Cathy the CPA, chimed in, prompting a few knowing chuckles.

"So what's your story?" Cathy asked Ivy point-blank.

"My story?" she said, twisting a curl around her finger.

"Yeah, the reason you're here. My husband died of lung cancer. Funny thing is he never tried tobacco in his entire life. Ironic, right? I bet he's looking down, smoking a pack of Marlboros, and laughing his ass off right now."

Cathy zeroed in on Ivy again. "Your turn."

"Only if you're ready to share. Nothing here is mandatory," Toby said firmly.

"That's okay. I can share," Ivy said, steeling herself for the interaction. "I'm Ivy, well, I said that already. My husband, Will, died in a bike accident—bicycle, that is, not motorcycle—four months ago. I'm just trying to get through this however I can."

Given her natural reticence, Ivy wasn't prepared for the outpouring of compassion that followed in the form of understanding head nods and comforting coos. She felt her cheeks flame in embarrassment as she tried to process the unexpected attention. *How do these people do this? They walk in here each week to spill their guts and still have something left over to give to the others. I don't know if I'll ever get there.*

But when she left the meeting, Ivy noticed that the knot between her shoulder blades had loosened an infinitesimal amount, and she thought she just might return.

11

Conrad's Mercedes crawled northbound on Pacific Coast Highway, known by the locals as PCH. It was almost noon and a gorgeous fall day, which meant the sun worshippers were already slowing the flow of traffic in both directions. In another couple of hours, the Friday crush of commuters heading home for the weekend would make the otherwise beautiful beach route nearly impassable.

His cell phone rang, and seeing his agent, Billy's, name pop up, Conrad tightened his grip on the wheel and answered.

"Good news, Con," Billy said.

Conrad inhaled sharply. "You closed the deal on the pilot?"

"Not yet. But we're getting closer."

"What does that mean?"

"I'm holding out for a series deal. With your track record, you're way past the stage where you shoot a pilot and then wait while the network decides if it goes to full series," Billy said.

"Billy, I need a deal, any deal. Are you sure we shouldn't grab the pilot if they offer it?"

"Relax, Conrad, and let me do my job," Billy responded. "Go blow off some steam."

When the conversation ended, Conrad exhaled audibly, not

realizing he'd been holding his breath until that very moment. On impulse, he hit his blinker and made a fast right turn off the highway, an exasperated driver behind him honking in annoyance at the sudden move.

A few minutes later, Conrad pulled into the parking lot of a cozy mock Craftsman with wooden rocking chairs on the front porch. A sign out front ringed with brightly painted handprints proclaimed MALIBU VILLAGE PRESCHOOL. Conrad unfolded his long legs, climbed out of the car, and paused a moment as the high-pitched chatter of preschoolers on the playground behind a row of tall privacy hedges washed over him. He listened for a beat, then went inside the building.

"Oh, Mr. Reed. It's nice to see you again," said a flustered teacher in a denim smock and leggings. Whether her statement was a greeting or an indictment, Conrad wasn't sure.

"Hello, Miss—" he faltered.

"Rachel," she said dryly.

"Of course, Miss Rachel."

"It's actually great timing that you're here today. Headmistress Nancy was planning to speak to Fernanda, but she can talk to you instead," the teacher said as she directed Conrad into the main classroom. He stopped short just inside the doorframe, caught off guard, as always, by the tiny tables and chairs, lilliputian next to his lanky frame, painted in soothing pastels. It all came back to him, how Dawn had had her heart set on this place the minute they moved to Malibu. Overpriced and precious, Conrad had thought at the time, but now he was glad that Hudson had the familiarity of kids and classroom for a few hours each day.

Miss Nancy, glasses dangling from a chain around her neck, was wiping down tabletops with antibacterial cleanser and brisk efficiency. She ceased her cleaning when she saw Conrad, a warm smile brightening her face.

"Welcome, it's nice to see you back at the Village."

"Nice to be back."

She stepped a little closer and looked into his eyes. "Tell me, Conrad, how are you doing? Really."

"Really? I'm hanging on for dear life. Throwing myself into work, probably too much."

"I'm truly sorry."

"How's Hudson doing?"

"Please sit," Miss Nancy said, leaning against the edge of the teacher's desk as she gestured for Conrad to take a seat in one of the preschool chairs. He sat awkwardly, stretching his legs out in front of him and then, as if he were taking up too much real estate, pulled his knees up under his chin.

"The truth is, we're having a few problems. For the last couple of weeks, it seemed that Hudson was starting to feel a bit better; he was beginning to participate and have fun with the other children again. But the past few days, we've noticed some regression. Not a surprise with all he's been through, of course. But I was wondering if there was anything else going on at home that we should know about."

"Not really. Just missing his mom, I think." Conrad reflected for a moment. They'd both lost the center of their universe with Dawn's death. But Conrad could only imagine how much more catastrophic it was for a child than for him. "Why? What's been happening?"

"Well, he seems more withdrawn, and he's wet his pants three times in the past two weeks. It happens with the littles, of course, but I was concerned that the frequency of the, um, incidents could be a sign of some new stressor. Even good stress—changes at home, new people around—could cause it."

"Our handyman, Fernanda's nephew, is doing some work at the house, but that's nothing new. And we've got a gardener doing some landscaping, but that's about it."

"I know you can't watch him every second, no parent can, and it may seem a little helicopter-ish, but try to keep a close eye on him. And if I haven't mentioned this before now, I always recommend background checks on anyone spending any length of time in the home. I don't want to complicate your life further. Just food for thought."

Conrad looked startled. Had he been too lax about what could be happening right under his nose? Or was this how any anxious four-year-old who'd just lost his mother in a tragic accident that was all over the news would behave? Miss Nancy saw his concern and patted him on the shoulder, as though soothing a cranky toddler.

"If there is anything else we can do, I hope you'll let us know. And please do tell Fernanda that it happened again," she said, pulling a paper bag out of a cubby and handing it to Conrad.

He took the bag, looking at her quizzically.

"His things. Not to worry, they're in plastic wrap. We gave him some loaners to wear home. Fernanda will know what to do."

"Of course," Conrad responded, unconsciously holding the bag a little further away from his pristine chinos. "I'll see if I can get to the bottom of it. I appreciate your concern, Miss Nancy. I really do."

A gong sounded outside and a crowd of kids surged into the classroom with the energy of a small army. Giggling and chattering, they collected artwork and sweaters, sun hats and hair bows, as they chirped goodbyes and bestowed hugs on their teachers.

Right behind them, the moms of Malibu paraded into the classroom backlit by beams of sunlight, dripping with diamonds and privilege. Like a casting call for coiffed and cared for upper-class moms, they came in yoga pants and tennis skirts, highlights and French manicures, with breast implants and Botox to greet their little Chloés and Coopers.

One pretty auburn-haired woman with twin girls hanging on either arm caught Conrad's eye and gave him a big smile and a forward thrust of her chest. "Conrad, how are you?" she cooed a little too suggestively. "I was so sorry to hear about your wife."

"Thank you," Conrad said, not wanting to engage but not wanting to be rude to a preschool parent either.

"You don't remember me. Jenny Marks. We worked together on that episode of *Bittersweet*."

"Oh, of course. Hi, Jenny. These beauties are yours?" he asked, glancing down.

Jenny laughed breathily at the unintentional double entendre.

"The twins . . . the girls . . . that is, your offspring," he clarified, chuckling.

"Well, I'm not a nanny, darling," she said, flashing her left hand with its neon-blue nail polish and cushion-cut diamond that had to be at least three carats. "Glad you got to see my twins. Call me if you ever need a shoulder to cry on."

Conrad nodded, trying to get away without seeming too obvious. Jenny smiled, blowing him a kiss and making a slow exit so he could check out her heart-shaped ass, twins in tow like pretty little props.

As the other moms began to eye him and smile, Conrad made a beeline for Hudson, casually tucking the paper bag behind his back.

"Hudson. Hey, man!" Conrad said, putting up his palm for a

high-five that went unreturned as Hudson looked up at him in surprise.

"Where's Fernanda?" he asked with a little frown.

"I told her I wanted to pick you up and take you to lunch. Come on, it's a gorgeous day for a drive," Conrad said, giving Hudson an awkward little one-arm hug.

"Okay," Hudson said uncertainly. "But we'll go home after that?"

"Sure, if you want," Conrad said, glancing back in hopes that Miss Nancy hadn't heard the boy's hesitation.

They headed to the Mercedes, where Conrad discreetly slipped the undies bag in the back seat. "Want the top down?" he asked cheerfully.

"Up. Sun gives you cancer," Hudson replied emphatically.

"Whoa. Who told you that?"

"I saw it on TV. That's why you have to wear sunblock."

"Well, that's true. But that's only if you're out in the sun every day without a hat or anything."

"Anyone can get cancer."

"I'll take that as a no," Conrad said, leaving the top up and revving the engine.

Ten minutes later, they were seated beachside on the elegant outdoor patio at Nobu, waves crashing just beyond the deck.

"Remember when we came here last time? You loved their sushi."

"Dr. Harvey says it has mercury."

"Not today," Conrad said, trying to retain some semblance of cheer as his favorite waitress approached.

"Hi, Yuki. Let's start with some edamame and an order of the yellowtail sushi. A Sapporo for me, and you want lemonade, Hud?"

Hudson nodded.

"Sure, Mr. Reed. Coming right up."

"Do you want to know what we're celebrating?" Conrad asked, as Hudson distractedly fiddled with the condiments in their little earthenware bottles.

"Okay."

"I got some good news today. I might have sold a television pilot. You know what that means, right? The first episode or maybe, if I'm lucky, an entire season."

"Uh-huh," Hudson said, intently focused on pouring soy sauce from one bowl into another.

"Be careful, honey. You're going to spill that," Conrad said, a little more sharply than intended. Hudson stopped abruptly and reached for his chopsticks instead. "And if it's good, it will be on all year and maybe the year after that."

"But you don't know yet," Hudson said.

"Well, no, not yet," Conrad admitted.

"What's it about?"

"It's about two lady cops who chase bad guys."

Hudson stared at the ocean silently. Pondering the universe or just watching the waves, Conrad had no idea. *Man, it's impossible to read this kid.*

"So what do you think, Hud? Could be good, right?"

Hudson broke a chopstick in half, his eyes wide at his unexpected display of strength.

"Honey, those aren't the kind you break apart. They're already separated," Conrad admonished, grabbing the delicately carved chopstick, now in pieces.

"Mommy would have been good on that show."

Conrad felt his heart drop out of his chest. He bit his lip, willing the tears away as he tried to wrap his head around the unfathomable depth of his stepson's pain.

"You know, you're right," Conrad said softly. "Your mom was such a great actress; she would have been amazing on the show. What if we name one of the characters after her? Better yet, what if you come down to the set when we start shooting? Maybe I can even write a part for you. Would you like that?"

The waitress dropped off the drinks and starters.

"Thanks, Yuki," Conrad said as he took a big swig of his Sapporo, then another. Hudson poked at a piece of yellowtail, then picked it up warily between two fingers, sniffing it suspiciously.

"It's raw."

"Of course, it's raw. You've had sushi before. You love it."

"No, I don't. You love it," Hudson yelled angrily.

A couple of young businessmen in their Friday uniforms of designer jeans and button-down shirts looked over to see who was interrupting their serene expense-account lunch. They rolled their eyes at each other—*Who brings a kid to Nobu?*—then turned back to discuss the latest IPOs.

"Hudson, calm down. I can get you something cooked," Conrad assured him. "How about a shrimp tempura roll?" Conrad glanced around the restaurant, hoping there wasn't a CAA agent or studio exec dining nearby. That thought was quickly expunged by a pang of guilt. *Dawn would be furious if she thought I was more worried about my reputation than Hudson's feelings.*

Hudson slammed the sushi back on the plate, closed his eyes, and pinched his nose shut in disgust.

"What's wrong? I thought you liked it here."

Hudson opened his eyes wide and glared at the offending yellowtail.

"We came here for your mom's birthday. Remember?"

"But Mommy's not here," Hudson said, bursting into tears.

"You are not my parent," he screamed, standing up so suddenly he knocked his chair over backward.

Conrad righted the chair and reached over to console the boy, but Hudson pulled away, weeping violently.

"You are not my parent, you are not my parent, you are not my parent," he sobbed.

Conrad looked at him in utter bewilderment, a hazy recollection of the phrase stirring in his memory. He vaguely recalled Dawn having to sign a consent form for the preschool allowing Hudson to take part in a "Stranger Danger" lesson meant to inform kids about predators, in the Village's age-appropriate way. Conrad remembered now that Hudson had been very keen to show them what he'd been taught to say if anyone ever grabbed him, but he had no idea the accusation would ever be used against him. *Thank God Dawn isn't here to see how pathetic a stepfather I am.*

By now, all the diners on the patio and a few inside the restaurant had turned to see what the ruckus was all about. The waitress hurried over to the table and asked Conrad if he needed the manager's assistance, which he took as a polite suggestion that they take their lunch to go.

"No," Conrad said through clenched teeth, slapping a $100 bill on the table rather than waiting for a credit card transaction. He turned to face the other diners and, through gritted teeth, said, "Apologies for the disturbance. Enjoy your fish."

12

The evening sun was just hitting the horizon when Ivy returned home from a visit to Healing Haven. Though she had yet to use the pool, she had a sudden desire for a swim, as though the chlorinated water might wash off the emotional residue of the meeting. She made her way up the brick path from the cottage, past the little patch of reclaimed rose garden, and through the still-scraggly grove of lemon and orange trees. The pool looked inviting, with its lacy sheets of water spilling into it from the adjoining spa.

Ivy stuck a tentative toe into the pool and, satisfied with the temperature, slid into the shallow end, luxuriating in the warm water. On one hand, she was grateful that Conrad kept the pool heated six months out of the year, but simultaneously aggrieved at the wastefulness. *Perhaps a discussion of solar panels might be in order*, she thought. Nah, Conrad didn't seem the type to be concerned about his oversize carbon footprint. With that thought, she realized she hadn't set eyes on her employer in days, other than an occasional Mercedes sighting as he headed down the driveway. She wondered where he'd been—and how long it would be before she saw him again.

Ivy began an easy breaststroke, surprised to discover that swimming was still as simple as ever, though the rest of her world had become so complicated. Stroke, breath, stroke. She imagined herself dissolving into the liquid like one of her lab experiments, flesh melting off the bone and body fluids blending with the pool water until there was nothing left of her except her arms hovering above the water's surface, toggling effortlessly from sidestroke to butterfly to backstroke and then to sidestroke again.

Better to swim than think, she decided, focusing on her breath, counting her laps, and letting her tears salt the pool water. But it wasn't possible to blot out her thoughts of Will. She pictured him swimming beside her in his old red college Speedos, with his cocky smile and confident Australian crawl. She longed to tell him about Fernanda, who seemed to rule the household with an iron fist, her boss included. To tell him about sad-faced little Hudson, who seemed so profoundly alone yet simultaneously underfoot, like a dog combing the kitchen floor for scraps.

Forty laps later, Ivy's muscles were as spent as her emotions. She pulled herself out of the pool, toweled her hair dry, and wrapped herself in her terry robe. She was about to head back to the cottage when Conrad called out to her as he came down the back steps, carrying a bottle of wine and two glasses.

"I saw you out here. Nice to see someone using the pool. Come join me when you're done. If you'd like to, that is," he said, holding up the wine bottle and gesturing to the back of the garden, where she'd noticed an outdoor pergola with a rattan couch and chairs.

A few minutes later, in her robe with a towel over her shoulder,

Ivy headed down the path toward the bluffs. She stopped short when she heard Conrad's voice, wondering if someone else was out there with him.

"What do you think, angel?"

When she didn't hear a response, she continued on to the little patio where Conrad was seated alongside an empty chair, the bottle of wine and two glasses on the table.

"Are you okay with red?" he asked her.

Ivy nodded and pulled her robe a little tighter as she looked at Conrad, slouching comfortably as he gazed at the ocean. He'd traded in his daytime black T-shirt and jeans for a black cashmere sweater and jeans, apparently his outfit for a fall evening at home. Conrad poured her a glass of wine, and when he looked at her, the fading sunlight behind him, Ivy stifled a gasp at the blueness of his eyes, bluer even than the Pacific down below.

"Are you sure I'm not intruding?" she said, before tentatively taking a seat.

"Not at all. It's going to be a beautiful sunset."

Handsome men had always made Ivy a little nervous. In her experience, they got so used to being fawned and fussed over; they grew to expect it. Will was good-looking, of course, but in a sturdy, comforting kind of way. Not in a movie star way like Conrad.

"I like to ponder the universe out here," Conrad said. "This is my contemplation spot whenever I have trying issues to, well, contemplate."

He turned the label on the wine bottle to face Ivy, as if she'd have any clue what she was drinking. White, red, or pink was all she knew about wine.

"Nice," she said, taking a sip.

"It's a Barolo from one of my favorite regions in Italy. The Piemonte. Do you know it?" She noticed he used the Italian word, instead of saying Piedmont like Americans usually did.

"Is that in the north?" Ivy asked.

"Indeed it is, foothills of the Alps. One of the best food and wine regions in the entire world. Dawn and I wanted to go for our honeymoon but she was in production for a film at the time and we couldn't get away for that long."

Ivy watched Conrad swirl the crimson wine in his glass, as if savoring the color in the fading light. With anyone else, she would have thought it was a pretentious wine snob gesture, but with Conrad it looked perfectly natural. Like he was used to enjoying the good life, maybe even sharing it with others.

"Did you and your husband honeymoon?" Conrad paused, frowning slightly. "Sorry, so rude asking personal questions right off the bat. Old writer's habit."

"It's okay," she said, hoping the wine would take the edge off her nerves. "We didn't have much time either, or money for that matter. Academics, you know," she murmured, half explanation, half apology. "So we went to Yosemite and stayed at the Ahwahnee, our one big splurge. Will wanted to hike Half Dome."

"Sounds like heaven. All that natural beauty."

"All those tourists," Ivy replied, smiling at the recollection.

"Ah. So you communed with nature alongside hundreds of Belgians and Chinese and Texans?"

"More like thousands. Where did you end up going?"

"I borrowed a friend's ranch in Montana, just outside of Billings. Dawn wanted to see Big Sky country and we only had a four-day weekend, so it seemed like a good solution."

"Must have been beautiful. I've never been to Montana,"

Ivy responded, thinking that life really was different for the wealthy.

"It was. Dawn had her heart set on learning to ride a horse. She'd never had the chance growing up."

As Ivy watched Conrad relax into the memory, she felt herself relaxing too. Funny that he'd sidestepped small talk and plunged into actual conversation. Not at all what she expected.

"Our first day there, I'd just gotten breakfast started and went looking for Dawn, who I thought was still asleep. I finally found her out behind the barn feeding the chickens. We were staying in the most luxurious ranch house I'd ever seen, and all she wanted to do was hang out with the critters," Conrad reminisced.

"So we both spent our honeymoons communing with nature."

"Yes," Conrad said, his eyes fixed on the horizon. "Though this is my favorite communing spot now."

"I can see why," Ivy said, glancing surreptitiously at Conrad before shifting her gaze toward the streaky hibiscus-colored sunset.

"So here we are, widow and widower stumbling through life. Though perhaps I should speak for myself," Conrad mused.

"Stumbling sounds about right for me too. I keep thinking . . . Well, never mind."

"Thinking what?" Conrad asked, giving Ivy a gentle smile.

"That I'll get my footing one of these days."

They sat in silence for a while, and Ivy thought about how peculiar this day had been. Waking up in Malibu, working in someone else's garden, Zooming with her lab colleagues, attending a grief group, and now talking to a near stranger with unexpected intimacy. Afraid she might laugh, or cry, depending on where the conversation went next, Ivy prepared to take her leave when Conrad suddenly turned to her, his deep-blue eyes boring into hers as he confessed, "This will probably sound crazy to you, but I come out here to talk to Dawn."

Ivy smiled. "Actually, it doesn't sound so crazy. I look forward to falling asleep in case I dream about Will." She realized the truth of her statement even as she said it.

Conrad nodded in understanding.

"The crazy part is that she talks back," he said.

"Ah, that is a little crazy," Ivy agreed.

Conrad nodded, a smile playing on his lips.

"Were you talking to her just now?" Ivy asked.

"I was. I was asking her thoughts about a television project."

"And she was talking back to you?" *Maybe it's a learned skill*, Ivy thought fleetingly.

"She was."

"I hope she gave you some good advice. I've barely watched any television since my grandmother and I used to watch reruns of that cop show, something about Miami."

"*Miami Vice*."

"Yes, that's the one. Even as a kid, it just seemed so stupid to me." Ivy paused awkwardly for a moment, thinking about his profession. "But then what do I know? I've been locked in a lab half my life."

Conrad smiled. "And I haven't set foot in a lab since . . . hmm . . . since I shot an episode of *Tricked Out* set in a hospital. The lead character was a prostitute turned private eye."

Ivy rolled her eyes.

"Don't even say it," Conrad said, laughing as he poured them each a bit more wine. "But to your question, yes, Dawn did give me some advice, actually. Same thing she always said about the business. 'Dumb it down, Connie. No one wants Eugene O'Neill anymore.' She always insisted I tried to be too highbrow when what people wanted was fun, escape, titillation. And just so you know, Dawn was the only one who ever called me Connie."

"Wouldn't dream of trying," Ivy assured him as they watched the last chalky smears of color fade below the horizon.

13

"A ttention, ladies and gentlemen, we are having our circle time outside today," Headmistress Nancy called to her charges, who were gathered in the playground area. "Because we have a very important guest."

Ivy thought back to the week prior, when Fernanda had oh-so-casually mentioned that outside experts frequently visited Hudson's school to teach special classes. Part of their "enrichment education," which apparently came along with the Malibu price tag.

"Why don't you come to the school and teach the children about plants? I'm sure they'd find it very interesting," Fernanda had said. Ivy had the distinct feeling that she was being tested, but it seemed like a good opportunity to atone for what Fernanda perceived as gossip about their mutual employer, so Ivy rose to the challenge.

Now, she was looking on as the children shuffled, jostled, and tugged at one another until they eventually formed a lop-sided semicircle. Miss Nancy raised her hand in the air, calling for silence, then continued, "Our good friend Fernanda has brought a visitor who's going to give us a lesson about plants today—"

"It was my idea," Hudson shouted, wriggling excitedly.

Ivy saw Fernanda shush him with merely a look.

"So let's use our best Village manners to welcome Ms. Bauer."

"Welcome, Ms. Bauer," a chorus of high-pitched voices sang out.

Hudson opened his mouth to say something, and Fernanda shot him an even sterner warning glance. *She is formidable*, Ivy thought, watching the two of them. *I hope my lesson is good enough to get me back in her good graces.*

Ivy stepped up to the front of the group, holding her gardening kit. "Hi, everyone. Thank you for that nice welcome. I, that is, we—Hudson, Fernanda, and I—thought it might be nice for me to teach you all a little bit about plants."

Ivy hesitated as if unsure where to start the lesson.

"Have you ever heard of pho-to-syn-the-sis?" She said the word very slowly as if that might help the little ones understand.

The children stared at her blankly and Ivy stared back at them, panicked by the sea of tiny faces. She wondered why it had occurred to her just now that she had no idea how to teach anyone younger than a college freshman. But it couldn't be that hard, right?

"Maybe you've helped your mom or dad in the garden?" Ivy asked tentatively.

Another confused stare from the kids and a stifled laugh from a couple of the moms in attendance.

Ivy glanced at Fernanda in hopes she might throw her a lifeline, but Fernanda remained stolid. *Oh my gosh*, Ivy thought with a start, *these Malibu parents don't tend their own gardens. And they certainly don't expect their kids to do yardwork. What was I thinking?*

Ivy looked around at the kids, who were beginning to fidget, then took a deep breath and started fresh.

"Never mind," she said. "Let me show you what I brought. Hudson, hand me that pot and I'll start the demonstration."

Beaming with importance, Hudson handed Ivy a bushy marigold in a nursery tub.

"Today we are doing something really cool," Ivy said to the group. "We are planting a butterfly garden."

The kids oohed and aahed, and even a few of the mothers began to show some interest.

"We're going to plant a garden that is a good home for butterflies to live in and to lay their eggs, so we'll have even more butterflies. First, we need a place that gets plenty of sun to help the plants grow and to keep the butterflies warm. Miss Nancy has picked out this nice, sunny spot alongside the wall here. What do you all think?"

The kids snuggled up near the wall, nodding and cooing their approval. Ivy took out her garden tools and held them up for everyone to see, as the preschoolers started to chatter curiously.

"But butterflies are very picky," Ivy told the kids, who cracked up at the idea of picky butterflies. "So I've chosen plants that they really, really like. These are marigolds, salvia, yarrow, seaside daisies, and asters." Ivy pointed out the different flowers from among the dozen or so plants in garden store pots that she had placed along the wall.

"Each of you gets to plant one. So I want you to pick out a plant and stand in front of your pot, but don't touch it yet, because I want to show you how to very gently wiggle it out of the container and plant it in the ground."

The kids jockeyed for a place in front of their favorite plant, Hudson smiling as he claimed the spot at the very front of the line.

"Wait until you see the caterpillars, which are butterfly babies, start to gobble up these plants. It'll be like feeding day at the zoo."

Ivy watched as the kids laughed and picked out their plants. Then, much to her relief, she caught a hint of a smile on Fernanda's face.

14

This is my favorite part," Hudson said, trailing a kid-size broom across the kitchen floor and sweeping an invisible cloud of dust out the back door. Fernanda watched as he stepped onto the patio and shook out the little broom, just like she'd taught him.

"I'm a good cleaner, aren't I?"

"You are an excellent cleaner. I don't know what I would do without you," she said, smiling. "Would you like some music? I think it makes chore day more fun."

"Yeah. That western story one you like."

"Ah, *West Side Story*. That's a good choice," Fernanda said. She cued the music on her cell phone, picked up a mop and bucket, and began swabbing the ceramic tile floor, which would have been completely spotless to anyone's eye but hers. She started at the hallway, mopping each rectangle in rhythm to the soundtrack. Hudson stayed one step ahead of her, making a little game of staying in the dry part as she tried to catch up to him.

Pobrecito. Someone's going to have to teach the little one his life skills, Fernanda thought as she watched him squeal with delight each time her mop made a near brush with his sneakers. *With his mama gone and Conrad working all the time, I guess it will be me.*

The "Officer Krupke" song started to play and Hudson began to hopscotch back and forth between the last dry tiles, as he made up his own nonsense lyrics to go along with the boisterous melody. He finally reached the back door and went outside on the patio, giving Fernanda a mischievous grin.

"All done now. Bye, gotta go," Hudson hollered, laughing as he sprinted off and disappeared around the side of the house.

This boy never stops, Fernanda thought as she backed through the kitchen, pulling the mop behind her so she wouldn't leave any marks. A moment later, the doorbell rang, then Hudson came running full speed through the house, magically appearing in the inside hallway just beyond the kitchen door.

"Ta-da!"

She laughed, relieved to see Hudson having fun, then announced, "Let's 'ta-da' to the next room, por favor!"

Fernanda picked up more cleaning supplies and a big feather duster and led the way into the living room, which Fernanda had always considered somehow grand and informal at the same time. Dawn had chosen the décor, including a Chesterfield couch and divan in a regal navy velvet, each with a cashmere blanket thrown casually over the back, as if someone were about to snuggle up with a good book and a cup of tea. Modern wingback chairs in a geometric print of silvery blue and leather side chairs sat across from the couches, an intimate conversation pit for a mere sixteen guests.

Fernanda handed Hudson the feather duster, and he went to work on the baseboards, his favorite job, and not coincidentally, the ideal one for his height. Meantime, Fernanda removed an old-fashioned paisley shawl—one of Dawn's theatrical touches—and several family photos from the top of the grand piano and placed them on the glass coffee table. She began polishing the piano with lemon oil until it gleamed, the fragrance reminding her of earlier times cleaning houses with her big sister when they first moved to Los Angeles.

"Can you wipe this very carefully? It has glass in the frame," Fernanda said.

Hudson nodded his head yes, and she handed him a clean cloth and a photo of himself with Dawn and Conrad on an oceanside patio. He stared at the picture for a moment.

"Was Mommy a good cleaner?"

"Oh, yes," Fernanda replied, knowing that this was not the real question. What it was, however, she wasn't entirely sure. "Your mama loved a clean house. She liked everything to be very pretty for your family and friends who came to visit. And always the flowers."

Hudson nodded somberly as he studied the photo.

Fernanda pointed to the image. "That was her birthday party at the beach."

"I was little."

"That's right. And you were eating sushi at that restaurant right by the ocean."

Hudson wrinkled his nose.

"I don't like that place."

"It was your mama's favorite. She used to hold up her fish with her chopsticks and you would *chomp, chomp* like you were a big shark and you were going to eat it. Then she would plop it in her mouth before you got a single bite. And you would laugh so hard."

"But I wasn't really gonna eat it, 'cause I didn't like sushi when I was little."

"And she would say . . . maybe by your next birthday you'll like sushi."

Hudson looked glum.

"Conrad said you didn't like the sushi when you went there the other day."

"I like it now that I'm big. I just wasn't hungry."

"I see. Anything you want to tell me, hijo?"

Hudson thought for a moment, then grinned. "Can I do Conrad's office now?"

15

*I*vy sat on the chintz-covered couch in her living room as the last of the afternoon sun glinted through the sheer curtains of the cottage. Her laptop was propped up on a couple of pillows as she Zoomed with Ed and Marlena at the lab.

"I was thinking I might try HydraHold on some residential gardens," Ivy said to her assistants. "I know that's not in the road map until year two, but since I'm here . . ."

"Why not?" Marlena agreed. "It would be interesting to see some results from another microclimate."

"Right, we've been pretty limited to the Bay Area so far," Ed added. "And it will be closer to the arid climate conditions we'll be testing soon."

"Great, I'll put the protocol and data in our Google docs. Talk to you tomorrow and I'll see you next week at the lab," Ivy said, signing off.

She closed her laptop, set it on the coffee table, and flipped through a stack of books—*Fundamentals of Soil Science*, *Hydrate the Earth*, and *The Sixth Extinction*—which she'd brought with her from her personal library back home. Having nearly finished the cleanup of the fruit trees and perimeter hedges, she was hoping for some inspiration for the restoration phase of the main garden, but clearly none of these books would fit the bill.

Ivy tossed the books aside and headed for the kitchen, where a nice California Cab from Conrad's everyday shelf was waiting for her. As she poured herself a glass of wine, she remembered that Conrad had mentioned a stack of gardening books and a schematic that Dawn herself had drawn up, but Ivy had yet to come across them. Naturally, she'd looked through the little built-in bookcases when she'd first arrived. What self-respecting scientist doesn't start a house inspection with the bookshelves? But she didn't find anything garden related among the novels and books on films and fashion.

She suddenly remembered a cardboard box in the bedroom closet that she'd shoved aside when she'd moved in to make room for her scant wardrobe. Had she needed more space for her clothes she might have moved the carton elsewhere, but the box had literally blended into the woodwork, so she'd never given it a second thought.

Ivy wiped her hands on a checkered dish towel, set her wine on the end table in the living room, then tore into the bedroom and dragged the box out of the closet. She smiled with anticipation on seeing a big stack of gardening books. Sitting on the bedroom floor, she eagerly began plowing through them. *Shit*, she thought after a few minutes, seeing titles like *The Well-Tempered Garden*, *Down the Garden Path*, and *Secret Gardens of the Cotswolds*.

Was this where Dawn got her inspiration? All these grand manor gardens? How can I possibly work this into an eco-friendly environment?

Nonetheless, she pulled an oversize coffee table book from the bottom of the box and plopped herself onto the living room couch to look through it. Maybe it would give her some inspiration or, at least, some insight into what Dawn loved about these gardens. Ivy wanted to honor Dawn's vision, but these over-the-top gardens weren't going to make it easy. She looked at the jacket flap, which read "Shakespeare's Garden: Botanical images inspired by the Bard."

She thumbed through the first few pages showing lush vignettes of massive gardens laid out in meticulously formal patterns. Each photo was accompanied by Shakespearean verse about the plants that were featured there.

Ivy sighed. *Why can't people see the beauty of native grasses and indigenous plants instead of all these gardens with their water hogs and chemically forced blooms?*

She reached for her wine on the side table and the big book accidentally slipped off her lap and onto the floor. She leaned over to pick it up and saw that a small cloth-bound journal had fallen out of the larger book. She looked at the cover of the journal and saw an ornate calligraphy title that read *Dawn's Shakespeare Garden*, along with an ink sketch of a garden with a brick path and wooden arch covered in climbing roses over the door to a storybook cottage.

Ivy gasped as she recognized the drawing as her current residence, the very cottage she was sitting in right now. She opened the journal and found pages of delicate botanical sketches: lemons hanging from a tree branch, a single gardenia, a row of marigolds, lavender in a pretty pot. Beautiful little drawings in ink and watercolor and pencil, accompanied by handwritten notes and signed *Dawn Delaney* in dainty cursive.

Ivy flipped through the rest of the book and saw sketches of herbs, hearty rosemary with its tiny blue flowers, dainty spirals of oregano, and wide-leafed sage. The last two pages showed a layout of an herb garden with all the plants cited throughout the journal penciled into their spots, Shakespearean references in the margins.

Bay for fame and reputation from *Pericles: Prince of Tyre*.

Primrose for your first child, pale and fair from *The Two Noble Kinsman*.

Marjoram for giving to men of middle age from *The Winter's Tale*.

Ivy was jolted out of her research when she saw her own name:

Ivy for faithfulness from *Romeo and Juliet*

written in Dawn's hand. It sent a little electric tingle down her spine, a feeling that Dawn was telling her that she had faith in Ivy's vision for reshaping the garden.

Ivy glanced up at the Dawn's portrait, and for the briefest moment, she was sure that Dawn had smiled at her.

16

*T*he thing about grief, Ivy thought as she settled onto a floor cushion, *was that there was always a fresh supply.* On the days when no one new joined the group, Ivy imagined she could feel all of Healing Haven let out a collective sigh of relief that someone had been spared the heartbreak that brought this hodgepodge of humanity together.

But today, a newcomer named Penny picked up a pillow and set it gingerly on the floor next to Ivy. Ivy glanced sideways at the olive-skinned brunette, recognizing the expression on the woman's face. It was that look of bewilderment, as though she'd meant to stop off at the dry cleaners and had somehow ended up sitting on a faux kilim floor cushion with a bunch of strangers welcoming her with hushed tones and gentle handshakes.

Ivy waited for Toby's standard opening about grief being a personal journey, which she knew would come next. She took a deep breath, clasped the newcomer's hand, and closed her eyes. As heavyhearted as she felt, especially at night when the loneliness pricked at her like a million little needles, she was grateful to be at the point where she could now function on a daily basis. At least if she didn't think too far into the future.

"Let's talk about our past week. Ivy, would you like to start us off?" Toby asked, once the opening ritual was completed.

"Okay, I guess. I dreamed about Will last night . . . his accident again. He's on his bike, pedaling really fast, picking up speed downhill, when he runs the red light."

Ivy paused, not realizing that she had actually wanted to share this information with the group until the words were out of her mouth. It hit her just how much comfort this grief-stricken little menagerie had brought her over the past weeks.

"Usually I see this car come through the intersection and hit him broadside—which is pretty much how it happened—but this time, just as he's about to get hit, this huge lion runs out into the middle of street and stops right in front of the oncoming car.

"And instead of running the yellow, the car just stops. Then somehow Will is in the driver's seat, and he pulls the car very carefully over to the side of the road, where I'm sitting cross-legged on the sidewalk. And I watch him parallel park right in front of me. Will always joked that if he had an inch and a half on either side, he could park anywhere."

A wistful little smile crossed Ivy's face.

"So he parks the car and just sits there in the driver's seat smiling at me as the lion comes over. The lion is really huge, and I'm not sure if I should be afraid, but then he kind of nuzzles me and lies down on the sidewalk and puts his head in my lap. And I start stroking his mane. His fur is really rough and matted, and I try to untangle some of the knots with my fingers, really carefully so it doesn't hurt him, and he starts to purr like a house cat. Then the lion sort of morphs into Will. I try to tell him I'm sorry, I shouldn't have made him rush, but I can't seem to form the words. And then I wake up."

No one spoke for a moment, as if they are all coming out of their own dream states.

"Um, I don't know if this is appropriate," the newcomer Penny spoke up, "but I'm a psychologist, and I often work with dream interpretation in my practice."

"Ooh, can you tell us what the dream means?" asked Cathy.

"No, nothing like that. I just wanted to say that in dreams lions often stand for family, the pride. This lion seems to be protective, trying to save your . . . husband?" Penny looked at Ivy, who nodded. Ivy noted Penny's composure, understanding from her time with the group that it was often easier for people to remark on someone else's grief than talk about their own, especially at first.

"And what about not being able to get her words out?" another group member asked. "Is that like when you try to scream but can't make a sound?"

"That's pretty common. It can occur when we have something we want to express, or wish we had said already. Or it can be a feeling of helplessness; we want to scream or run, but we can't. But those are only generalizations," Penny cautioned.

"No, that all fits," Ivy said, tears welling. "Will wanted to start a family, and I wasn't ready. I didn't even know if I wanted kids. But instead of being honest with him, instead of telling him I was afraid it would ruin my career or I might be a lousy mother, I got resentful and rude to Will, who was the most loving guy in the world."

She nodded her head and let the tears spill.

· · · · ·

*I*vy was the first to arrive at the Culver Hotel, Mak's favorite Westside watering hole. She staked out a poufy flowered couch in the corner and glanced around the quirky lobby lounge with its eclectic mix of vintage furniture, enormous grand piano, and floor-to-ceiling sepia-toned movie stills. Ivy smiled; it was so Mak to hang out at a retro-hip historical landmark famous for having housed the notoriously raucous Munchkins during the filming of *The Wizard of Oz* back when the nearby Sony lot was still MGM.

It was just after five, so the crowd was still sparse, the clientele ranging from a few young hipsters to a handful of neighborhood seniors who looked old enough to actually have known the Munchkins. *Definitely not in Kansas*, Ivy thought to herself as she ordered two draft beers from a waitress with pink-tipped hair and a tattoo sleeve running the length of her right arm.

A few minutes later, Mak made her grand entrance. Ivy watched her friend lean across the marble bar to plant a kiss on the handsome, shaved-headed bartender's cheek before turning her attention to a young waitress with braids pulled up in a funky chignon. Ivy listened to their laughter as Mak spotted her from across the room.

"You must live in this place. You certainly seem to know everybody," Ivy said, greeting Mak with a kiss as she slid her beer across the table.

"What can I say? People flock to me," Mak replied, taking a big swig of her beer. "So how was the meeting?"

"I don't know," Ivy sighed. "Strange. Sad."

"No shit. That's why they call it grief group and not comedy improv."

Ivy rolled her eyes.

"It's all these brokenhearted people sitting around trying to figure out how to be alone for the rest of their lives."

"They won't be alone forever."

"Maybe not, but it sure seems like a long way off before they, *we*, rejoin the human race."

"Give it time, honeybunch. They'll get there. And so will you," Mak said, giving Ivy a maternal pat on the shoulder.

"I guess," Ivy said, pushing a bead of condensation down the side of her mug with her fingertip.

"What did you all talk about? No names, I know, just give me the gist."

"There was this shrink who just joined . . . nah, never mind," Ivy said, realizing she wasn't ready to replay her dream for Mak and shifted gears. "There's this young guy whose wife died in childbirth. Can you believe it? It's like something out of a Victorian novel. He doesn't get along with his own parents, who are some sort of fundamentalist wackos, so his late wife's parents are helping him raise his daughter. He moved into their basement apartment with baby Madison."

"Oh my God. That's about the saddest thing I've ever heard. How could he name his baby Madison? It's so nineties," said Mak.

Ivy shot her a *Be nice* glare, then changed the subject. "How's the love life?"

"You think grief group is sad, try online dating. Last night, I went out with a tax attorney who spent forty minutes talking about himself before we even ordered drinks," Mak laughed as she made a *knife across throat* gesture, then downed the rest of her beer.

17

*L*ater that evening, Ivy opened a bottle of wine and checked the freezer to see what she had on hand for dinner. As she was poking around, she heard a *meow*. The cat, a striped tabby she'd seen lurking around the garden a few times, was back. This time, right on her front stoop.

She opened the door to give the cat some water and it barged past her and ran right into the living room.

"Okay, I get it. You think you own the place."

Unfazed, the cat looked up at her, meowed again, then marched into the kitchen and staked out a spot next to the refrigerator, as if commanding Ivy to open up and fix him a snack. *Like now.*

"Sorry, pal. I'm a little short on groceries right now. You're not going to find anything in there except some expired yogurt and a couple of overripe avocados."

The cat didn't look like it was leaving anytime soon, so Ivy decided she'd better find something edible for him. She grabbed her key off the hook by the front door and started up the brick path toward the main house. She let herself into the dimly lit kitchen and headed straight for the Sub-Zero. As she was rooting around in hopes of locating some suitable cat fodder, she was startled by a low voice from across the room.

"Hungry?"

Ivy gasped, then saw Conrad sitting at the table by the window, the last bit of daylight illuminating the room. Rory was snoring at his feet.

"I'm sorry, I didn't realize anyone was in here. I was looking for something to feed the cat."

"We have a cat?" Conrad reached over and turned up the dimmer switch on the kitchen lights.

"He seemed right at home. I thought he might live here," Ivy said.

"I think it belongs to my neighbor. Dawn used to feed him, but I didn't know he was still coming around."

Ivy nodded and closed the fridge, not sure what to do next.

"Why don't we feed you first? I've got some linguine with Fernanda's homemade pesto here."

"That sounds fabulous, if you're sure I'm not disturbing you," Ivy said uncertainly.

"That's what you said the time I offered you a glass of wine by the pool."

"I did? You remember that?"

"I do, and you did," Conrad replied with a grin. "Trust me, if you were disturbing me, I would let you know. And you're not, so grab a bowl and a wineglass."

"Well, since you insist . . ." Ivy realized that other than that poolside glass of wine they'd shared nearly a month ago, she'd hardly seen him. She certainly hadn't shared a meal with him. But the pesto smelled so good and the invitation seemed so sincere, she opened the cupboard he pointed her toward and grabbed some dishes.

"I've got a nice Chianti too. Hold the fava beans," Conrad said as Ivy slid into a chair opposite, giving him a puzzled look. "Never mind, bad joke. Probably not your kind of movie anyway."

"What are you reading?" she asked, noticing a stack of magazines in front of him.

Conrad fanned them out so she could see the covers.

Ivy tried to restrain herself, but couldn't help but laugh. "I wouldn't have pegged you a for a *Teen People* guy," she said, noticing that magazine along with *Us Weekly*, *People*, and *In Touch*.

"Hey, no making fun. I have to keep up with who's hot and who's not. All part of the job," he responded.

"In other words, it's research."

"Precisely. Not as heady as yours, I grant you, but research just the same."

Ivy chuckled and helped herself to some pasta, while Conrad poured her a glass of wine. "In my defense, we'll be doing a lot of guest casting for my new series, so it's good to see who has the kind of following that can pull in some new viewers. Building a younger audience base and all that."

"Right, your show. So how's it going?"

"Well, we're working twelve-hour days, staffing the writers' room, scouting for locations, and getting ready to shoot the first episode of a thirteen-episode order. But overall, I'd say it's going pretty well, though it sort of feels like déjà vu all over again."

"Really? Why's that?"

Conrad thought a minute before giving her an answer. "There's this memoir, a Hollywood tell-all book called *You'll Never Eat Lunch in This Town Again* written by a rather caustic film producer. In it, she famously warned the wannabes of Hollywood that they should be very careful what they first succeed at because that's where they'd be stuck for the rest of their careers."

"And that's you? Stuck in what you first succeeded at?"

"Pretty much. Viewer-friendly police procedurals, that is, mindless cop shows," Conrad said, taking a sip of his wine. "Never mind. I'm just kvetching. I'm very grateful to have a show on the air at all, especially since it went right to a full series order instead of having to shoot a pilot and then wait around while the network twiddled their thumbs," he said, brushing the topic and the magazines aside. "How about your work? And I don't mean the garden, I can see that it is blossoming, literally."

"I'm a little stuck myself," Ivy admitted.

"How so?"

Ivy heard the sympathy—or was it curiosity?—in Conrad's tone but when he looked at her with those probing blue eyes, she felt her heart skip a beat.

"Well . . . at some point in the near future, I have to finish my dissertation. It's mostly done, but I've been dragging my feet about bringing it before my doctoral committee. And even though I handed off teaching my seminar to a colleague, I'll need to pick it up again next semester. But all I really want to do is focus on my product research."

"Which, as you'd said, is in a lab in Northern California while you're down here in a garden in Southern California?" Conrad asked gingerly.

Ivy sighed and nodded. "I know it's crazy. But it feels like if I don't clear my head first, I'm not going to get the research right. And if I don't get the research right, then the product won't succeed and I'll be right back where I started."

"Which is where?"

"Teaching science to college kids. Don't get me wrong, teaching is a noble career. My husband, Will, changed people's lives as a professor."

"But it's not what you want to do?" Conrad asked, a little more emphatically.

Ivy looked at him, surprised how easy it had been to share the career struggles she rarely discussed with anyone but Will. "Exactly."

"It's hard enough to sort out all this work-life stuff when you haven't just lost your best friend and partner," Conrad said.

Ivy sighed, and they sat in silence for a moment.

Conrad suddenly looked Ivy straight in the eye. "Grief is a fucking bitch, isn't it?" He hadn't meant it to be funny, but suddenly they were both laughing at the absurdity of living without their partners, of beating their grief, maybe of life itself.

"I don't really know what your product is," Conrad confessed, after they had composed themselves.

"Ah, well . . . it's an irrigation solution, a gel that retains water in the soil so that plant roots can tap into it and stay hydrated. It's designed to help increase crop yields. If we get it right, it could be an enormous benefit to agriculture, especially in drought-impacted areas."

"Wow," Conrad said, genuinely impressed.

"If you're interested, you're welcome to come to a lecture I'm giving about it at UCLA. One of my former professors asked me to talk to his climate science class. UCLA was one of the first universities to offer climate studies as a major."

"Very California of them," Conrad said drolly. "I'd love to hear more about your creation, it sounds fascinating. Besides, I'm obviously one of those people who needs to get educated. As you can see from this eight-thousand square foot monster, I'm woefully ignorant when it comes to the environment."

Ivy smiled and took a sip of wine. "While we're on the subject, I'd like to try my product on your garden. I hadn't planned to test residential applications for another year or so, but if you have no objection. . . ."

"Be my guest."

"Great. I'll draw up a design plan for the geo-thermal panels later," she quipped.

"Hey, I never said I was an early adopter."

"Oh, you're way past early," Ivy said.

"Ouch," Conrad laughed.

"So who owns the product? You or the university?" he asked.

"I'm working with a private investor at a lab she funds, although the university is tangentially involved. I guess we'll all share in the patent. I haven't really thought that far ahead," Ivy said vaguely, hoping Conrad couldn't see her blush in the dim light. Will had been such an active force in the business side of her work, she'd always assumed he'd be there to help her. She looked down at her pasta, praying the tears wouldn't start to flow as she added one more thing she missed about Will to the mental list that grew longer as the days went by.

Conrad cleared his throat, waiting for Ivy to look up at him.

"I don't want to be a buttinsky, as my mother used to say, but let me give you a little advice. You need to own the IP, the intellectual property."

"I know what IP is," Ivy said, trying not to bristle. Men had condescended to her throughout her academic career and she wasn't about to let Conrad start.

"Of course you do, sorry. I never went to college, but one thing I've learned in my career is that he or she who owns the underlying rights to the intellectual property has the control."

"Well, my investor is taking care of all that . . ."

"Right, right," Conrad said, backing off. "I'm sure you know what you're doing. I guess I've been around show-biz math, not to mention morality, for so long, I don't trust anyone—even academics and investors out to save the world. Ignore me."

Conrad stood and headed to the pantry. He opened a cupboard, took something out, and came back to the table.

"For the cat," he said, placing a can of sardines in Ivy's hand.

18

Ivy and Mak sat on the ground next to a broad patch covered in dark brown mulch. Just three months after she'd moved to Malibu, Ivy's handiwork was evident, with newly planted purple fountain grass shimmering alongside the pathway. Ivy jiggled bright orange marigold plants out of their little plastic pony packs and planted them in rows nearby. Mak sprawled on the ground beside her, her face upturned to catch the half-hearted autumn rays.

"Explain to me again why you're off on a Monday," Ivy said.

"We're on hiatus."

"Meaning what, in regular people speak?"

"Every few weeks the writers need some catch-up time to work on new episodes, so the cast and crew get a little time off," Mak said.

"Gotcha, I think. What are the leading ladies like?"

"Gorgeous, of course, a little high maintenance considering this is the first series for both of them. The diva stuff doesn't usually pop up until season two or three, but these girls are ahead of schedule. They're going to keep Conrad on his toes for sure."

"I'm sure he can stand his ground with a couple of beautiful young actresses," Ivy said, laughing as she patted the soil around a marigold's crown.

"How's the dragon lady investor?" Mak asked.

"Alexandra? I saw her at the lab on Friday. It's kind of weird, though . . ."

"What's weird?"

"I thought she'd be all over me to get back to work full time. But she doesn't seem to care that much."

"Maybe she trusts you and your team."

"I guess. One thing's for sure, though, if I worked in a university lab instead of a privately funded one, they'd have booted me out already," Ivy said, surveying the expanse of resuscitated garden with a sense of satisfaction that surprised her.

"Look who's coming," Mak said, nodding toward the main house. Hudson, wearing crisp cargo shorts and a khaki bucket hat, strode purposefully down the pathway, Rory trotting along behind him.

"Hey, Hudson," Ivy called. "How're you doing?"

"I'm here to help," Hudson announced.

"Really? And what exactly do you plan to do?" Mak asked.

"Dig," Hudson replied, pulling a kid-size trowel out of his back pocket.

"Great idea," Ivy said, handing him one of the pony packs. "You can start over there with these salvias. They're pollinator plants."

"They attract good bugs," Hudson said to Mak.

"Isn't that special," Mak replied, ruffling Hudson's hair. "Well, I've got to run. I've got a date with a realtor tonight and it's going to take me all afternoon to get ready."

"Wait, what happened to the tax attorney? Or was it the ER doctor?" Ivy asked.

"Yesterday's news," Mak said with a dismissive wave.

"You know you're too picky, right?" Ivy said, to which Mak gave her a *moi?* face and headed up the path.

"What are you waiting for?" Ivy said, turning to Hudson. "Start digging."

Hudson broke into a grin and stuck his trowel into the ground.

"There you guys are," a male voice called out a few minutes later. Ivy had been so busy supervising Hudson, she hadn't noticed this new intruder until he was right next to them. He looked like he was about thirty, five foot ten with dark brown hair, and just short of handsome.

"I'm JP Ortiz, fix-it guy. Fernanda's nephew," he said with a broad smile that showed startlingly white teeth against his dark complexion. He rubbed a hand through his thick hair, and Ivy felt a pang of lust pass through her, the gesture was so reminiscent of how Will used to brush his long hair back off his forehead.

"Ivy Bauer, gardener," she replied.

"She's fixing Mommy's garden," Hudson said, with a twinge of unconcealed wistfulness that sent an unexpected chill through Ivy.

"Mr. Reed asked me to stop by to check out the sprinkler situation. Looks like you're going to need a low-volume drip irrigation system," JP said.

"An adjustable gear-drive system would be great," Ivy said, impressed. "It's pretty dry out here."

"Worse every year. I'll be back with the stuff tomorrow. I've got to get to school now."

"You have kids to pick up?" Ivy asked politely, not sure if she really wanted to learn about his family as much as she wanted an effective drip system. But Will had taught her that when you made people feel good about themselves, you usually got what you wanted.

Hudson laughed and JP joined in. Even Rory seemed to get the joke.

"He doesn't have kids," Hudson said. *Duh*.

"No, *I'm* the student, master's program in engineering at UCLA," JP said with a self-deprecating little smile. "Lucky for me UCLA is on the Westside or I never could have kept this job. Amazing how geography defines everything in LA. Have you noticed that?"

"That and traffic," Ivy responded dolefully.

"And money, of course. But I guess that's true everywhere," JP said. "Gotta run. Let's get you out of Ivy's hair and back inside to Fernanda. She's got your lunch ready," JP said, hoisting Hudson in the air like a sack of potatoes.

"Be careful. I have tools here," Hudson yelled.

"Call your mutt," JP added, jostling him high up in the air.

Ivy watched as Hudson broke into a big belly laugh, that deep, unselfconscious sound that can only come from a small child.

"She's not a mutt," he gasped between giggles. "And if you don't believe me, you can call the American Kennel Club."

"Come on, mutt," JP called, and Hudson laughed even harder.

Ivy watched the flex of JP's biceps as he clasped Hudson's twiglike torso and placed him across his shoulder, the pair of them looking like a happy two-headed beast as they disappeared up the path.

19

*H*i, everyone, I'm so happy to be back. Your garden is really coming along!" Ivy said as Hudson's schoolmates gathered around her in the Village's backyard, proud to show off their flowers. "And I've brought someone who's made something very cool for you."

"His name is JP," Hudson yelled excitedly, waving to JP and Fernanda nearby. JP had a big wooden planter box that he placed along the garden's shady back fence.

"Hi guys," JP said, waving to the happy little gaggle. "I made this planter out of cedar for you. Wait until you see what Ivy has in mind!"

"Thanks, JP," Ivy said, smiling at her new friend. "It's going to be perfect for what we're planting next. Any guesses, anyone?"

"I know, I know," Hudson hollered, waving wildly.

"But you can't tell," Ivy said, shushing him.

The kids called out their answers: bug garden, puppy house, wading pool.

"Nope," Ivy said. "Who here loves veggies?"

Little hands shot in the air. *Gotta love California kids*, Ivy thought.

"That's good. Because we are planting—wait for it—a salad garden!"

"And when it's grown we get to make a salad and eat it!" Hudson said importantly.

The kids went wild, though Ivy suspected there were at least a few non–veggie lovers in the crowd.

"JP is putting soil in our planter box, then we're all going to plant these seeds. Take a look." Ivy gathered the children around and read the names of seed packets, and the corresponding garden signs, for lettuce, Swiss chard, spinach, and carrots.

"Check this out," JP added, pushing a wire trellis into the soil. "We're going to grow beans that will climb up this pole."

"Like Jack and the Beanstalk?" one of the kids asked, others echoing the question.

"Exactly!" Ivy replied, throwing JP a thumbs-up as Fernanda looked on with a giant grin.

20

onrad slid quietly into a seat in the back of the amphitheater-shaped classroom. A stickler for punctuality, which he considered a lost virtue as well as a show biz necessity, he was annoyed at himself for being five minutes late. The parklike UCLA campus with its beautiful ivy-covered brick buildings pocked by a random mix of contemporary structures was so vast that he'd gotten lost despite the maps mounted at nearly every walkway intersection. He'd finally hailed a student with a skateboard tucked under his arm and asked him to point out Young Hall.

Fortunately, Ivy had just been introduced and was stepping up to the front of the class of a hundred or so students when he took his seat. In her jeans and blazer with her hair in a neat topknot, Ivy looked more like a scientist than a gardener, yet Conrad felt strangely nervous for her. *These kids*, he thought glancing around, *so self-assured in their T-shirts with the ironic sayings and their hipster glasses, staring at laptops purchased by their parents. Will they even appreciate what she has to share with them?*

Ivy nodded to her hosting professor. "Thank you. And thank you for letting me borrow your desk," she added breezily to a male student sitting in the front row as she placed a small cardboard box on his desktop.

"So, there's a pretty funny story about the origin of my product," she said, taking two glass Mason jars out of the box. "My husband's sister had just given birth to twin girls, and we were visiting them in Fresno. And I'm a little embarrassed to admit this, but I'd never changed a diaper in my life."

A few people chuckled, and Conrad smiled to himself.

"Hey, in my own defense, I am an only child," Ivy said as she opened one of the jars and held it out to a student. "Give this a sniff and tell the class what it is, please."

The student dutifully stuck his nose close to the jar. "Water?"

"Correct. Proves my theory that A students always sit in the front row."

A few more students chuckled.

"Anyway, while everybody was oohing and aahing over the twins, who I must say for the record are pretty darn cute, two things struck me. First, that tiny babies could pee so much. And second, that disposable diapers could hold so much urine. I was so intrigued that I immediately took a box of Huggies into the kitchen and spent the next three hours experimenting by increasing the water level to test the diaper's retention. It struck me that if I could eliminate the polyacrylate in the gel—which, I'm proud to say, I've done—we'd have an amazing product. I got so excited, I didn't even realize how much water I was adding until the diaper—"

"Exploded?" a student in the back row yelled and everyone laughed.

"You got it. Drained all over the kitchen counter," Ivy said. She held up another jar and shook it to show the class the white powder inside, then poured the powder into the water, screwed the top back on and began shaking the jar as she talked.

"I'm sure you all know that there are two branches of soil science: edaphology is soil science as it relates to living plants—my specialty; and pedology, which looks at soil profiles and classification. But really, who wants to classify soil samples when you could be hired by a winery to cultivate grape vines?"

Conrad saw the growing curiosity in the room as students gathered near, coming along the sides of the tiered classroom to see what she was doing with the jar. He was relieved, and then surprised at his relief, to watch the students become more and more engaged as Ivy spoke.

"This is HydraHold," Ivy said, holding the jar up high for everyone to see, like the Lion King holding baby Simba aloft. "It's a nontoxic gel solution that absorbs two hundred times its weight in water. After it's distributed at the root bed, the plant roots find it and it provides slow and steady hydration to crops. It's far more sustainable than sprinkler or subsurface irrigation techniques."

I'll be damned, Conrad thought, *she may not want to be a teacher, but she's awfully good at it.* He was impressed with her smooth delivery and skillful storytelling, like an actor who could recite dialogue and manage props, from cocktail shaker to defibrillator, at the same time. It looked simple enough, but he knew how much practice it took. As if reading his mind, Ivy glanced up at the back row and caught Conrad's eye. She gave him a nearly imperceptible eyebrow lift. *You actually showed up.*

"Okay, I think we're good. Would you stand up here next to me and cup your hands together?" She nodded to the second row and a Bruin-shirted student joined her at the front of the class and held out her hands. Ivy unscrewed the Mason jar and carefully turned it upside down into the student's cupped palms. At first, nothing happened.

"Wait for it . . . wait for it . . . here we go."

After a moment, a wobbly gel slid into her hands. The students crowded around to get a closer look. Ivy began pouring out small globs of the clear gel into their palms. They rolled, patted, and sniffed at it as she continued. One student even gave it a lick before grabbing a paper towel from the stack Ivy had placed on the desk.

"The powder absorbs the water and the reactants trigger the chemical reaction, which rearranges the constituent atoms to create the gel. Yield rates have been really promising in our test lab up north and at the UC Davis co-op. By the way, I'm getting ready to field-test the product on a private ten-acre citrus orchard in Malibu if anyone wants to join me."

Ivy tossed Conrad an inquiring glance, as if to say, *I hope it was okay that I just invited a class of students to hang out in your backyard.* Conrad gave her a little head nod in return, intrigued that he was feeling both pleased and proud to have become her test case.

Turning back to the students, she said, "Fair warning, though, I will put you to work. After all, exploiting students, from under-grads to postdocs, is a time-honored tradition. But at least I pay in beer and pizza."

Winter

21

A few days later, Conrad settled into his director's chair in front of a video monitor to watch as cameras rolled on a deserted stretch of highway near LA International Airport. It was chilly at six a.m., and he was glad he'd remembered to grab his Lakers jacket from the car. *What am I doing out here at the crack of dawn? This really is a young person's game.*

They'd gotten lucky with the marine layer, which shut out the harsh shadows and created an eerie haze for the morning's shoot.

"Here you go," Mak said, handing Conrad a metal thermos.

"What's this?"

"Coffee. Black. I know how much you loathe those little cardboard cups from craft services."

"So glad you're out here calling the shots," Conrad said, smiling as he twisted open the thermos.

"Drink up, boss. It's gonna be a long one."

Conrad watched as two burly guys rigged a camera on the hood of a police car, while a couple of uniformed motorcycle cops looked on. *Only in Hollywood,* he thought, *actual cops watching the setup for a scene with fake cops.*

"Yeah, and you know how I love stunt days," he said sarcastically. "The bar's set so high with all those fucking *Batman* and *Superman* and *Whatever-Man* movies, a mere network series doesn't stand a chance."

"This isn't a *series,*" Mak corrected him. "This is a ReedWorks production." She'd gotten a permit to film in a remote area behind LAX that had been closed long ago because as the airport expanded over the years, the neighborhood was eventually directly under the flight path, not only noisy but dangerous, with the runways so close to the houses. It was a spooky spot, an urban ghost town of unused streets and buildings a mile or so square, surrounded by a massive chain-link fence. Perfect for their purposes.

As the creator-writer-producer, a "triple hyphenate" in Hollywood parlance, Conrad could have stayed in the production trailer or even back in his office on the lot working on the script for the next episode, while he let the director handle the shoot. But there was a tone he was determined to get right—stylish contemporary with a hint of throwback irony. Otherwise the show was going to be just another cheesy procedural. He had more riding on this series than he cared to admit. Not just his livelihood, but his dignity. And there was no way he was about to let a hotshot young director jeopardize that.

Dexter Roberts was a twenty-nine-year-old USC film school

wunderkind who'd shot a series of award-winning commercials for luxury brands like Mercedes and Cartier. He had a beautifully liquid filming style that was elegant, spare, and undeniably hot all at the same time. The network suits "had to have him," even though he'd never directed a series before. Conrad was more cautious, concerned that Dexter still had a lot to learn. *Shooting stunt cars with actual people in them was a lot more challenging than shooting parked cars for commercials.*

Conrad leaned back in his chair and focused intently on the monitor. He knew to watch the screen rather than the live action, as that was the true barometer of how the show would look when it was eventually televised. Only rookies got caught up in anything that lived beyond the box.

"Hey man," Conrad shouted as a clean-cut college-aged guy drifted in front of the monitor. The kid swiveled around, thrilled to see that he was needed after all the hurry-up-and-wait of the early morning production setup.

"Yes, sir. What can I do for you?"

"You can get the fuck out my sight line, that's what you can do for me."

"Sorry," said the young man, visibly deflated as he sunk behind an equipment trailer.

"Glad he's getting a quality internship. What the business is really like and all," Mak quipped in the straightforward style that Conrad pretended to loathe but secretly admired.

"Yeah. Whatever," Conrad replied sourly, shifting his focus back to the small screen. Finally, the shot was framed, the stunt drivers were prepped, and everyone was ready to go.

"Action," Dexter yelled over the PA system.

"Action," the assistant director repeated through his mic.

Conrad felt a stabbing pain pass through his abdomen. Nerves, he thought, surprised that he was having such a painful physical reaction to a shoot. Then again, this was the first car crash he'd filmed since Dawn had died in a very real one, so maybe it wasn't so surprising that he felt triggered. The stunt would be followed by an emotional scene that the two young stars had to carry. Conrad wasn't sure which one would be harder for Dexter to pull off. He took a deep breath and steeled himself for the car chase.

On camera, a black-and-white cruiser with two women inside raced up the street that doubled as a freeway on-ramp in pursuit of a souped-up Chevy. After numerous stops and starts so the camera could capture different angles, the cruiser made a wild hairpin turn, swung around in front of the other car, and screeched to a stop, forcing the Chevy to ram into a center divider and flip on its side, with the help of a crane and a dozen crewmembers.

"Cut! And we're out," the assistant director called. "Thanks, guys. Nice job. Stunt crew, swap out, please."

The two stuntwomen jumped out of the cop car, high-fiving each other for a perfect performance, while two stuntmen carefully extricated themselves from the upended Chevy. The AD and first assistant cleared the stunt crew and steered the male actors, already made up with their postaccident scrapes and scratches, to their marks, while another makeup artist touched up the two female leads, Ceci Lindstrom and Nakia Williams. Conrad watched the two costars chatting amicably as they got their touch-up and sincerely hoped that they'd remain friends as their stock grew in the business. Not always the case when the competition set in.

He had interviewed nearly three hundred young women for the leading roles, a task that some might have envied but that he found painfully tedious, sorting through all the pitiable hopefuls looking for some genuine spark of talent. Ceci, who played Pulaski, was a former Miss Wisconsin. She had creamy skin and stick-straight blond hair, and was from an honest-to-God farm family. When Conrad had read through some scenes with Ceci at the audition, he'd been thrilled to discover that not only could she deliver straight dialogue, but she also had a knack for comedy. If he could develop that sparkle—and he was sure he could—he'd be able to inject some humor into the show.

Nakia, aka Jones, was a Yale drama school grad with an athlete's body, glowing brown skin, and an Afro worthy of Angela Davis, at least when she wasn't shooting. Total opposites, it was uncanny how much the camera loved the two women and how well they complemented each other on-screen. Conrad had been ecstatic at the pairing, breathing a huge sigh of relief when he finally convinced the network honchos that they'd be better off *creating* stars than *casting* them.

"Dex, let's talk through this next scene before you roll. Why don't you give everyone a ten?" Conrad said into his headset.

"I've got this, Conrad. We're ready to roll," Dexter's peevish voice came back through the mic from the production trailer.

"Actors to your marks, please," Dexter said over the PA.

"Roger that," the AD said as he steered the girls to their marks near the Chevy and placed them facing each other.

"Dexter," Conrad said more insistently into his headset. "This is a delicate scene where the tension has to mount. You can't start in a tight shot with the girls facing off against each other or there's nowhere to go. It's got to be deftly handled." *So that intelligent and discerning people—people like Ivy—will tune in and not want to throw up.*

Conrad was surprised to find himself wondering what Ivy would think about *Pulaski & Jones*. But there it was; he wanted her to like his show. Or, at least, not consider what he did for a living completely mindless horseshit.

"Let's talk," Conrad repeated through clenched teeth.

"Fine, let's talk," Dex whined.

The AD called a ten-minute cast and crew break. Conrad took off his headset and looped it over the arm of his chair. When he stood, he felt an even sharper pain suddenly shooting through his midsection. *It must be all this sparring with Dexter that's got me tied up in knots*, he thought. *It's not like I haven't gone through shit like this a hundred times before.*

He took a couple of steps toward the street and stumbled, reaching back to steady himself on the chair arm. As if she possessed eyes in the back of her head, which Conrad had long suspected, Mak caught Conrad's stagger and was at his side in an instant.

"It's nothing. I took a long run yesterday and I'm a little stiff is all," Conrad lied.

"Why don't you sit a sec, boss?" she suggested, half easing and half forcing Conrad back into his chair.

"I'll be fine. Quit fussing." Conrad started to stand, but took one step and clutched at his side, his face turning white. Mak grabbed him by the arm before he hit the ground and helped him back into his director's chair. He took a few deep breaths and tried to regain his composure, aware of a conversation buzzing somewhere on the periphery.

"Hey, Mak. You on a break?" the twentysomething network publicist called. "I've got Tasha with me for her interview with *Teen Ink*." She came a little closer, holding a very cute little girl by the hand. Tasha was nearly eleven, but she'd been cast to play Jones's six-year-old daughter so her small size worked in her favor. When she became a legal adult at eighteen and the child labor laws were lifted, she'd likely work nonstop playing thirteen-year-olds.

"We're taking a ten," Mak shot back to the publicist, giving Conrad a glance, as if to say, *We've got a problem*. Thinking fast, she called over to the intern that Conrad had blasted earlier in the day.

"Hey, Brian. Can you please escort Tasha and our network publicist, Alyssa, over to the craft services table to check out the Red Vines? I'll join you ladies in a minute. I just have to sort something out here," Mak said.

The intern—grateful to finally have something to do—led the little girl and the publicist away. A gaggle of extras and crew members followed along, chatting up the child as though she were already a superstar.

And people wondered why so many kid actors became felons.

"How you feeling?" Mak asked, giving Conrad the once-over. "You want to lie down in the makeup trailer for a minute?"

"Thank you, no," Conrad grunted, his breathing labored as he eased back into the director's chair. "I don't want the vultures to start circling prematurely."

22

hoever said nobody walks in LA wasn't a hiker, Ivy thought as she and Hudson headed toward a trailhead in the hills above Conrad's house, Rory loping along behind them. Conrad had told her about the hiking trails that snaked through the foothills of Malibu, and ever since, she'd found a sort of peace walking the eucalyptus-lined paths, the foliage mottling the glare of the afternoon sun.

She glanced down at Hudson, trying to shake her nervousness about being solely in charge of a little human, though he seemed fine trudging along beside her without complaint. Anyway, it wasn't like Ivy could have refused Fernanda's request to keep an eye on Hudson after she'd come flying out of the house saying Conrad was in the hospital.

Now that she was the designated babysitter, Ivy thought maybe a hike and some fresh air might distract Hudson. So here she was, walking in LA with a kid and a dog and hoping that it was a false alarm and Fernanda would be home, Conrad in tow, before dinner.

"We need to be prepared," Hudson had told her once they'd settled on going for a walk in the hills. He'd led her to a closet just off the kitchen where flip-flops, tennis rackets, and golf clubs were all neatly labeled and stacked in the cupboards. Fernanda's handiwork, of course. What guy would label his sports crap?

"You have to drink a lot of water on the trail. Rory too," Hudson said, extracting a couple of reusable sports bottles from a bin. "You can die of thirst in three days, you know."

"I've heard that," Ivy said, taking the bottles back into the kitchen. While she was filling them at the filtered-water spigot, she noticed that the names *Hudson* and *Dawn* were scratched into the plastic. The unexpected realization that she'd be drinking out of Dawn's water bottle, a bottle that had probably been used by Dawn not so very long ago, sent chills of grief down her spine. Not just for herself, but for Hudson and Conrad, who she knew were as rocked by the daily reminders of their loss as she was of hers.

"And this is super important," Hudson said, grabbing a whistle strung on a lariat hanging on the closet doorknob. "I always take this baby with me. If you get lost, you blow it really hard. And stay in one place, don't move around, or people can't find you."

"Good to know, thanks."

A few minutes later they were on the trail, hiking through the leafy mélange of greens and browns. After a few minutes, they came to a point where the path split in two, the righthand trail going uphill and the other downward.

"Which way?" Ivy asked.

"You might like this way," Hudson said pointing toward the downhill path. "It's a little easier, and you can always tell it's the path to the left if you do this." He pointed his left forefinger straight and opened his thumb to make a 90-degree angle. "See, it makes an L. That's the first letter in left."

"I see," Ivy said. "So no school today?"

Hudson nodded.

"All day?"

He nodded again.

"Why not?"

"Teacher training."

"I see," Ivy said. "You like to hike? You seemed pretty prepared for the trail."

"Uh-huh. Mommy and me used to walk up here sometimes.
And Conrad says it keeps him and the damn dog from getting fat."

Ivy glanced over at Hudson, hearing the wistful tone in his
voice. Her pain was as familiar to her now as her own face in the
mirror, but she couldn't begin to fathom what loss felt like to a
four-year-old.

"Look, Ivy," Hudson called, pausing in a clearing beside a
massive growth of leathery cacti. "Do you know what kind of
cactus this is?"

Ivy instantly recognized the beavertail cactus with its broad,
flat appendages, commonplace throughout California. "Hmm, let
me see," she said, moving closer to inspect the plant through her
imaginary microscope.

"Don't get too close," Hudson cautioned, throwing a protective arm across her torso like a carpool parent who'd braked too
swiftly.

"Good point," she said.

"Ha! You made a joke!"

Ivy chuckled at his reaction to her unintentional pun.

"I give up," she said, shaking her head in defeat. "What is it?"

"It's a beaver-butt cactus."

"A beaver-butt cactus? I don't think I've heard of that one."

"That's 'cause I made it up," he laughed. "But it's somethin'
like that."

"Maybe a . . . beavertail?" she asked.

"That's it," he said excitedly. "Ding, ding, ding! And you are the grand-prize winner!"

"Gosh, thanks. What did I win?"

They walked a few minutes in silence, Ivy watching as Hudson examined sticks and weeds along the way. They came to a cairn on the side of the trail, one of those little rock piles that people place as location markers, or, perhaps, just as confirmation of their own existence. *I was here. I matter. I left rocks to prove it.*

Hudson stopped, scoured the earth for a suitable stone, scraped it clean, and balanced it carefully atop the pile. Ivy wondered if he'd ever paused in this exact spot, picked out the perfect rock, and added it to the stack, his mother gazing on in awe at the flawless little creature she'd produced. She stifled an unexpected sob, unable to stop herself from picturing the child she and Will might have had.

Ivy took a big swig from her Dawn bottle, as Hudson finished with his rock pile, dusted his hands together, as if to say, *Mission accomplished*, and motioned for them to move along.

"Are you a real scientist?" he asked.

"I will be if I ever finish school."

"You're too old for school."

"Don't I know it," Ivy groaned.

"I have a friend at my school named Kenny. He says I'm a worrywart."

"A worrywart? I never studied one of those. Is it a plant or an animal?"

"Nuh-uh. It's a kid who worries all the time." Ivy noticed Hudson's chin beginning to tremble as he stopped to inspect a clump of toadstools on the side of the path.

She took a step toward him, but stopped, more comfortable offering logic than hugs. "That's not very nice of Kenny. Besides, I would say you were more of a planner than a worrywart."

Hudson looked at her, about to say something, then suddenly began to stomp on the toadstools, pulverizing them until there was just a little puddle of grayish mush.

"When I was little," she told him, "I went to a slumber party where the other girls waited until I fell asleep, and then they connected all the freckles on my face with a Magic Marker. It took me three days to wash it off."

"That's not very nice."

"No, not nice at all."

They continued on, each pondering their childhood wounds, until Ivy felt a little nudge. Hudson had wiggled his fingers into her hand, sharing Rory's leash between them.

"It gets easier," she said, wishing she could channel Toby. *What would a grief counselor say to a four-year-old who'd lost the center of his solar system?* "Losing someone you love."

"How do you know?"

"My husband died around the same time as your mom."

"Oh. What was his name?"

"Will. His name was Will."

"He's never coming home."

"No, he's never coming home." Ivy flashed on Conrad lying in a hospital bed, and even though she was pretty sure she didn't believe in God, she said a little prayer that he'd be home soon and no one would have to tell this boy any more bad news, at least not for a very long time. She realized with a start that she wanted Conrad to come home, too, and not just for Hudson's sake.

"Do you miss him? Your dead husband?" Hudson asked, pulling her out of her thoughts.

Ivy didn't think even Toby would know how to field this one. What could she possibly tell him? That she missed him so much it felt as if someone had taken an axe to her chest, cleaved open her heart, and left her bleeding? She stopped on the trail and turned to face Hudson.

"I miss him all the time. Just like you miss your mom. But I have this nice group of people that I talk to who help me get used to missing him. If you ever want to talk about your mom, you can talk to me," she said softly, as afraid as she was hopeful that he might take her up on her offer someday.

23

The temperature had dropped along with the setting sun as Ivy and Hudson pulled up in front of JP's garage-top apartment in a neat, working-class neighborhood. As they got out of the car, Ivy noticed that the building was freshly painted and had a close-trimmed front lawn. She trudged up the stairs behind Hudson, grateful that Fernanda had enlisted JP's help with the evening portion of her Hudson duty. *My reward for playing sitter,* she thought, *though it turned out to be a fun day aside from concerns about Conrad.*

"Welcome," JP said, flinging open the front door as a string of f-bombs exploded from the rap music playing inside. He glanced at Ivy, embarrassed at the lyrics, then clapped his hands over Hudson's ears, sending the boy into a fit of giggles.

"You didn't hear that, Hudster."

"We went to the Santa Monica Pier," Hudson said, showing JP a stuffed mouse. "Ivy won it for me."

"Cool," JP said as he ushered them inside, turning off the music as they entered.

"Thanks for having us." Ivy's mouth began to water at the tangy fragrance of herbs and onions. "Yum. What is that? It smells amazing."

"Specialty of the house. Chicken pepián."

"I told you he was a good cooker," Hudson crowed triumphantly to Ivy.

"I didn't mean for you to go to so much trouble. When you said 'come over for a bite,' I thought you meant we'd go out for a pizza or something," Ivy apologized, trying to smooth her hair back into its ponytail.

"It's no trouble at all. I love to cook, and I never have anyone to cook for except myself."

"See? He loves to cook and never has anyone to cook for 'cept himself," Hudson echoed. "Fernanda taught him."

"That's right. She says food is to a Guatemalan what air is to everyone else."

Ivy handed him a bottle of wine. "I wasn't sure what to bring. It's Rioja, from Conrad's everyday shelf," she said.

"Nice, let's open her up." JP headed into the kitchen.

"Can I help?" Ivy called after him.

"Nope, just make yourselves at home."

Ivy looked around the space, deceptively large once you got past the entryway. The interior was an artful blend of simple contemporary pieces and original features like built-in nooks and hardwood floors, scuffed with age to a rich russet. Above the worn leather couch hung a striking metal sculpture, twisted wire and steel that vaguely resembled a city skyline. And in the corner, a spiral staircase led to the level below.

Hudson was already making a beeline for the stairs when JP emerged from the kitchen with the wine and a juice box.

"Hey," he said firmly. "You know the rule. You don't go downstairs without me."

"But I want to show Ivy."

"Okay, then we all go together."

If the apartment's upstairs was a surprise to Ivy, the downstairs was a revelation. What looked like it had once been a two-car garage had been completely revamped as a workshop. Tables were littered with welding tools, wire cutters, even an oxy-acetylene torch. On one side of the room was a bin filled with scrap metal in more shades of rust than Ivy realized existed. In the center of the room was a table unlike any she'd ever seen. It was heavy steel plate, at least an inch thick, with a grid of holes in the center.

"It's an acorn table," JP said, catching her gaze.

"For squirrels?" Hudson asked. He reached for a hunk of metal on the table, and JP gently redirected his hand to a piece with smooth edges.

"Why do they call it an acorn table?" Ivy asked.

"You know, I have no idea. Have to look that up, I guess."

"What's it for?"

"You put the steel pieces in these holes and then apply heat and pressure so you can bend them into different shapes. Here's what I'm working on now," JP said, guiding them to the back of the workshop. There on a steel bench was a sculpture about four feet tall, strips of aged metal braided together like vines that opened up like a blossoming flower.

"You made this?" Ivy said, wondering how the metal piece could be so delicate and substantial at the same time. JP flipped a switch, and Ivy gasped as she heard water beginning to gurgle up through the fountain. A couple of drops spilled over the side onto the leaflike base and then the water stopped.

"It's a fountain!" Hudson shouted.

"It will be when I get the water pressure working," JP said, annoyed.

"I think it may be the most beautiful thing I've ever seen," Ivy said, staring at the piece in wonder.

"You're obviously food-deprived," JP laughed, though clearly touched by the praise. "Let's go upstairs and eat."

After dinner, Ivy and JP sat at the table drinking wine while Hudson watched *Toy Story*.

"What'd you tell Hudson?" JP asked, as the voices of Buzz and Woody drifted in from the other end of the room.

Ivy lowered her voice. "I told him that Conrad was having a checkup and that the doctor needed him to stay overnight. I'm not sure he believed me, even though it's more or less the truth."

"Sounds good. Fernanda said they were waiting for some results to come back. There wasn't really anything she could do but hang out."

"Doesn't he have any family?"

"Not really. His parents have passed. I think he might have a cousin somewhere back East, but no one who's going to come rushing to his bedside."

"That's so sad. It's a good thing he's got Fernanda."

"And believe me, she's not going anywhere as long as he's in the hospital. She is mad loyal to him."

"If he stays in, what will, what should . . ." Ivy let the thought trail off, embarrassed to admit that she was afraid she'd get stuck with Hudson.

JP poured them both a little more wine and let the moment pass.

Ivy glanced at the sculpture on the wall, wondering if JP had made it. "I didn't know you were an artist," she commented, happy to change the subject.

"It's just a hobby."

"Hobby? That fountain is incredible."

"Thanks, still a work in progress."

"What got you started? In art, I mean."

"Fernanda. When I was a kid she gave me a little toolbox, and I'd go to work with her and try to fix things. I'm sure I broke more stuff than I fixed. But I've always loved seeing if I could build things that were beautiful and functional. This place has been my biggest project to date."

"What do you mean?" Ivy asked, puzzled.

"Fernanda owns this building. She bought it and I renovated it. She owns another property too."

"I had no idea she was a real estate mogul."

"Looks can be deceiving."

Ivy blushed in embarrassment. "I'm sorry. I didn't mean—"

"I'm just giving you a hard time," JP said with a smile.

"So when do you finish your degree?" she asked, switching topics.

"Another year. Feels like forever," JP sighed.

"I know what you mean." Ivy thought grimly about how much she still had to do to finish her dissertation and launch Hydra-Hold. *Sometimes it seems so much easier to keep my hands in the dirt in Conrad's garden.*

She rose and started to clear their plates.

"Let me do that," JP said, standing and taking the plates from her. "You look tired. Go sit with Hudson."

"I think I'll just sit right here for a few more minutes," she said.

"Good, then I will too. The dishes can wait," JP said, setting the plates back on the table and sitting down again. "So how do you like it down here? Must be a big change from the Bay Area."

"I can't think of anything that hasn't changed lately," she replied, with a *what are you gonna do* shrug.

He paused, giving her a sympathetic smile. "When I moved to the States as a kid, I thought my whole world had turned upside down and that I'd never adjust. But somehow I figured it out. Just like you will."

"Thank you. I appreciate that," she said, returning the smile. They sat in silence for a moment, as though wanting to continue the conversation but not sure where to go next.

"Ivy," Hudson called out from the other room.

"Yes, honey?"

"Can we go home now? I'm tired."

"Of course," she said. "I think you're on your own with those dishes."

"No problem," JP said, standing.

Ivy watched as he stacked the dishes, noticing how strong his forearms looked as he reached across the table. She wondered how it would feel to have arms like those hold her again.

24

*M*ak heard the familiar *irasshaimase* greeting when she sat down at the sushi bar at Sugarfish in Hollywood. She opened her menu and, as usual, grimaced at the prices. It was only a chain restaurant, but it was an LA Westside chain restaurant and sticker shock went with the territory.

With Conrad in the hospital and production shut down for a few days, I might as well treat myself, she thought, fully aware that she was stress eating.

As she powered her way through a rainbow roll, a good-looking, dark-haired guy with a throwback Tom Selleck moustache slid onto the stool next to her. He shoved his phone in his jacket pocket, greeted the chef, and placed an order for yellowtail and an Asahi.

"Something else for you?" the chef asked Mak as he cleared her plate.

"A couple of pieces of California roll and an order of eel, please."

The man watched her for a moment, then leaned over with a conspiratorial wink.

"That stuff's not fat-free, you know," he said.

Mak looked at him, surprised that this total stranger was negging her. He grinned, white teeth showing under his bushy moustache. Mak thought there was something deliciously mischievous about him and burst into laughter.

"Don't I know you from somewhere?" he asked.

"Oh, come on. Does that line really work on anyone these days?"

"No, seriously. You look really familiar to me. You live around here?"

"Uh, no. Santa Monica," Mak said, wondering if he was flirting with her or just one of those chatty kind of guys.

"That's it. The Farmers Market, right? I love going there on Saturdays," the man said, then leaned over and reached out his hand. "Sal Horner."

"Makayla Suarez. Mak. So now am I supposed to ask if you come here often?"

"Ha! Funny, but no. Just grabbing a bite in the neighborhood before I drop off some photos nearby. I'm a news photographer."

"Really? That sounds interesting."

"You'd be surprised how boring it is waiting for the light to be just right so you can get your shot."

"Tell me about it. I'm a unit production manager."

"Now that definitely sounds interesting. Are you working on anything now?"

"I'm working on a new show for Conrad Reed at ReedWorks," she said.

"I think I've heard of him," Sal said. "The action guy, right?"

"Yeah, the action guy," Mak said.

Mak launched into a description of *Pulaski & Jones* with its car chases, fake cops, and production hijinks. Sal listened, egging her on with his boisterous laugh, for nearly an hour.

"Listen, it was great chatting with you," Sal said, checking the time on his phone. "But I've got to run. I've got a gig over in Beverly Hills this afternoon and I don't want to be late."

"It was nice meeting you," Mak said, a little disappointed when their impromptu lunch date ended.

"But first I'm gonna pick up your lunch tab. This was the most fun I've had in a long time," Sal said, grabbing both of their checks from the counter and plopping down his credit card.

Mak looked at him in surprise. "You don't have to do that."

"Sure I do," Sal said, with a grin. "That way you'll have to reciprocate by taking me to lunch."

25

The morning was brisk and the sky decidedly blue. Ivy tilted her chin upward to catch a bit of midday sun, extending her arms, trowel in one hand, high above her head then down along the sides of her body, then out in front of her to give her back a good stretch. She smiled when she realized she'd just performed the sun salutation pose she'd learned in a yoga class Mak had dragged her to. Ivy had made the mistake of telling Mak that Toby had suggested in grief group that everyone find new sources of comfort—massages, walks on the beach, poetry readings. That's all Mak had needed to strong-arm her into trying yoga. All those relentlessly fit women in their tight pants and slinky tank tops made Ivy anxious, but she had to admit the stretching made her work-sore muscles feel good.

Now if it could only get rid of the anxiety she was feeling about the lab and HydraHold. On one hand, she felt she should be back at the lab full time; on the other, she loved being outside and putting her hands in the soil every day. And since Alexandra didn't seem too worried about her progress, why hurry back? Ivy rolled up the sleeves of her denim work shirt and plunged her hands into the earth, hoping that the rich texture of the organic matter and the soothing buzz of the insects could push aside all thoughts of Alexandra, the lab, and the random thoughts of JP that kept popping into her head. It was bad enough that she couldn't keep her mind on her work, but it was even more disturbing to discover that she could find someone, anyone, attractive again.

First Conrad, now JP, what is going on with me? Am I that starved for affection?

Ivy heard a crunch on the path behind her.

"Don't move," a voice said quietly.

She froze. When she finally cocked her head sideways, she saw that Conrad had come up the path and was nearly beside her.

"Look," he said softly. "Three o'clock. There's a hummingbird right by that flower."

"You're home," Ivy said smiling.

"So it seems."

"How are you?"

"Minor heart thing," Conrad responded. "Nothing to worry about."

"I'm not sure you can have a *minor* heart thing, but I'm glad you're feeling better."

Ivy followed his gaze and saw the tiny green Anna's hummingbird doing its crazy helicopter dance just a few feet away. No matter how often she saw them, hummingbirds would always be a source of fascination for her. Apparently, Conrad felt the same way. She noticed the quiet look of pleasure on his face as he watched the little bird furiously pumping its wings.

"Red trumpet," she said, standing up slowly so as not to scare off the creature.

"What?"

"That's a red trumpet vine. Invasive species, they'll take down an entire wall if you don't trim them, but hummingbirds love the nectar." They watched in silence, sharing the moment until the bird revved its engine, lifted off, and disappeared into the sky.

"I wanted to tell you how much I appreciate your watching Hudson," Conrad said. "Fernanda was at her wit's end. You really helped out in a pinch."

"My pleasure. JP helped too."

"Yes, I heard," Conrad said. Ivy thought she detected a shift in his tone. "Did he make dinner for you?"

"He did, a Guatemalan dish. It was delicious."

"Did he walk you and Hudson out to the car?"

"There was really no need. We left around six thirty."

"Still, it gets dark early now," Conrad said.

Ivy was puzzled by his questions. *Is he teasing me? Or could he be jealous of JP? No, that's ridiculous, he's just being protective of Hudson. Or of both of us . . . ?*

The thought occurred to her that JP *was* a very nice guy, but her attraction had been a passing fancy brought on by loneliness. There was nothing between them but a good dinner, a garden, and a shared interest in comforting Hudson on a night that could have turned out very differently.

"Okay, just making sure you had a good night. And . . . I wanted to thank you properly for taking care of Hudson." Conrad paused and Ivy had the distinct feeling he was trying to decide how to phrase the next bit. He always seemed so confident; she was surprised to see him hesitate. "And if there's anything I can do for you in return, please let me know."

Conrad started back up the path, but Ivy called after him and he turned.

"If you really don't mind, I have a work issue I'd like to bounce off you. I'm in a kind of a quandary about my investor, aka the Dragon Lady, which pretty much—"

"Conraaaaad!"

Hudson came charging out of the house and running full tilt down the brick pathway, flinging himself into Conrad's arms.

"Whoa, take it easy there, kid," Conrad said, hugging him warmly.

"Careful, honey. You know Conrad just got out of the hospital, right?" Ivy said.

"I know. Did you get any shots? Did you get Jell-O?"

"No on the Jell-O. Yes on the shots. But I am one hundred percent okay," Conrad assured the boy. "I'm taking off work for a few days to rest up, so we can hang out in the den and eat dinner in front of the TV together."

"Yayyyy! Ivy too?" Hudson asked.

"Sure," Conrad replied, smiling. "Ivy, too, if she'd like that."

"I would love to, but I may have go out of town for a few days."

"Okay. When you come back," Hudson insisted.

"I think that can be arranged," Conrad said, giving Ivy a little wink at Hudson's exuberance.

"Ivy took me to the Santa Monica Pier. We went on the Swinging Ship. Ivy said she might puke but she didn't."

"That's a relief," Conrad said.

"I thought you were gonna die," Hudson said to Conrad.

"I wasn't the one who went on the Swinging Ship," Conrad said.

"No, in the hospital. That's where people go to die."

"Also where people go to get well," Ivy said. Conrad shot her a grateful glance.

"Let's go see Rory," Conrad said, propelling Hudson along the path. He looked back at Ivy. "Come up to the house later. I'm happy to help with your work problem, if I can."

As she was wrapping up for the day, Ivy spotted Hudson sitting on the edge of the bluff. Something about him seemed so forlorn, a little lump of a figure sitting with his legs folded one over the other in a position he'd informed her was called crisscross applesauce. She'd been on her way to the cottage, but had a sudden change of heart and headed in Hudson's direction instead.

"What are you doing out here? It's going to be dark pretty soon," she said gently, as she saw him looking up at the sky.

"I like coming out here now because my mom said that whenever I look at the sun going down and the moon coming up, wherever I am anywhere in the world, it'll always be the same sun and the same moon she's looking at."

"I see. It's pretty, isn't it?" Ivy asked, gazing up at the sky.

Hudson nodded solemnly. "I don't remember her so much. "

"What do you remember most?" Ivy asked, sitting beside him in crisscross applesauce.

"Well, um, she let me brush her hair. And she always tucked me in, if she wasn't working too late. And she loved pictures."

"You mean like the photos of you and your mom and Conrad?"

"No, like paint pictures. You know, like art and stuff. The hockey picture was her favorite," Hudson said.

"A hockey picture? I don't think I've seen that one."

"It's famous," Hudson assured her. "It's in Conrad's room. It used to be my mom and Conrad's room, you know."

"I know." Ivy watched as the sun began its descent and the moon appeared, a faint sliver of light high above the horizon.

26

onrad and Mak sat at the wrought-iron table on the patio near the pool, Conrad's ever-present leather binder parked in front of him. Despite being in the hospital for less than forty-eight hours, he felt exhausted but pressed on.

"Get rough cut for episodes five and six, book Graphics Garage for opening titles, remind Dex not to be an asshole. I've got it, boss," Mak summarized back to him, slapping her laptop shut. "Now, what about you?"

"What about me?" Conrad asked warily.

"What did the doctor say?"

"You're asking for official insurance purposes?"

"No, I'm asking because I care about you, even though you're an a-hole."

Conrad sighed. "He said to eat more fruits and vegetables, cut back on sodium, red meat, and booze, and avoid climbing stairs and lifting heavy objects for a while."

"That's it?"

Conrad glanced away, avoiding Mak's laser-focused stare. His gaze landed on the flower beds, planted with what looked like kale or cabbage, that bordered the patio. *Were those always there or did Ivy plant them? Who knew vegetables could be so pretty?*

"What else? I know there's more."

He sighed, looking back at Mak. "Yeah. Eliminate stress and be prepared for the depression and anxiety that can follow a cardiac event, even a minor one."

"I'm so sorry," Mak said somberly.

"Oh, and also that people who've had a first heart attack have a one-in-five chance of having a second one within five years."

"Yikes. Forget the rewrites and edit notes. They can wait. Just get well."

"There's too much to do," he said, concern clouding his voice.

"Come on, Conrad. We'll cover for you. That's a TV show, this is your life."

"I guess," he conceded. "No need to be a hard-ass. Just keep the suits happy for me for a few more days. I don't want Adam and the network guys thinking they don't need me around."

"Stop fishing for compliments. You know we only run like a well-oiled machine when you're there to crack the whip."

"Hmm . . . triple mixed metaphor, but so true," he agreed, breaking into a rueful smile.

Conrad looked at Mak intently.

"You look different, Mak. What is it? Did you lose weight?"

"I saw you four days ago, boss." Mak snorted dismissively.

"Seems like four months. It's the earrings, right?"

Instinctively, Mak reached up to touch one of her gold hoops. She shook her head. "Same ones for the past decade."

Conrad examined her more closely. Still the same old Mak, tough, funny, capable, but something was definitely different. *What is it?* It was driving him crazy.

"Anything else you need?" Mak asked self-consciously, turning away to shove her laptop into her backpack while Conrad continued to stare.

"Yes, for you to tell me what's different about you."

"Oh, all right," Mak said, putting her hand to her cheek and smirking for a pretend close-up. "I'm just wearing a little—"

"Makeup," Conrad practically yelled.

"Just a little lipstick and blush . . . and a dab of mascara."

"It looks great on you. You look so pretty and . . . happy," he replied, realizing as he said it that it was actually true.

Mak shrugged off the compliment, but she was beaming.

"Please tell me you're not going for the Botox and Juvéderm next."

"No. And no ass lift or spray tan either," she replied. "You know me better than that."

"Mak, are you seeing someone?"

Bingo! Conrad couldn't believe that Mak, who could shut down the most arrogant actor or aggressive publicist with barely a glance, could actually blush. But there it was.

"Okay. I met a guy," she confessed, rolling her eyes in embarrassment.

"That's great, Mak." Conrad said. "Dish!"

She smiled. "It's actually pretty funny. Sal, that's his name, and I were both eating alone at Sugarfish in Hollywood. I'd seen him around, he kept popping up in my neighborhood. He's a news photographer; seems like a pretty cool guy."

"News photographer, huh? Sounds downright dashing," Conrad interjected, giving Mak a suggestive eyebrow raise.

"Puh-leeze. Anyway, I guess I was packing away a lot of sushi, because he leaned over and said, 'That's not fat-free, you know.' It cracked me up. Next thing I know, he takes me up to Yamashiro for cocktails and tonight we're going out for dinner."

"Wow, quite the whirlwind. But if you're happy, I'm happy," Conrad said.

"I am. He's like this gift that came out of nowhere. God, I sound giddy."

"No, it's nice. Hey, why don't you bring him to the premiere party?"

"Slow down, Dad. I only just met the guy."

"Sorry, you're absolutely right," Conrad said, brushing his palms together—*fini*—and sinking back into his chair. "This is me buttinskying out of your love life."

· · · · ·

A little later, Conrad was back outside in the yard near the kitchen. He'd placed a putting cup on a strip of grass and was lining up a shot with his favorite TaylorMade putter.

"Hey, just the person I was looking for," Ivy called out cheerfully as she walked up the brick path toward the house, gardening basket in hand.

Conrad scowled as he missed the cup by more than a foot.

"Sorry," Ivy said. "You're supposed to be quiet when a golfer is driving, right?"

"Putting. And yes."

Conrad glanced at her as he went to retrieve his ball.

"I just wanted to let you know that the landscape installers are coming next week. They're adding some ficus trees on the south side of the house where the hedge is a little spotty."

"Great," Conrad replied indifferently, as he lined up another shot.

"I decided to go with red chokeberry shrubs. I didn't want to use common Ligustrum, even though you see it all over California, since it's an invasive plant that's wiped out a whole list of native species. Anyway, I thought you might want to see a photo," Ivy said, pulling a printout from her basket.

Conrad looked over, nodding his head in the general direction of the photocopy. "Fine."

"I used a wholesaler," Ivy rambled on. "The commercial nurseries always want to sell you cultivars and I really wanted the straight species so it would help our ecosystem. Not to mention, their rates are better."

Ivy put the photo back in her basket, gazed out across the yard toward the ocean, then back at Conrad.

"I'm also going to have the landscaper plant some bamboo near the pergola for a little extra shade. It'll be beautiful in the breeze. Bamboo has a bad rep, but only because people plant running bamboo instead of clumping bamboo, which is noninvasive and easy to control. Amazing what a little education could do."

Ivy looked over at Conrad, noticing his gloomy silence for the first time.

"Are you okay?"

Conrad shrugged as he lined up a row of balls to putt. Concerned now, Ivy started up the path toward him.

"What's going on?" she asked.

Conrad dropped his putter on the grass and looked at her. "It's just a little hard for me to get quite as excited about noninvasive species and clumping bamboo as you are."

Ivy stopped short, a look on her face as though she'd just been slapped.

"Whoa. Sorry. I thought you were interested in what I was doing to your yard."

"Interested, maybe. Riveted, which it seems like you're expecting, no."

Ivy yanked at a piece of her hair, trying to get her simmering anger under control.

"Okay, I get it. You don't want to be bothered. You just want me to enhance the curb appeal," Ivy said, walking away.

Conrad called after her, "Wait, I'm sorry. It's just . . . I'm just."

27

*I*vy tried to settle gracefully into a chair shaped like a giant hand in Alexandra's office in San Francisco's financial district, but it was hopeless. It almost seemed as if Alex had chosen her artsy décor to throw people off their game. It certainly had that effect on Ivy.

Alexandra, clad in gunmetal gray pants and a matching cashmere sweater, leaned across her sleek desktop and gave Ivy a smile a degree or two warmer than the setting.

"It's good to see you. In the flesh, that is," she said pointedly.

Ivy nodded, but said nothing.

"Are you ready to get back on track?" Alex asked.

Ivy swallowed hard, preparing herself for the pressure to return to the lab that she was sure was coming. "I know I've taken more time off than you expected."

"Come on, I hardly expected you to come racing back after losing your husband. And I appreciate your online check-ins and lab visits."

"And I appreciate your flexibility," Ivy responded cautiously.

"But now we've got to get moving. We're behind schedule for test results, which means we're behind schedule for the next round of funding. We can't very well claim 'less water, more yield' if we don't have the data to back it up."

Ah, here it comes.

"I know this is taking longer than either of us wanted," Ivy responded. "But it's not because I've been away. Developing an organic product like ours is an iterative process. Adding constituent chemicals in the right balance takes time and tweaks and testing and retesting."

"Duly noted. Now how do we speed it up?"

Ivy thought for a moment. "It's not really feasible unless we hire a huge number of lab techs and cultivate more land to sample, which is financially prohibitive and might not speed up the process anyway. And we can't add synthetics to the formula. That would take us completely off mission."

"But it might work, right?"

"Sure, possibly. But then we wouldn't be creating an organic irrigation solution at scale."

Alexandra stared out the window of the high-rise for a moment, then turned back to Ivy. "Of course, you're a hundred percent right. But even if adding technicians to the team doesn't make sense, I think I'll bring in a lab supervisor to help out until you're back full time. Maybe even a postdoc or two."

Ivy was aware of a subtle shift in the room, as if someone had just turned down the thermostat. Was Alexandra actually trying to help? Or was this a warning of some kind?

Alexandra's face softened into a smile. "And if you need more time off, you just say the word. You've been through so much."

• • • • •

*I*t was late afternoon when Ivy slid into the passenger seat of Mak's red Mini Cooper outside Terminal 1 at LAX. She took off her pantsuit jacket and tossed it into the back seat along with her briefcase.

"Spill, chiquita," Mak said, pulling away from the curb and heading north on Century Boulevard toward the 405 Freeway.

"Nice to see you, too, and thank you for picking me up."

"Yeah, yeah. So what did Alexandra have to say?"

Ivy sighed audibly and sank back into the seat. "It was strange."

"How so?"

"Well, we talked about test results and the next round of funding, stuff like that . . ."

"And?"

"And she told me *again* to take off all the time I needed."

"That bitch," Mak joked. "How dare she?"

Ivy was quiet for a few minutes, until Mak nudged her with an elbow and demanded, "Speak."

"Something is off, I can feel it. Plus I had a stupid fight with Conrad."

"About what?"

"Landscapers. Bamboo. I don't know."

"Yeah, I have arguments about landscapers and bamboo all the time. Anyhoo, my surprise will put you in a good mood," Mak said as she passed the exit for the 10 Freeway westbound and continued north.

"Why? Where are we going? I need to get back to work."

"Well, I was thinking about what your grief guru lady said about finding multiple means of comfort. So I planned a little outing."

"Do we have to do it tonight? I just want to go home and crawl into bed." She'd learned to be wary of Mak's surprises ever since Mak had "kidnapped" her for a birthday weekend in Las Vegas, the one place on the planet that Ivy loathed the most.

"It's all set. And it will be so relaxing, like a big warm hug. I've been a few times and it's awesome."

"If you say so." Ivy leaned her head back against the headrest, knowing it was a waste of energy to argue with Mak when she was in one of her helpful moods. Besides, maybe it was a deep tissue massage or something actually relaxing.

Mak swung through a gated entry and down a long driveway opening onto a sleek midcentury house nestled among a cluster of trees. The house had the kind of clean, simple lines that probably cost a fortune.

"We're here. The Clearing."

"The Clearing? You haven't signed us up for a cult, have you?"

Mak snorted. "No, it's a movement meditation class, very neurosciency. You'll love it."

A few minutes later, Ivy and Mak—now barefoot and wearing loose white pants and T-shirts—joined a group of women outside on a circular swath of lawn surrounded by jacaranda and liquidambar trees.

"See? A clearing?"

"Yeah, I get it," Ivy replied, her voice tinged with annoyance.

She looked around the circle. All women, all different shapes and ages, all wearing the same loose pants and tees. Ivy noticed that all their tops, including her own, were embossed with little pink scripted words. Hers said JOY, Mak's SERENITY. She also saw HOPE, PEACE, HARMONY, PURPOSE, and GRATITUDE among them. Catching Mak's eye, she pointed to the word on her shirt and gave her a *WTF* look. Mak flashed a big smile in return.

A beautiful tan and toned woman of about forty, with no

apparent makeup or facework, strode into the center of the clearing.

"Welcome ladies, to the Yancy Method of Integrated Movement Therapy. I'm Jenna, and I'll be your instructor. Now, who's been here before?"

About half the women, including Mak, raised their hands.

"This class is the brainchild of Dr. Miyaki Yancy-Shwartz and it combines simple moves with sound therapy to help you clear stress and regain balance. A sort of restorative mini retreat. Ready to get started?"

The women nodded and smiled enthusiastically, and as if by magic, the sound of temple bells and heartbeat-like drum sounds wafted through the air.

"Just follow along and remember to breathe," Jenna said as she began to glide around the circle, the women following after her. She raised her arms high into the air, then reached low to the ground, stretching and swaying in time to the gentle drumbeat.

"Now move freely any way that feels good. Let your body carry you, no need to think, edit, or worry about what you look like."

Mak took off with the rest of the group, spinning and swooping with abandon, while Ivy began to move self-consciously around the perimeter of the circle. She thought about the ballet class she took the summer she turned ten, then quit when she overheard her friend tell another girl that Ivy was as graceful as a cow on ice.

After a good twenty minutes of free-form movement, Jenna stepped into the center of the circle. "Excellent work connecting the breath to the movement. Now, let's get down on all fours and move through the grass like jungle cats. Let go of inhibition and thought, and feel your inner power. And no need to worry about grass stains. We've got an excellent on-site laundry."

Jenna crouched down on the lawn and begin to slink along like a jaguar. Ivy looked on in amazement as the women followed suit, some crouching down on hands and knees and others slithering upright as they transformed themselves into imaginary cheetahs and tigers.

That was it. Ivy pulled out of the circle, nearly trampled by the pride of lithe jungle cats as she moved to the outer edge of the lawn. She signaled Mak, subtly at first and then more overtly. But Mak was having none of it. She continued to slink with catlike stealth, glaring as Ivy walked off the lawn and pushed open the door to the dressing area.

She can't actually enjoy this jungle cat crap, Ivy thought. *It looks like something Hudson would do at preschool.*

Ivy changed clothes and sat down to wait on a bench outside the dressing room. After a while, the music quieted and Mak came bursting through the door. She threw herself onto the bench, her face within inches of Ivy's.

"You think you cornered the market on grief? You think nobody suffers but you?"

Ivy looked at her friend in shock. "No, I just didn't—"

"My mom died when I was eleven years old. I just went on my first decent date since . . . since forever, and it's scaring the shit out of me. And my employer—and the only decent boss I've ever had—just had a heart attack putting not only his health but my career in jeopardy."

Mak's face turned a deep crimson and angry tears rolled down her face, soaking through the little serenity logo on her white tee. Ivy reached out and put a hand on her shoulder, but Mak shrugged it away.

Oh my God, Ivy thought, *this is Mak's grief group.*

She reached her arms around Mak, holding her tight and rocking her as if soothing a toddler in the throes of a tantrum. Neither noticed as the other ladies began quietly tiptoeing past them on their way to the changing room.

28

erfect, Ivy thought, spotting the one decent outfit she'd brought with her to Malibu, a pearl-gray sweater dress, in the back of the closet. She hadn't expected Conrad to invite her to the house for his *Pulaski & Jones* premiere party, especially given his snarky state the last time they'd spoken.

Maybe this is his way of making it up to me.

When she'd asked Fernanda what to wear, Fernanda had put her head back and howled with gleeful disdain. "Believe me, you can wear whatever you want. You'll see everything from Target sweatpants to sequined cocktail dresses so short they leave nothing to the imagination. And I mean *nada.*"

Ivy pulled the dress over her head, pleased to see how it draped on her body, muscles toned from weeks of yardwork. If she dabbed on a little lipstick and pulled her hair into a loose bun, she might actually be presentable. Peering into the little mirror over the bathroom sink and seeing her cheeks flushed with anticipation, she was glad she'd said yes, despite her initial hesitation. Will had always had to twist her arm to go to faculty events, but she was curious about this party and, to her surprise, looking forward to it.

Ivy headed up the path to the main house, the muscle memory of wearing low-heeled sandals instead of sneakers starting to kick in. Conrad had told her he was under strict orders from Fernanda and his doctor not to overexert himself, so she hoped it would be a smallish, laid-back gathering. She opened the kitchen door and saw a swarm of activity—chef, waitstaff, bartenders—all buzzing under Fernanda's watchful eye. Ivy followed the flow of white-jacketed traffic across the hall and into the dining room. The waitstaff was stocking the portable bars and placing trays of grilled vegetables, charcuterie, and pasta on the dining-room table. Watching the preparations grow more lavish with each platter—cheeses, sliced meats, poached salmon—it occurred to Ivy that the massive house, the revamped garden, the party itself were all part of Conrad's image. Maybe even more than his image, they were a necessity of his livelihood, a carefully cultivated persona that was required if he wanted to continue to succeed in his field, no less than a published doctoral thesis and funded lab were part of hers.

As if on cue, Conrad stepped into the dining room, handsome in black jeans and a dark-blue long-sleeved shirt that set off his eyes.

"Just the person I was hoping to see," he said. Ivy stopped short a few feet away.

"I owe you an apology," Conrad said with a self-deprecating shrug. "My behavior the other day was . . . unacceptable . . ."

Ivy's didn't say a word.

"Inexcusable?"

She stared at him with a straight face, as he began to fidget.

"Deplorable? Reprehensible? Disgraceful? Should I continue . . . ?

Ivy started to laugh. "No, that'll do it. I just wanted to see how far you'd go with the groveling."

"Ah," Conrad said, smiling as he breathed a sigh of relief. "I really am sorry. I actually called my doctor to see if I was losing my mind."

"And are you?" Ivy asked, enjoying having the upper hand.

"Maybe a little. He told me that between the minor heart thing—I know, I know, there is no *minor* heart thing—and the medication, I might experience some mood swings." He took a step toward her. "Am I forgiven?"

Ivy hemmed and hawed for a moment, as if making up her mind. "You are forgiven," she finally, then looked around the room. "Am I the first one here?"

"No one comes to an industry event on time. It's an unwritten rule, like never hiring your friends."

"I can come back later."

"No, please, I'm afraid you might not return," Conrad said, laughing. "Anyway, I'm glad you're here on time. I need an impartial opinion."

"I'm surprised that you would think any of my opinions could be impartial," she joked.

Ivy followed him into the adjacent media room, outfitted with a big-screen TV and sleek leather chairs and couches, softened by colorful pop-art pillows. Fancy wooden folding chairs were squeezed in wherever they could fit to accommodate what looked like it would be a sizable crowd. *So much for the casual get-together.*

"Wow. I'd forgotten about this room. I haven't been in here since Mak gave me the grand tour," Ivy recalled, glancing around.

"Really? We'll have to screen a movie in here sometime."

"*Screen* a movie? Is that anything like *watching* a movie?"

"Touché. You look lovely, by the way, I don't think I've seen you in anything but head-to-toe denim."

"Not true, but thank you anyway," Ivy replied. "You needed an opinion?"

"Right, big decision to make." Conrad poured two glasses of champagne and handed one to her. "Should I have the television already on when people arrive? Or have a ta-da moment and turn on the TV right at nine o'clock?"

Ivy laughed. "So glad I could be here early to consult on strategy."

"Well, you are the gardener with the PhD." He clinked his glass against hers.

"In that case, since you are deferring to my expertise, I would say TV on, sound off, hit the volume at nine sharp."

"Perfect, thanks." Conrad turned on the TV with the remote, silencing the sound. "This party may be a little different from your academic soirees."

"You mean where we gather in front of a roaring fire in the dean's drawing room drinking sherry and debating the theorem of Pythagorean triples?"

"Exactly. And I should warn you, these entertainment do's tend to get a little self-congratulatory."

"What do you mean?"

"You'll see."

There was a noisy shuffling outside the media room.

"Ah, the teeming masses are arriving," Conrad said. "Join me?"

Conrad opened both doors, and he and Ivy joined the growing crowd in the dining room. Ivy spotted Fernanda and Hudson, the latter of whom was in a tuxedo-printed T-shirt for the occasion, and went to join them.

They chatted, watching Conrad happily back in the frying pan of fame, as he sprang to greet each guest, kissing, hugging, and escorting them to the bar and buffet. Within minutes, the room was packed with Hollywood folks, from writers in their jeans and flannel shirts to glittery young women in bodycon dresses that looked like Band-Aids stretched across their lean torsos.

"Does everyone in Hollywood have flat abs and perfect teeth?" Ivy asked Fernanda.

"Maybe not everyone," Fernanda said, nodding her head to where Mak was standing with a guy with an overgrown moustache.

"That's Mak's date! I've got to go say hi," Ivy said, heading across the room.

As she filtered through the crowd, she heard fragments of conversation in the foreign tongue of show biz floating past— *biopic, hip-pocket deal, tentpole movie.* A murmur went through the dining room as a large man entered, flawless in dark trousers and an untucked monogrammed shirt that almost managed to hide his girth.

"Billy, you showed." Conrad greeted him with a handshake, but Billy pulled him into a big bear hug.

"Of course I showed. You're the man of the hour," Billy bellowed.

Billy looked around the room, as if taking note of who he'd need to schmooze before the night was over. Conrad saw Billy's gaze stop on Ivy, who was chatting with Mak and Sal nearby. Conrad motioned her over.

"Ivy, let me introduce you to Billy Greene, my agent for more years than I care to count. Billy, this is Ivy Bauer."

"Nice to meet you," Billy said, giving Ivy the once-over.

"You, too," Ivy smiled.

"You're not an actress, are you?" Billy asked.

"Ivy is an edaphologist," Conrad said proudly.

"An eda what?" asked Billy.

"A soil scientist," Ivy explained.

Billy stared at her blankly.

"A gardener," she clarified.

"Right, you're the gal who's tarting up the grounds," Billy said. "Excuse me, I see . . ." And with that, he was off to greener pastures.

Ivy and Conrad heard female voices from the foyer, and Conrad was suddenly as alert as a hunting dog who'd caught a scent. "The divas have landed," he stage-whispered to Ivy.

He turned to the group at large. "Hey everybody, grab your plates and drinks and head on into the media room."

The guests went silent, but no one made a move.

"Did I mention there are two more bars inside?"

Everyone laughed and began to surge into the next room, plates and glasses in hand.

"Excuse me, I'm on leading lady duty. Grab a seat and I'll see you inside," Conrad told Ivy, then disappeared toward the foyer, shutting the doors behind him.

Ivy entered the media room and saw Mak waving her over to a couch she'd commandeered near the back of the room. Mak was chatting with Sal, pointing out who's who in the crowd in a discreet whisper, hardly necessary since the hum in the room was reaching a fever pitch.

"Wait a minute. I don't know that guy," Mak said, gesturing toward a man near the bar.

"That's JP," Ivy said.

"That dishy guy is the handyman?" Mak asked, lifting her eyebrows.

"Hey, aren't you supposed to be on a date with me?" Sal asked Mak.

Mak laughed. "Just stating the obvious, honeybun." She turned to Ivy and said, "No wonder you volunteered to take Hudson over to his house. Dinner, my ass!"

Before Ivy could protest, the double doors swung open. Conrad stood in the doorway, a star on each arm. Ceci was perfection in a sapphire cocktail dress that matched her eyes, while Nakia looked impossibly chic in a leather miniskirt and silky tank.

Mak and Ivy watched as the threesome entered the room. "Nicely done," Mak whispered to Ivy. "Equal billing."

Ivy gave her a questioning look.

"One girl on each side, neither one gets the final movie star entrance," Mak explained.

"People actually care about stuff like that?" Ivy asked.

"Celebrities—and aspiring celebrities—definitely do."

"Hiiiii," Ceci giggled, giving the crowd her dazzling former-beauty-queen smile.

"Hey bitches," Nakia said with a grin.

"Five minutes, everyone. Grab another drink and take a seat," Conrad shouted as he led the leading ladies to a reserved couch in the center of the room. With a chivalrous bow, he seated them on either end of the couch, then took the middle seat. Waiters hustled over with champagne and truffle cheese puffs as people scrambled for last-minute refreshments and prime seating.

"It's showtime, everybody!" Conrad announced, remote in hand, as he dimmed the lights and turned up the sound on the network logo. When the title card for *Pulaski & Jones* appeared on the screen, the crowd went crazy, hooting and hollering in appreciation. Conrad glanced around the room and, spotting Ivy sitting in the back, gave her a little wink.

The first half hour was filled with improbably sexy women, hot perps, and plenty of trash-talking in the squad room. The crowd cheered at each actor's entrance, laughing raucously and applauding furiously as the action unfolded. Ivy was amused at their outsize reactions, chalking up their enthusiasm to their proprietary sentiments after having worked together for so many weeks. It was harder to banish the notion that this was just another formulaic cop show like the ones she'd watched with her grandmother as a kid. Obvious setups, stock characters, and some clever dialogue—but with a little updated psychobabble and casting diversity thrown into the mix.

So much for the new golden age of television.

When the show came to the half-hour cliffhanger, it looked like the lady cops had been double-crossed by a sleazy informant. Conrad turned the lights up and the sound down for the commercial break as Fernanda signaled the waiters to circulate with fresh drinks and finger foods.

"We're trending on Insta," someone hollered. '*Pulaski & Jones is red hot.*'"

"This is from Reddit. '*Love seeing women cops with brains bigger than their boobs!*'"

Commercial break over, Conrad cranked the sound back up and everyone settled in for the second half. Predictably, the show ended in a blaze of glory with the two gorgeous cops solving the case, arresting the bad guys, and jumping into their squad car. As they peeled off into the mean streets, actually a backlot in the San Fernando Valley, final credits rolled, and the crowd exploded in deafening applause.

Conrad brought the lights back up to a soft glow as the group started to chant "Conrad, Conrad, Conrad" like drunken fans at a college football game. Looking slightly embarrassed at the effusive reaction, he faced the group and raised his hands to quiet them.

"As most of you know, it's been a tough time for me the past few months. And I want to take this opportunity to thank each and every one of you, especially our beautiful—and, of course, brilliant—leading ladies for hanging in there. I know how hard all of you have worked, and I stand before you humbled and grateful for your faith, your diligence, and most of all, your talent, for which I plan to take full credit."

The room burst into applause once again.

I guess this is what Conrad meant about the self-congratulation. Not exactly PBS, but maybe this is what people want these days.

Dexter stood up next, raising his glass to Conrad.

"Here's to Conrad Reed, the king of cop shows," he said with a grin. "We weren't sure you had another one in you, but what do you know, you proved us all wrong." Dexter raised his glass as the crowd chuckled, joined in the toast, then immediately began helping themselves to more free food and booze.

Conrad gave Ivy a subtle *follow me* head nod and, grabbing a couple of glasses, they slipped away from the crowd in the media room, through the adjoining dining room, and around the corner into the hallway just beyond. Out of sight of the party guests, Conrad stopped and leaned against the wall, sighing with relief. Ivy felt a little giddy being singled out by Conrad, especially in the midst of his celebrity crowd.

"I need a breather. A little too much good cheer."

"You deserve it," Ivy replied.

Conrad gave a sardonic laugh. "I don't know, but if my guess is right, the fans will love it and the critics will skewer it. As they should."

"Why do you say that?"

"Look, I'm not complaining. I'm thrilled to have a show on the air. God knows I needed it. But I didn't expect to be producing this kind of crap. Not at this stage of my career."

"Oh my gosh, so you think it's crap too?" Ivy asked, visibly relieved.

"You do keep it real, don't you?"

"I'm sorry, that came out a little more bluntly than I intended."

"Don't apologize for honesty. It's a rare commodity in this town."

"So why don't you do something that's not crap? Something that you're really proud of?"

"That is the hope," Conrad said. "And it will happen . . . eventually."

He leaned in, looking Ivy square in the eye.

She didn't move a muscle, but she felt like every cell in her body was on fire.

Conrad reached out and gently took her hand, kissing a fingertip.

Ivy gasped as a jolt of something like electricity jumped from her finger to a spot behind her knees. Conrad moved closer, tipped up her chin, and touched his lips to hers. She took a sharp intake of air as, from out of nowhere, a thought leapt into her head. *What lips my lips have kissed, and where, and why.* It was a line from an Edna St. Vincent Millay poem that Will loved for its haunting beauty.

Ivy pulled back almost imperceptibly. *Go away, Will. Please.* She heard a faint murmur, tinged with amusement. *If that's what you want.* She exhaled, not realizing she'd been holding her breath, then kissed Conrad back. She parted her lips slightly and felt Conrad's mouth press on hers, gently at first, then more hungrily.

When they pulled apart, Conrad and Ivy were grinning at each other like two teenagers, their faces still close together as they stared into each other's eyes. The crowd on other side of the wall was still humming like a swarm of honeybees foraging for food and hookups. Conrad suddenly cocked his ear, and Ivy could hear Hudson's voice talking to someone close by.

"You're Hudson, right?"

"Yeah. Who are you?"

"I'm Sal. I knew your mom."

"You knew my mom?"

"Yeah, I took that picture of her with her hair down over her shoulder. You know the one I mean?"

"Yeah," Hudson said, his croaky little voice beginning to quiver.

"That's a pretty famous photo, you know. I'm a professional photographer."

"Um, okay," Hudson stammered.

"We were real good friends, me and your mom. Maybe I can take your picture someday."

Conrad dropped Ivy's hand. Even without the physical connection, she could feel his body tense up, his muscles growing taut as he listened.

"My picture?" Hudson asked, confused.

"Sure. We get it out on social media. Maybe you'll find out you've got a whole big family out there. Wouldn't that be cool?"

"What family?" Hudson sounded like he was about to cry.

Conrad turned the hallway corner and burst into the dining room like he'd been shot out of a cannon. He went straight for Sal, Ivy on his heels.

"Can I help you with something, pal?"

"No, just talking with the boy here," Sal replied. A few people turned to see what was happening, but most were focused on food and small talk.

"Tell me your name again. I'm not sure I caught it the first time," Conrad said with the warmth of a coiled cobra.

"Sal. Sal Horner. Mak's friend."

"Well, Sal Horner, I don't know why you are interrogating my stepson but I think it's time for you to leave."

"Hey man, I'm sorry. I didn't mean anything by it. Just chatting the kid up," he said, giving Hudson a friendly ruff on the top of his head.

"Like I said, the party's over."

"I'll just go find Mak," Sal said.

"That won't be necessary. I'll see that she gets home," Conrad said, looking like he was about to strangle Sal. Ivy saw the situation escalating, so she quietly opened the front door, Conrad half shooing, half shoving Sal outside.

"Who was that? Why did he say that stuff?" Hudson asked Conrad, tears starting to well up and spill down his cheeks. Conrad kneeled down and wiped Hudson's eyes.

"I don't know, buddy. He's probably just one of your mom's fans. You remember how many people loved her, right?" Conrad asked gently.

Hudson nodded, "'Cause she was so special."

"That's right," Conrad assured him. "You couldn't help but love your mom because she was so special and so kind and so beautiful."

Hudson nodded his head, still confused but calming down.

"There will never be anyone like your mom. They'll never be anyone in the whole world who could even come close."

Ivy watched, touched by Conrad's tenderness but surprised to feel a sudden ache somewhere in the region of her heart.

29

Conrad sank back into what he'd come to think of as the pitching couch as he organized his thoughts for his meeting with the network development team.

"Congratulations," Adam said, taking his customary power seat. "We just got the green light to start developing the *Pulaski & Jones* franchise."

"Franchise? I thought we were only discussing season two. I brought beat sheets for the first six episodes," Conrad replied, his mouth twisting into a frown as he took in the news. Having a spin-off series on the air would give him financial security. More than security, it would give him wealth. He could keep his team employed, pay off the house, send Hudson to any college he wanted. But it also meant being tethered to *Pulaski & Jones* indefinitely.

"We'll get to season two, but first let's talk franchise ideas," Adam said, smiling so broadly Conrad thought his pearl-white veneers might blind him.

"And later we can discuss selling the format rights into international territories. Cha-ching!" Lonnie added, rubbing his hands together with childish glee.

"I really hadn't thought that far ahead," Conrad said. He sighed, knowing he should be enjoying this moment more.

"Luckily for you, we have. We've been kicking around some great ideas," Sara jumped in.

"You're the expert, of course," Adam said. "But what we've observed is that the audience will follow you to the next incarnation of the series as long as you stay true to the core creative elements."

"Fascinating observation," Conrad replied dryly.

Adam gave him a quizzical glance, but plunged ahead. "So let's see which of these spark your interest."

Dial back the annoyance, Conrad cautioned himself.

He'd tried so hard to get a smart series on the air, something with depth that he could really be proud of, not just with this group, but with all the networks. The one truly poignant drama series he did manage to sell, about a homeless kid who hooks up with a Faginesque con man, only lasted two seasons. And it was great, but apparently too much of a "downer" for the average viewer. *Please.*

"Sure. Shoot," Conrad said, mustering a lukewarm smile.

The trio breathed a collective sigh of relief at Conrad's amenability, and Adam flipped open his MacBook Air and threw a snazzy PowerPoint up on the big-screen TV, advancing to an image of two muscular, handsome men in uniform.

"Cop partners, one straight, one gay. We're thinking San Diego PD, cool beach vibe, a little edgy," Adam said.

"Of course, we'll run it by our LGBTQ-plus consultants to make sure it's realistic but not offensive," Lonnie added.

Adam advanced the slide to a firehouse with an overlaid image of two attractive women, one young and dewy eyed, the other middle-aged and toned. "Two firefighters. Seasoned vet and first-year rookie."

"It could also be guys, of course," Lonnie said. "But we think that audiences will love the contrast of the older-younger leads like they do the biracial casting in *Pulaski and Jones*."

"And female audiences loooove seeing smart women at work. I have been advocating for powerful women leads for-e-ver," Sara added.

"Or we go the relevance and responsibility route," Adam said. "Two plastic surgeons, best friends, one fixes droopy wattles in Beverly Hills, the other repairs cleft palates in Zimbabwe."

"Or India. Or Mexico," Lonnie mused. "Huge taste for American shows there."

"Plus it'd kill on social media," Sara said.

Conrad had heard enough. He leaned forward, intentionally encroaching on Adam's personal space and closed the laptop lid. As if feeling the power shift, Adam inched back uncomfortably in his chair.

"Why not a good-looking gay cop couple, one older, one younger, plastic surgeons and members of their volunteer fire department?" Conrad asked.

The wind now fully out of their sails, the three execs stared at Conrad awkwardly. "I get it," Conrad said finally. "You want me to cannibalize, I mean build upon, the relationships and storylines of *Pulaski and Jones*, then slice and dice them into multiple formats before it fades away."

"We don't see it fading anytime soon," Sara protested.

"Look, Conrad," Adam said. "I'll lay our cards on the table. The chief wants another series, if not several, with the *Pulaski and Jones* sensibility."

"Which is what? In the chief's view?" Conrad asked, putting air quotes around the word *chief*.

"Pretty people and plenty of action." The *duh* was implicit.

"That's what the chief wants, and that's what the audience wants."

"Especially from you. This is your oeuvre."

"Hey, let's stick to English, I'm just a kid from Jersey," Conrad replied.

Adam sat forward in his chair, puffing out his chest and dropping his professionally cheerful demeanor. He looked like he was prepping for the network executive's equivalent of a barroom brawl.

"Conrad, I have great respect for your body of work and for *Pulaski and Jones*. It's an honor working with you. But I've got to tell you, I feel like you're fucking with us when all we want to do is get your next series on the air. Is there a problem?"

That's enough, Connie, he heard Dawn warn him. *This is your future, and more important, it's Hudson's.*

"Hey, I'm sorry, guys. You caught me off guard. What if I mull these ideas over and get back to you in a day or two?"

Adam smiled, creative crisis averted. "Sure thing," he said. "Just keep the chief's mandate in mind."

"I know," Conrad reassured him. "Pretty people and plenty of action."

After the ritual handshaking and a bit of cautious backslapping, Conrad strode down the carpeted corridor, passing the rogue's gallery of network cast photos mounted on the wall. He stopped in front of the recent addition of *Pulaski & Jones*: Ceci and Nakia standing in front of the cruiser in too-tight uniforms, pistols drawn absurdly, *Charlie's Angels*–style. Conrad grabbed a marker from his notebook and drew mustaches across the girls' grinning faces. He gave the ladies a little salute and marched down the hallway, exiting into the midday haze.

· · · · ·

*S*teering the Mercedes out of the parking lot, Conrad started to call Billy to report on the meeting, then thought the better of it and hung up, turning onto Sunset. Twenty minutes later, he was parked on the shoulder of Mulholland Drive, high above the city.

He looked across the street at *Dawn's Descanso*, the little shrine built in her honor, faded now with only a few sun-bleached teddy bears and bedraggled bouquets alongside her famous photo.

"I did it, Dawn. I dumbed it down—I mean lightened it up— just like you said," Conrad said out loud. "I've sold my soul to the devil, but at least I can keep the house and take care of Hudson. That's what you wanted me to do, right?"

He stared at her photo for a long while, then dropped his head in his hands and leaned against the steering wheel, his shoulders shaking as big soundless sobs overtook him. The tsunami of grief washed through his body until, finally, he lifted his face, a tiny indentation from the steering wheel imprinted on his cheek.

Breath now under control, Conrad got out of the car and crossed over to Dawn's shrine, squaring his shoulders as though bracing for a difficult conversation.

"I'm sorry I didn't bring any flowers." Conrad gave her photo a wry smile, squatting down on his haunches at eye level. He looked up at the sky, as if for guidance, then back again at Dawn.

"Dawnie, I need to tell you something."

He paused, reaching for the right words.

"There's . . . a girl. Sorry, a woman. She's nothing like you. In fact, she may be your total opposite. But I think you'd like her. I like her. I like her a lot."

He sank to his knees in the dirt and began clearing weeds and brush away from the homemade monument.

"There's more. I don't even know how to say it."

Conrad hesitated. After a moment, he picked up the least mangy of the mangy stuffed bears, knocked the dirt off its little round butt, and moved it closer to the shrine, closer to Dawn. "This guy showed up out of nowhere. The thing is, the thing is . . . he's making noises like he knows you, maybe even knows something about your birth family. It could be total horseshit, of course, but I'm checking him out. I thought you'd want to know."

Just then, a banged-up yellow Volkswagen bug pulled onto the shoulder and parked in front of the Mercedes. Three chattering girls climbed out of the car and scooted across the road in a tight little teenage pack. Conrad backed off a few feet, giving them access to the shrine when he saw that they were headed over, but they barely noticed him.

"I told you," said a chubby girl with a know-it-all tone. "Her shrine is right over here."

"She was so beautiful," said a girl with Friday the 13th tattoos running up her left arm, as she deposited a new yellow teddy bear next to Dawn's photo. "I've seen every single one of her films."

"Dude, she's only been in three. But they were all amazing."

"Okay, let's go now," said the third girl. "This creeps me out."

"What are you talking about? She totally gave foster kids a good name. I heard she was even starting a charity to get more fosters placed."

Conrad was vaguely aware that Dawn had a subset of fans among girls in foster care, but he'd never seen them in close proximity. A stray thought floated through his mind about shooting a documentary about the broken foster care system. Dawn would like that.

"Hey, remember when she played that inner-city teacher and one of her students pulled a gun on her?" the tattooed girl asked the others.

"Yeah, she was great in that." She flipped her frizzy hair over one shoulder with theatrical flair and said, "'Kid, what I'm about to tell you may be the most important lesson you'll ever learn.'"

The other girls applauded her Academy Award performance. They turned when they saw that Conrad was clapping too.

"She would have been a huge star," Conrad said, venturing gently into their conversation. The girls eyed him with varying degrees of interest and suspicion.

"You've seen her movies?" one asked, seemingly curious as to why this middle-aged guy would be visiting a dead movie star's shrine.

"I was supposed to work with her," he answered, wondering for a moment if that would ever have happened.

"You're a director?" one of the girls asked doubtfully.

"Writer, actually," Conrad said, to which the girl responded with a skeptical *sure you are* look.

"Would you take our photo?" one of the girls said, hovering over Dawn's photograph.

"Sure. Why don't you get on either side so I can get Dawn in the picture with you? I bet she'd have liked that." Conrad framed the photo on the girl's cell phone, remembering how touching he'd always found Dawn's genuine affection for her fans.

They huddled around the shrine, a happy-sad little bundle of hormonal angst, as Conrad stepped back a couple of feet to get a good angle. One girl draped her hair over her shoulder like in

Dawn's famous photo, then the others followed suit, and soon all of them were smiling for the camera as Conrad snapped several photos.

The girls thanked him and then immediately forgot he was there.

"Bye, Dawn. We love you."

The girls whimpered away, zigzagging across Mulholland and squeezing back into the Volkswagen, which *pfutt-pfutted* off down the highway.

Conrad watched them go and then turned back to Dawn's photo.

"Okay, Dawn," he said softly, smiling. "No need to lay it on quite so thick. You know I could never forget you."

30

*I*vy heard a dog bark, a kid holler, and then the tromping of feet down the brick path toward the garden. Rory sprang into view, paws and tail swinging, with Hudson sprinting behind.

"Ivy! Where is it? Where's my surprise?"

Ivy now regretted telling Hudson that she had a surprise for him the night of the premiere party, but he seemed so left out of all the adult hubbub, she'd felt sorry for him. She'd spent the last two nights at Mak's, and if she'd kept her mouth shut, she'd still be there drinking tequila sours and reviewing their relationships—hers potentially promising and Mak's dead on arrival. And even though Ivy felt like an insecure teenager retreating to her best friend's house, she needed to put a little distance between herself and Conrad to sort out what she was feeling about him, about Will, about getting back to her real life. In short, about everything.

Mak had been none too pleased to hear that Ivy had kissed her employer.

"What were you thinking, girlfriend?" she'd said. "First of all, you work for him. Second, did you ever think this might be some crazy kind of widower's rebound crush for him? Or you? Or both of you?"

"Ivy, where's my surprise?" Hudson repeated, jogging her back to the present.

"It's right over here. But you'll have to be patient because it's not quite finished yet."

Ivy led him past a border of three awn, a native grass she loved not only for its drought tolerance but also its purplish flowers and tall spikes that swayed in the breeze.

"Where is it?" Hudson asked, doing a little happy dance as he followed Ivy into the recently planted vegetable garden, carefully sidestepping the beds.

"You're looking at it," Ivy said, gesturing toward a small square plot with six thin bamboo poles tied together at the top to form a tent shape. At the bottom were green bean shoots, each about a foot long, that she'd tied in place to grow upward along the tall poles.

Hudson looked at her questioningly, not sure what this open-air thingamajig was supposed to be.

"Huh?" he asked, disappointed.

"I know it doesn't look like much now," Ivy told him. "But check out this picture and you can see what it will look like in a few weeks." Ivy handed him a color printout of a structure smothered in bountiful pole bean foliage with a little flap for the front door.

"I'll have my own veggie tepee!"

"Right. I thought you might like a playhouse out here."

"Hideout," Hudson admonished.

"Sorry, hideout. It's similar to the shape of the tents that Native Americans used to live in, but it's also like the trellises that farmers used as planters when they didn't have a lot of space."

"Cool," Hudson exclaimed. "When it's all grown, I can hide inside and no one can see me. And then I could come out to help you when it's time to pick the vegetables."

"Sure you could," Ivy said lightly, unsure if she should be making any commitments about the future. Especially to Hudson.

Ivy recalled the first time she'd met him in the garden. He'd been such a prickly kid, with his perpetual scowl and nonstop questions. Now he seemed more, well, kid-like. Rough around the edges with his uncombed hair, dirty knees, and gap-toothed smile.

He's healing, Ivy thought. *Maybe there's hope for me too.*

"Let's go have some cookies to celebrate. Fernanda made white chocolate chips!"

Normally the mere thought of Fernanda's fresh-baked cookies was enough to lure Ivy into the main house. But today the thought of running into Conrad made her pause, his comment *There will never be anyone like Dawn* still burning in her memory. She knew intellectually, of course, that Conrad still loved Dawn just as she would always love Will. And she knew intellectually that someday she might be ready for a new relationship. But was it now? Was it him? Just the mere thought of all these things made her feel like her head was about to explode.

"Why don't you go inside with Rory? I worked up a sweat out here. I think I'm going to take a dip in the pool, and I'll see you a little later."

"Okay," Hudson said. "Rory, let's go."

He stopped suddenly and looked at Ivy.

"I almost forgot the manners stuff," he said solemnly. "Thank you, Ivy."

"You're welcome, Hudson."

He turned back to her once more, grabbing her in a big hug around her waist. "I love you, Ivy."

"I . . . I . . ." Ivy faltered, not sure she could trust herself to speak without crying.

But it didn't matter. Hudson and Rory were already gone, up the path toward a kitchen fragrant with the smell of comfort and white chocolate chip cookies.

· · · · ·

*N*ow that she'd used swimming as an excuse to avoid going into the house, Ivy decided she might as well take a dip. Her muscles were aching after her work in the garden, but she welcomed the physical labor after her alcohol-soaked stayover at Mak's. As the warm water enveloped her body, she began her slow rhythmic crawl to ease the tension from her shoulders and the insecurities from her head. Usually, Ivy could lose herself entirely in the water, giving way to a deep sense of calm. But today her thoughts refused to quiet, rattling noisily around her brain like the raccoon she'd spotted in a garbage can a few nights ago.

Ivy switched to a fast crawl, picking up her pace as she slapped her arms hard against the water. Sooner or later she'd have to sort out her feelings about Conrad. She wasn't even sure how to think about him, their worlds were so far apart. She finally understood why people referred to Los Angeles as La La Land. Everyone in this nutty town seemed to be an aspiring something else. A rapper. A reality star. A film director. Will, a die-hard Northern Californian, had always loved the Woody Allen quote about LA's only cultural advantage being able to turn right on a red light.

She and Will had been different in taste and temperament, but they both valued the same things: intellectual pursuit and academic rigor. *What does Conrad value, and how could I possibly fit my work and research into his crazy world? And what was that kiss about? Was it just a bit of drunken flirtation, or did it actually mean something?* Ivy came to the pool wall for a flip turn and jumped as a hand reached down into the water. Lost in thought, she hadn't noticed Conrad's approach. Now there was no escape; he was there leaning down next to her by the pool. She grabbed on to the edge for support and popped her head out of the water, giving him a faint smile.

"I thought you might have gone back to San Francisco," he said. "You didn't return my call."

"Sorry, I was hanging out with Mak," she said, though both of them knew it was an excuse.

They stared at each other, neither knowing what to say next.

"Did I do something to scare you off?" Conrad asked after a long pause.

"No, it's not that."

"What then?"

"I just . . . it just . . ."

"Talk to me."

She pushed off the wall a foot or two and treaded water for a moment.

"Your life doesn't make sense to me," Ivy blurted, lowering herself into the water a bit to cover her blush-stained cheeks.

"How do you know? We're just getting to know each other."

Ivy looked away, toward the garden, toward the ocean, toward anything but Conrad.

He waited.

"You're words and I'm data," Ivy said finally, reaching for the pool edge again. "You tell stories with your imagination, and I tell stories with statistics. You create all these crazy characters and situations out of thin air, and I live by precision and replication."

"Isn't that what makes romance so exciting?"

She turned back and looked him directly in the eye. "And . . . I heard you. I heard you tell Hudson that no one could ever come close to Dawn."

"She was his mother. For him, that's true."

"And for you?"

"It's true for me too."

Ivy inhaled sharply.

"There will never be anyone like Dawn. But there could be someone like Ivy."

"But you don't know that. It could take years before you're ready—"

"You mean before *you're* ready?"

Conrad moved closer, kneeling on the tile and reaching both hands into the water, clasping Ivy's hands tightly between his.

"It's so soon. And we're just so . . . so different," Ivy said uncertainly.

"I'm not so sure about that. We've both had plenty of pain, plenty of loss. And even if we are different, it's the differences that make life exciting. Maybe it's time to take the leap."

"I don't know if—"

Conrad abruptly dropped Ivy's hands, stood up, and jumped into the pool, clothes and all.

"Your watch," Ivy exclaimed.

"Water resistant to a hundred meters," he responded, holding his Rolex above the water line.

"Your shoes?" Ivy asked,

Conrad laughed as he took them off, shook the water out, and threw them up onto the tile.

"Replaceable."

Conrad scooped her into his arms. Ivy shuddered as she felt his powerful arms encircling her and his hot breath on her face as he pulled her close.

"You're right. We don't know if this can work. But isn't it worth finding out?"

31

Conrad Reed Conrad@ReedWorks.com

To: IvyLBauer@gmail.com

Re: Entire week?

Hey, how's it going at the lab? And why are you in SF for an entire week? If I am remembering correctly, you usually do an overnight or maybe a couple of days. Is it me?

Was it the jump in the pool? The kiss at the party? I can work on the kissing thing. Just as soon as you return. Pinky swear.

Ivy Lynn Bauer IvyLBauer@gmail.com

To: Conrad@ReedWorks.com

Re: Entire week?

It's not you. In fact, you're giving yourself a bit too much credit. 😊 Actually, my team and I are working on an abstract for an agricultural conference. The data has to be spot-on.

Conrad Reed Conrad@ReedWorks.com

To: IvyLBauer@gmail.com

Re: 3 things

1. I had no idea ag folks were such sticklers for accuracy. Would you be open to asking them if they could use their depth of knowledge to improve the taste of store-bought tomatoes? 2. I did not know scientists were allowed to use emojis. Did they teach you that in soil school? 3. I look forward to seeing you when you return. Mostly for Hudson's sake, of course. He misses you and Rory does too. Btw, how is the Dragon Lady (henceforth known as DL) treating you? Are you staying at the DL's luxury SF penthouse?

Ivy Lynn Bauer IvyLBauer@gmail.com

To: Conrad@ReedWorks.com

Re: 3 things

Hardly! Staying at my parents' place. 😣 To answer your queries: 1. Ag folks are picky and no I will not ask them about tomatoes, which they might find insulting. 2. I am not a native emoji user, but my students have shamed me into learning the rudiments. 3. Yes, I would like to see Hudson and Rory—oh, and you, too. As for how DL is treating me— maybe I can talk to you about it? Seriously. She's pushing me to speed up production, which doesn't make sense. How are you? Hudson? Show?

Conrad Reed Conrad@ReedWorks.com

To: IvyLBauer@gmail.com

Re: 3 things

Pulaski & Jones is moving apace (good word, right?). The network gang and I are in discussions about another iteration of the show for the international market (God help us), as well as ideas for season two, which I have mixed feelings about. (Arggh, did you see how I ended that sentence with a preposition? Not that scientists care about that sort of thing. Or do they?) I am very eager to branch out, spread my wings so to speak as I have none, and try something other than a cop show. An artistic stretch as they say, but I also don't want to bite the hand that feeds Hudson's college fund. I am thinking that once I have season two well under way, I might have the psychological and creative bandwidth to pitch a series idea to a new and different, i.e., more progressive, outlet. Outlet, for the "non-pro," means a network, cable company, or streaming service. Essentially, anyone who can put a television show in front of eyeballs. Btw, are you singing to your plants? I understand that corn prefers Barry Manilow while tomatoes are more team Aretha. And, most important, when do you return?

Ivy Lynn Bauer IvyLBauer@gmail.com

To: Conrad@ReedWorks.com

Re: 2 days

FYI, scientists rarely sing. We just hum quietly under our breath, although I have noticed my plants perking up when I hum anything by Mumford & Sons. Back in Malibu in two days. See you then!

Spring

32

*L*ooking at her reflection in the bathroom mirror, Ivy scrunched her hair into a low ponytail and pulled on a faded Warriors cap. *No, that's no good*, she thought, snatching off the cap and putting on her wide-brimmed sun hat. *Better.* She opened the medicine cabinet, reached for a lipstick, thought better of it, and tossed it into the sink, where it ricocheted for a moment and then settled on the drain.

Oh, for God's sake, it's only a hike. Or is it?

She laced up her boots, thinking it was fortunate that Hudson had come outside last week looking for Conrad and discovered him, fully clothed, in the swimming pool. If he hadn't, she thought, things might have progressed with Conrad . . . and she wasn't sure if she was ready for that yet.

"We're just testing the waters," Conrad had told Hudson, with a mischievous wink at Ivy. Hudson had laughed himself silly.

Conrad may have been ready to test the waters, but she needed more time to wrap her head around whatever it was that she was feeling. *Do I need a distraction? A reprieve from loneliness? Or should I just stop analyzing and let myself explore?*

She could practically hear Cathy and the others from the grief group inside her head, encouraging her to *move on*, but moving on also meant letting go. Of Will.

· · · · ·

*T*he spring morning held a hint of the summer heat to come as Conrad, Ivy, and Hudson ventured up the foothill trail above Malibu, Rory poking along behind. With the drought dragging on, the vegetation lining the dirt trail was nearly as brown as the path itself, but no one seemed to mind. The three traipsed along, content in one another's company, Ivy tingling whenever her fingertips brushed Conrad's, while Hudson zigzagged along the path happily prospecting for interesting bugs and rocks.

"Look, Ivy," Hudson said, eyeing a patch of cactus on the edge of the trail. He squatted down to inspect it more closely, pulling Rory's leash tight so she wouldn't wander off into the needles.

"Hey, Conrad. Do you know what this is?" Hudson asked excitedly. Ivy smiled to herself, knowing where this was headed.

"Looks like some kind of cactus to me."

"Yeah. But do you know what *kind* of cactus?" Hudson insisted.

"Saguaro?"

"No."

"Prickly pear?"

"No."

"Spikegantica gigantica?" Conrad asked.

"You made that up," Hudson said knowingly. "Give up?"

"I give up. But I bet Ivy knows."

"I'm not telling," Ivy shot back. "You really should be more familiar with your local flora, you know."

"I'll work on it, Doctor."

"It's a beavertail," Hudson cried out, unable to contain himself any longer. He grabbed Conrad's hand and dragged him over to the cactus patch. "See? You can tell because the leaves are super fat like a beaver's tail. Do you see it?"

"Oh yes, I can see that now," Conrad said.

"Isn't that cool? Ivy taught me. I'm gonna go to the climbing cave now," Hudson announced, taking off at a gallop with Rory right behind.

"Wait for us there."

"Don't go off the trail."

Conrad and Ivy laughed at their overlapping parental admonitions, as Hudson disappeared down the path.

"He's happy," Conrad commented. "There were times when I worried he'd never feel that way again."

Ivy looked at Conrad, wondering if he was actually talking about himself.

"He's resilient. A lot like his mom, I'd imagine," Ivy said. Once the words were out of her mouth, she realized how much easier it was to feel affection toward Dawn now that she was beginning to understand Conrad a bit better. As if reading her thoughts, Conrad reached for her hand and interlocked his fingers in hers, and they continued down the trail.

"Have you heard anything more about Sal?" Ivy asked, knowing she was poking a sore spot, but wanting to know the latest.

"Not really, but I have a feeling we haven't heard the last of him."

"Mak told me she was distraught about bringing him to the house. Did you know he tried to reconcile with her?"

"Yeah, she told me. But she wouldn't give him the time of day."

"What do you think he wants?"

"Money probably. But there's something else, I just can't put my finger on it."

"Can you report him to the police?

"There's nothing they can do. He hasn't broken any laws yet."

Ivy saw Conrad's jaw clench and thought about Toby telling the grief group how physical activity could change your emotional state.

"Race you to the climbing cave," she said suddenly, taking off down the path.

"No fair. I don't even know what the climbing cave is," Conrad responded.

"Sucks for you," Ivy yelled over her shoulder.

33

few days later, Conrad steered the Mercedes toward the Village Preschool. It was a gorgeous SoCal day and it felt good to be driving with the top down and the breeze blowing through his hair. He hadn't picked Hudson up from school since *Pulaski & Jones* started production, and he was surprised to feel so excited about seeing him with the teachers and other kids.

He turned into the parking lot and saw the wicker rocking chairs on the front porch sitting vacant as usual, as if Mimi or Gramps would be coming out with a pitcher of lemonade any minute. As he pulled into a spot, Conrad noticed a man in an old Acura pull in behind him and park in a space nearby. Probably another dad picking up his kid. Not typical in Malibu, the land of the stay-at-home mom, but not entirely unheard of either, with all the actors and musicians with free time between gigs. He started up the front steps, and his fingers knotted into fists when he saw that the man behind him, the man with the bushy mustache, was Sal.

Conrad turned on him and hissed, "What do you think you're doing here?"

"I wanted to speak with you, and I didn't think it was appropriate to disturb you at home."

"And you think *this* is appropriate?"

A pretty Malibu mom got out of her Range Rover and headed up the steps, doing a little two-step to get around them, as a preschool aide opened the door.

"Hello, Ms. Singh," the aide said, glancing at Conrad and the unfamiliar man.

"Let's take it away from the school," Conrad said gruffly, grabbing Sal by the arm and bolting down the walk and around the side of the building as a few more moms headed toward the preschool's front door.

"I just wanted to explain—" Sal said.

Conrad whirled around, backing Sal against the side wall of the preschool. "Where do you get off scaring my kid? *My* kid!" Conrad exploded, his old Jersey street sense rising unexpectedly to the surface. A few of the moms glanced warily in his direction, and Conrad shoved Sal farther around the side of the building. "What is it you want? Is it money?"

"I didn't mean to scare him. I was just curious if maybe Dawn had ever mentioned her photographer buddy from back in the day—"

"How much?" Conrad asked.

"How much what?"

"Don't fucking play dumb with me. How much money do you want?" Conrad had to stop himself from decking the guy. Just the sight of Sal's furtive expression and ridiculous moustache made his blood boil.

"Listen, man, you've got me all wrong. I just wanted to reconnect with the kid of an old friend. Maybe get to know you, share a little information."

"What information? You going to try to tell me you're the father? Don't you think I know who that is already?" Conrad was bluffing; he didn't know who Hudson's father was and neither did Dawn, but the last thing he'd do was admit that to Sal.

"Nah, that's not it. But I have some information that I think you'd be—"

"Get the hell out of here," Conrad said with a look that meant business. "Stay the fuck away from this school and my family. You have no idea what kind of shitstorm I will unleash on you if I ever see your face again," Conrad said, grabbing Sal by the shoulders.

"Okay, okay. Back off, I'm leaving," Sal said, pulling away from Conrad. "But if you change your mind . . ." Sal thrust his business card into Conrad's hand and hurried off toward his car.

Conrad felt his pulse racing as he crumpled the card in his clenched fist. He slumped against the side of the building, feeling like his heart might leap out of his chest. He waited until he saw Sal drive away, took a few deep breaths to steady himself, then headed into the school. He pushed his way through the front door, where the Malibu moms were cooing over one another's children, clad in the latest from Versace or Burberry Kids.

"Oh, Mr. Reed," said school owner Miss Nancy, who was in the front hallway overseeing pickups. "Just the person I was hoping to see. Rachel, take over for a minute, won't you, dear?"

The young teacher relieved her boss from door duty, and Miss Nancy led Conrad into the classroom. *Last time it was the soiled underpants, now I'm about to get reamed for causing a disturbance on the school steps*, Conrad thought glumly.

"I'm not sure what you're doing." The formidable Miss Nancy pulled herself up to her full five foot two inches and, as much as physically possible, looked him straight in the eye. "But Hudson seems so much better."

Conrad breathed a sigh of relief, touched at how much her words of praise meant to him. For a moment, Conrad felt like he was back in high school getting the highest mark in the class for something he'd written.

"He seems far less anxious; he's getting along with the other kids. And he's showing so much interest in our little garden," Miss Nancy said, gesturing to the small patch in the children's outside play area. "He's quite insistent that we learn the proper scientific names of the plants."

Conrad smiled. "Well, he's pretty enamored with our gardener."

"Of course, Ivy. Delightful lady. The kids love it when she visits."

Conrad wondered if he'd just given away the fact that he was the one who was enamored and smiled to himself. "Thank you for sharing Hudson's progress with me. It really means a lot coming from you."

"Of course. And I don't mean to sound patronizing, but I feel quite proud of you. We all do. Just let me know if there is anything else we can do to help."

"Actually, there is something," Conrad said cautiously. "I need you to watch out for this jerk who's popped up and started asking questions about Hudson's mother."

"The fellow on the porch?"

"You saw him?"

"I did. And of course, we would have captured him on our video cameras."

"Of course you would," he replied. "I'm not sure what he wants, possibly some kind of paternity claim, which is bogus. You know that his mother—"

"This is Malibu, Conrad. We're trained to deal with custody

disputes, parental kidnappings, ransom threats. Not to worry, they're rare. But I will alert the staff, and we'll keep an extra close watch on Hudson. Now go enjoy your little one," she said as Hudson burst into the room.

"Conrad!" Hudson yelled, jumping up to give him a high five. "Are we going to lunch?"

Conrad mentally regrouped, trying to let go of the altercation with Sal. "What'd you have in mind?"

"Pink's Hot Dogs."

"Pink's Hot Dogs? That's all the way back in Hollywood!"

"Kenny says they're the best."

"Well, in that case, Pink's it is."

They climbed into the car.

"Top up?" Conrad asked.

"No way. Top down. I love me a convertible!"

Conrad laughed and cranked up the Beach Boys. "Let's go get us some chili cheese dogs. We can puke our guts out later."

34

*I*vy squirmed uncomfortably in the pulsating spa chair in the posh Santa Monica nail salon. Mak, on the other hand, was basking luxuriously beside her, her feet in a tub of scented water and her hands wrapped in steaming towels.

"Why am I even doing this?" Ivy asked. "I'm just going to wreck my manicure as soon as I plant the new kumquat trees."

"It's the national pastime for women. Men have football, we have mani-pedis. Besides, now that you and Conrad are an item—and I still have my doubts about that, missy—you might want to consider looking like a girl once in a while instead of a field hand."

Ivy settled herself into the chair, attempting relaxation, as the manicurist began rubbing cream into her cuticles. She rarely frequented nail salons, relying on swimming and heavy-duty scrubbing to dislodge the deep-set dirt that was an occupational hazard of her profession. She looked around at the manicurists, some young, some old, all Asian, wondering if they felt as foreign in this town as she did. Ivy listened to the staccato soundtrack their voices made as they chatted back and forth in Vietnamese.

On the drive over, Mak had told her about the actress Tippi Hedren—*Melanie Griffith's mom to you*—who had introduced the art of nail design to a group of Vietnamese women refugees in Northern California. Now the Vietnamese owned 80 percent of nail salons in California and half the salons across the country.

Impressive, Ivy thought, looking around the chic salon. *Well, if they can start over, so can I.* She smiled at the manicurist, who returned the smile, then went back to work on Ivy's nails.

Mak jogged her out of her private thoughts. "So what's up with you and Conrad? Have you had sex with him yet?"

Ivy gave Mak a *shush* glare and responded in a quieter tone.

"Let's try another topic, shall we? Like what's happening on the set? When do you wrap production?" Ivy smiled. "Hey, did you hear that? I'm catching on to the lingo!"

"No fair," Mak whined. "If you guys are actually getting together, I expect regular updates."

"Don't hold your breath."

After all these months, Ivy was just starting to feel like a semifunctioning adult who could carry on a conversation without every other word sending her on a downward memory lane spiral. *But sex? A flirtatious kiss was one thing, but could I ever make love with someone who wasn't Will?*

"Scared, huh?" Mak commented, neatly summing up the entire issue.

"It's not the sex," Ivy responded. "Well, not *just* the sex, although that is pretty scary. It's all of it. Getting invested. Feeling responsible for Hudson. Betraying Will."

"Slow down, girlfriend. We're just talking about getting you laid."

Ivy's manicurist glanced up when she heard Mak's comment and said something to her colleague in Vietnamese, and they both laughed. The manicurist finished filing Ivy's nails and held up two bottles of polish, one clear and one pale pink. Ivy pointed to the clear one, but Mak pointed to the pink one, giving Ivy a *puh-leeze* look.

"I don't know if I can do it," Ivy said finally.

"The pink polish?"

"Funny. No, a relationship, sex, all of it."

"Of course you can. Just open your mind. And other parts. Speaking of, let's get you a bikini wax while we're here. When's the last time you deforested down there?"

Ivy let out a groan so loud that everyone in the shop, including the normally unflappable staff, looked up to see what the fuss was all about. Embarrassed, she settled back into her chair and let Mak's advice sink in.

"You're right," Ivy said.

"About the bikini wax?"

"Everything but."

· · · · ·

*T*he last flame of sunlight was dropping below the horizon as Ivy returned to the cottage and a text from Conrad dinged on her phone.

> Care for some vino?

> > > Twist my arm.

> Your glass and I await.

Ivy smoothed back her hair and washed her hands, rolling her eyes at her newly polished nails. She headed for the main house, considering what the appropriate greeting would be for her to give Conrad. *Give him a little peck? Throw my arms around him? Or just stand back and let him make the first move?* Silly, she knew, but she couldn't help it. It had been a long time since she'd been in this situation, heading toward a relationship but not yet in sync.

She was still pondering her options as she approached the kitchen, but she needn't have worried. The minute he heard her coming up the path, Conrad flung open the back door, giving her a warm hug and a kiss on the cheek. Ivy was instantly relieved that their mutual affection wasn't just in her imagination.

"Barbaresco?" he asked, pulling out a chair and pouring her a glass of red wine, a half-eaten plate of pasta in the center of the table.

"Lovely," she remarked, staring at the vibrant color. She took a sip and thought about all the times she and Will had sat at their tiny kitchen island, drinking wine and rehashing the day. She'd been surprised to discover that it was the loss of the daily interaction that she missed most acutely. Anniversaries, holiday dinners, summer vacations—those she'd expected to miss. But having someone you could share the little details of life with, the ins and outs of your day, someone you could sit in silence with, that was even more precious. She looked at Conrad, handsome in the dim light, with his blue eyes, long limbs, and sand-colored hair. He felt her gaze and smiled, taking her hand and kissing her fingertips.

"Pretty," he said, noticing her manicure.

"Mak said I was starting to look like a field hand."

"If you are what field hands look like, Ms. Bauer, we should cultivate another hundred acres."

"Thank you. But as satisfying as it's been playing gardener, I'll need to get back to my real job, my real life, soon," Ivy said with a wistful shrug.

Conrad frowned, then leaned closer to her.

"Maybe this is wildly premature, but I'll ask it anyway . . ."

He paused to think through what he wanted to say next, as Ivy drew back in alarm.

"Don't worry, I'm not proposing," Conrad said when he saw the look on her face.

"I didn't think that," Ivy replied, embarrassed that she had thought exactly that.

Conrad regrouped and started again. "So here goes . . . Do you think you would ever consider moving your business down here? I understand that UCLA has a pretty robust agriculture and business department. They'd be lucky to have you."

Ivy took a deep breath, grabbed at a curl, and began to twist it around her forefinger.

"You mean as a professor?" Ivy asked, concerned that he didn't seem to understand that that was the last thing on her list of career ambitions.

"No, I didn't mean that. Just that you could form a relationship with UCLA like you have with UC Davis. I think you'd find plenty of resources down here."

Does Conrad really think it's that simple? To pack up my lab and my plants and move down here? Anyway, aren't women past trading their ambition for a relationship?

"I don't think so. I have a lab, assistants, a grow space," she said.

"I understand. I'm not saying it would be easy. But you've managed it all so well from Malibu, I thought maybe you'd think about making it a more long-term arrangement."

They sat in awkward silence for a moment.

"I've talked to a few environmental experts, business consultants in your field," Conrad continued.

Ivy set her wineglass on the table and sat up a little straighter in her chair. "You're talking to people about my product?"

"No, no, not your product. Just about businesses in the sustainability sector, biodynamic farming, eco-friendly products, that sort of thing."

"Why?" Ivy asked, twisting her curl even tighter.

Conrad paused for a moment, as if caught off guard by the question. "Curiosity, I suppose. Initially, at least. About you and what you're doing. And the more I talked to the experts, the more blown away I was by how ahead of the curve you are. With global warming accelerating and arable land at a premium, you've got an incredible first-to-market advantage over the competition."

"I am aware," Ivy said, an icy edge creeping into her voice. "I've been at this for a while, you know. I'm getting my doctorate in this specific field. If you wanted more information about the science, you could have just asked me."

"Of course you're the expert, no doubt about that. I just wanted to look at the broader landscape and see if there were opportunities for you in Southern California. LA has a pretty innovative culture, you know."

"So you want me to give up everything I've worked so hard for just so I can move down here?"

Conrad winced. "No, I just thought that, well, if we were going to give this relationship a real shot, that your business was more mobile than mine."

"They don't make television shows in the Bay Area?" she asked, the heat rising in her cheeks.

"Yes, of course. But I've got Hudson and this home. And you seemed to enjoy taking some time off from your lab."

"So because I'm taking some time off, you think I've given

up? I've done nothing but think about my work—my real work—as I've been planting and pruning in your backyard," Ivy said, wondering if she could stop her train of thought, but the words kept tumbling out. "It seems to me that you have a lot more flexibility, more leverage than I do. I have to answer to investors, the FDA, and about a dozen other governmental agencies, not to mention potential customers."

She paused and looked directly at Conrad. "And you want to know what will happen in the end, no matter how hard I work or how effective my product is?"

Conrad shrugged in the affirmative.

"Odds are I'll finish the product development and the testing, we'll get it into the market, it will start to get some traction, and some Big Ag company will step in to buy it."

"Isn't that the start-up dream?"

She ignored his question and continued.

"Then they'll begin to change the formula, just a tweak or two at first, then more and more over time until it's no longer what I created. It's just another mass-market chemical soup."

"But it's your creation. You can make it whatever you want."

"And is that what happens when you write a brilliant script and the network gets ahold of it? Does it stay the way you wrote it? Or does it get a little tweak here and a little twist there until it barely resembles what you set out to create?"

"My business is collaborative by definition."

"But it's still a choice you make. You made the choice with your show, and I'll have to make the choice with my invention."

"It's not the same thing at all."

"Of course it is. You said yourself you could have taken *Pulaski and Jones* to a smaller outlet that would have given you more creative control, but you wanted a network hit. I have the same choice. Let a chemical company blow up HydraHold or keep it myself, assuming I can even do that, and have a nice, niche product for a handful of organic gardeners and regenerative farmers, and maybe, just maybe, a few enlightened agriculture companies."

Conrad stood up abruptly, walked over to the island, and poured himself a glass of water. Through clenched teeth, he said, "So what you're saying is that I'm a sellout."

"No, that's not what I'm saying. I'm saying you made a choice and you have to live with it. And so will I."

"You think I had a choice? I have a child, not to mention sixty-four people relying on me to keep them gainfully employed in a very fickle business." He banged his water glass down on the counter so hard it shattered.

"Shit."

The glass had opened a small cut and blood was dripping down his hand. He ran it under the faucet for a moment, then started to clean up the mess from the broken glass.

Ivy watched silently, not offering to help.

"I think I'd better go," she said finally, wondering if he would stop her.

He didn't.

"I'm going back to San Francisco tomorrow," Ivy decided on the spot.

35

*I*vy looked up at the lab's concrete façade, as an unforgiving blast of Bay Area chill blew against her bare legs. Had Will been there, despite it being spring, he would have repeated one of his favorite Mark Twain quotes about the coldest winter he'd ever spent was a summer in San Francisco.

She winced, wishing she hadn't worn a skirt, as she pressed the buzzer and stared into the aperture of a video camera, its metallic eye glaring back at her. The heavy door, new since her visit just a week before, opened with a menacing grate.

Was it just a year ago that I felt a thrill every time I walked into this lab? Like Madame Curie and Rachel Carson and Albert Einstein would all be waiting inside to greet me? Why am I feeling so nervous right now?

"Marlena," Ivy said, surprised to see her lab assistant poised like a security guard on the other side of the door. It swung back into place, locking with an audible clunk as a worker in a lab coat—a face new to Ivy—floated past them down the hallway. She'd known, of course, that there had been changes to the lab, and true to her word, Alexandra had added more lab personnel, but seeing them live twisted her stomach into unexpected knots.

Calm down, she told herself, *it just means we're on track to speed up the process so we can get to our next funding round.*

"Nice door," Ivy commented.

"Alex thought we should beef up security. Your badge," Marlena said, handing Ivy a clip-on security badge.

"Thanks . . . I think. Well, let's take a look at the latest," Ivy said, attempting to keep her tone upbeat. She was suddenly very grateful that she'd scheduled a late-afternoon visit with her former mentor Charlotte, who was still renting her house. Every time they talked, Charlotte managed to set the world right.

"We just got the results of the last UC Davis tests. Ed's got them in the office," Marlena told Ivy as she started down the hallway.

Ivy followed her down the narrow corridor, wondering once again whether to be thrilled or dismayed at the developments. The lab had once been her sanctuary, but it had been transformed into an unabashed factory, brimming with life, both vegetal and human. Where once there had been open floor space with plenty of room for expansion, now every inch was covered with potting beds, LED grow lights, and lab stations. More workers in scrubs, most of whom she didn't recognize, moved between the raised beds, ghostly figures silently making adjustments and adding notations to the logs that hung off each wooden platform like charts on hospital beds.

"Hang on," Ivy said as she stopped to grab a clipboard. She began skimming through the chart, her eyes opening in alarm.

"This can't be right."

"Afraid it is."

"What the fuck!"

A few minutes later, Ivy, Marlena, and Ed sat at a conference table littered with the detritus of strangers in the now-enclosed office. Ivy pored over a thick folder in her lap, her colleagues waiting in silence.

"We thought the Davis results would be better than the last round," Ed finally ventured. "But this is . . . too good. HydraHold is storing more than three hundred times its weight in water."

Ivy slammed the folder down onto the conference table, coffee mugs and tablets rattling in defiance.

"How could I not have seen this coming? Alexandra's added a synthetic, hasn't she?"

"Seems like it," Ed said quietly, as though he were afraid of being overheard.

"We agreed that we wouldn't use any synthetic chemicals. They might increase the water retention in the short term, but they'll contaminate the soil. We might as well dump industrial waste into the ground. And it's my name on this product," Ivy said.

"She cut us out of the loop weeks ago, Ivy," Marlena said. "There wasn't much we could do about it."

Ivy stopped scanning the chart and looked at her beleaguered colleagues, tears beginning to well up. She flashed on how excited she'd felt about the early results. *A minimum viable product*, Alexandra had called it, meaning there was just enough positive data to get the attention of other investors, and, ultimately, consumers. And that was only the beginning.

Ivy inhaled sharply, holding back a sob.

"I should have known Alexandra wouldn't wait until we got the formula right. No wonder she brought all these new lab techs on board. Not because we're scaling so quickly, but so that she could do whatever she wanted without our knowing about it."

"Maybe you can turn her around," Ed added.

"I'd like to think so, but I seem to have a knack for misjudging people."

· · · · ·

As Ivy's Uber pulled up in front of the little earthquake cottage she'd shared with Will, she felt her body sink into the car seat as if anchoring itself to the relative safety of her vehicular cocoon. She and Will had loved the house's quirky history as a relic of the 1906 quake, as well as its skinny trilevel footprint, but now the thought of going inside the home she hadn't seen for nearly a year—the home filled with memories of Will—filled her with dread.

"Ma'am?" the Uber drive said.

She thought of Toby's advice—*When triggered, seek support*—and slid wordlessly out of the car. Other than Mak, no one was more supportive than Charlotte and her husband, Randy. Charlotte, especially, would help her sort through her fears about Alexandra's attempts to change her formula as well as Conrad's zealous appeal for her to move to LA. Ivy had the distinct feeling that she was at a crossroad in both her personal and professional life and had no idea which way to turn.

"Come in out of the bluster, dear. It's about time we saw you at the old homestead," Charlotte called out, opening the door. She gave Ivy a sympathetic smile, as if to say, *I know how hard it is for you to come back here.*

Ivy walked up the steps and fell into her friend's embrace. Charlotte, more round than tall and wearing thick black-framed glasses, had been Ivy's first role model. Ivy adored her and Randy, a retired investment banker. Before she could protest, she was inside. Not much had changed—a blanket here, a stack of CDs there—but, of course, the house felt entirely different.

"Let's go upstairs, honey. Randy can't wait to see you and, as usual, he has a list of projects he wants to clear with you before he makes a hash of your house."

They went up, and with a little gasp, Ivy stopped short just inside the kitchen. Randy sat at the counter reading, his back to her. With his dark hair spilling over his collar, for a moment he looked just like Will.

"Ivy, so nice of you to drop by," Randy joked. "Here's my list."

"Rand, give her a moment, will you? She just walked in the door."

Charlotte and Randy exchanged a glance, noting Ivy's hesitation.

"Right, sorry. It must be a bit of a shock to be back after all this time," he said.

"This was my favorite room," Ivy said quietly.

"On second thought, I'll just email you the list," Randy said.

Ivy realized that she hadn't moved, and Charlotte and Randy were both staring at her, worried expressions on their faces. She shook her head, as though to wake herself from a stupor.

"No need, whatever you want to fix is fine. I'm sure it will be an improvement. You're still enjoying the neighborhood?" Ivy asked finally.

"It's delightful," Charlotte said. "There's so much variety, so much energy here."

"Who would have thought we could be transplanted at our age?" Randy added.

"Resurrected is more like it," Charlotte quipped.

"Like one of those resurrection plants you're so fond of," Randy said, laughing.

"Don't remind me. Ivy's sat through enough of my lectures."

"You couldn't possibly remember Charlotte's insane love of lycopods," Randy teased.

Ivy smiled and pushed her glasses up the brim of her nose. "'Lycopods like the commonly referred to Rose of Jericho and *Siempre viva* can survive at near total desiccation with five percent relative water weight, but spring back to life when rehydrated.'"

"That's us to a T," Randy said. "Plant us anywhere and we spring back to life."

"Well, it's true," Charlotte insisted. "Survival against all odds. One of the miracles of nature. You stick to your spreadsheets and I'll stick to my resurrection plants."

"I know when I'm not wanted," Randy said with a grin as he nodded to the ladies and left the room.

They settled on the kitchen stools and Charlotte said, "There's something's troubling you. And it's more than missing Will. Am I right?"

Ivy looked at her old friend and smiled.

"I never could fool you."

"You never needed to. You were the hardest-working student I ever had, not to mention the smartest. So what's on your mind?"

Ivy began to tear up. "Charlotte, I don't know what I'm doing with my life. I feel like I've worked so hard to get where I didn't want to go."

"And where is that exactly?"

Ivy gave a deep sigh. "Big Ag, commerce, chemical companies."

Charlotte took Ivy's hand in hers. "Tell me what's happened."

"My investor has introduced synthetics into my formula. Legal maybe, but not ethical, since the whole idea was to see if we could scale an organic product."

Charlotte listened patiently.

"But it's more than that. I really thought I could buck the trend and get through grad school and my product launch without surrendering to the chemical companies. Which is ridiculous, because they're the ones funding all the research programs. I was so naïve, so arrogant."

"So courageous, so idealistic." Charlotte reflected for a moment, then said, "I never even attempted anything like you've done. I was happy with teaching, publishing enough to get tenure, and coming home to Randy every day."

"That sounds lovely," Ivy said.

"Yes, but you can do so much more. You can have a groundbreaking career and . . . love? Is that what this is about?"

Ivy nodded, then shook her head. "Maybe. I don't know. There's a man, the owner of the estate where I've been working."

"Conrad, yes. You've mentioned him. What's going on?"

"I think . . . that is, I think . . ."

"You have feelings for him," Charlotte finished her sentence.

Ivy looked at Charlotte, surprised that her friend had gotten to the heart of it so quickly.

"Yes, but it's not even a year since Will . . ." Ivy said. "And how would we even manage it? I've got my lab and he's got his television show."

"Do you think you could love this man?"

Ivy's eyes began to well up with tears.

"I think I already do."

Ivy's phone dinged. Her face grew warm as she showed Charlotte that it was an incoming text from Conrad.

"Love is always an experiment," Charlotte said gently. "Answer it, dear."

36

*H*udson sat in a tall director's chair in the *Pulaski & Jones* makeup trailer, staring straight ahead as a pretty makeup artist examined his reflection in the big light-rimmed mirror.

"I think he needs eyeliner," Conrad said, winking.

"What's that?" Hudson asked, and when Conrad picked up a pencil to demonstrate, he squirmed away and let out a big laugh that traveled from his belly up and out through a lopsided grin.

Ivy stood nearby, wishing she didn't feel so awkward about her proximity to Conrad after their intense argument a few days before. But she was glad he'd tried to smooth things over and had invited her to join them for Hudson's debut on the show. She wondered, in fact, if Conrad had invited her specifically to smooth things over, since he'd apologized, then suggested they table their disagreement and discuss it after the day's shoot was done.

She watched Conrad, observing how comfortable he was busying himself with Hudson and chatting with various production team members as they came in and out of the trailer with their questions and updates. He was clearly in his element, in command but with a warm and casual style. As he worked, she nosed around the makeup trailer, fascinated to find it every bit as purposeful as any laboratory. Ivy herself had never been interested in clothes or cosmetics, but she was intrigued with the makeup artists' neatly compartmentalized stations, counters swathed in pristine white towels, rows of squishy cosmetic wedges, bottles of tawny foundation, pots of vibrant lipsticks, trays of blush, mascara, tweezers, eyelash curlers, hot rollers, curling irons, hair spray, and more.

"Yes, definitely eyeliner," Conrad said, leaning in to look at Hudson more closely. "And maybe some lipstick to brighten him up a bit. Red, I think."

"No lipstick!" Hudson squealed. "You promised me only a teensy bit of makeup so I wouldn't look like a zombie under the lights."

"Did I say that?" Conrad asked, chuckling.

Hudson nodded emphatically.

"Well, a good producer always protects his artists. Just a touch of antizombie base then."

"You got it," the makeup artist replied, smiling at Conrad in the mirror.

When Ivy had asked Conrad if he had any concerns about putting Hudson in the public eye while Sal was still creeping around, he'd told her that he didn't want to break his promise to Hudson. "Besides," he'd said, "by the time his episode airs, Sal will be long gone."

Ivy watched as Hudson scrunched his eyes shut, wrinkled his nose, and tilted his chin up to the makeup artist, who deftly dabbed a foundation-tinged sponge across his face. *How can you possibly improve on a preschooler's skin*, Ivy wondered as she watched the process. She was a little anxious that all the attention might be too much for Hudson. But he seemed to relish the spotlight, and Conrad was never more than two feet away from him.

The door swung open, and Mak, ever-present clipboard and key ring in hand, burst into the room. She winked at Ivy, then turned to Hudson. "Hey pal, you ready for your big debut?"

"Soon as we finish my makeup," he replied, mugging for the mirror.

"You're going to be awesome," Mak said. "We're ready in ten, boss. Just moving the cop car into position and we're good to go."

"Great, we'll see you out there," Conrad said as Mak headed out the door.

"You're the big boss, right?" Hudson asked Conrad.

"That I am. Which means I get all the big headaches. Like dealing with actors." Conrad made a fake groan and tweaked Hudson's hair.

"Was my mom a headache?" Hudson's voice was wistful.

"Never. She was always on time and not only knew her own lines, but everyone else's."

"So she was good at her job?"

"She was the best."

"She never got fired?"

"Never. Why do you ask?"

"I told Kenny I was gonna be on TV. And he said if I didn't do a good job, you would fire me."

"Well, did you show up on time?"

"Yeah. Ivy brought me," Hudson replied, turning around in the tall makeup chair to smile at Ivy behind him. She felt a slight stab, remembering how dismissive she'd been when she'd met the funny little loner that first day in the garden.

"And do you know your lines?"

"I only have one."

"Okay. Do you know your line?"

Hudson looked at himself in the mirror, his expression growing serious.

"WHERE ARE YOU TAKING MY DAD?!" Hudson shouted full voice as Ivy, Conrad, and the makeup artist all stifled chuckles.

"Excellent. Then you have nothing to worry about. And Kenny can eat his heart out 'cause he's not going to be on TV," Conrad told him.

Zeke, a tall PA in shorts, beanie, and headset hooked to his ear entered the trailer. "Hey Mr. R., we're ready for the Hudster."

"That's me," Hudson said, pleased at his new nickname.

"He's all yours," the makeup artist confirmed, giving Hudson's hair a final swipe.

"Okay, gang. This is it," Conrad said, as Hudson hopped down from the chair.

Ivy followed behind as Zeke led the group across the studio back lot to a faux city street where a corner was blocked off, the street dressed down with litter and graffiti. Dead center among a maze of lighting equipment, cables, and crew, Ivy saw the two stars, Ceci and Nakia, hair loose and uniforms tight. They spotted Conrad on the sidelines and waved him over. Conrad approached the two girls, Ceci flashing her Miss Wisconsin smile and kissing him on the cheek, Nakia giving him a big bear hug. Ivy watched, swallowing an unexpected pang of something that felt strangely similar to jealousy.

A ripple went through the crew as Dexter, in his signature Red Sox cap, came through the crowd, randomly giving orders to various crewmembers as he approached Conrad and the group.

"I came to greet our star," Dexter said, extending his hand to Hudson. "I see you've brought your entourage."

"Who are you?" Hudson asked.

"He's your director," Conrad replied as introductions were made, Dexter lingering a little too long as he greeted Ivy and gave her the once-over.

"Shouldn't you be taking it easy?" Dexter said to Conrad in a conciliatory tone. "I'll have one of the PAs bring you a chair." Dex turned and snapped his finger at a nearby production assistant.

"I'm fine," Conrad said, annoyed. "Just one for Ivy."

Dexter turned to Hudson. "Okay, champ. Don't let me down." The AD hustled Hudson up the steps of an apartment building façade while the assistant set up a chair on the sidewalk for Ivy. Conrad repositioned Ivy's chair and stood next to her. When his hand accidentally touched hers, she felt a tingle run down her arm.

"We need to be able to see the monitor," Conrad pointed out, as if explaining why he was so close to her.

"Places. Settle, please."

Ceci and Nakia got a final bit of powder from the makeup artist, morphed into their tough cop characters, and slid into the squad car.

"Quiet, please. Speed. And we're rolling!"

"Action!" Dexter yelled from beside the camera.

The two stars jumped out of the car and bounded up the sidewalk, the camera crew a few feet behind them, a grip unspooling coils of cable as they all followed.

"Should we call for backup?" Ceci asked in character as Pulaski.

"Nah, we got this guy. No priors, should be a pussycat," Nakia, aka Jones, responded.

They ran up the steps to the apartment building and started banging on the door.

"Police!"

"Open up!"

"Cut!" Dex yelled. "Next position, folks."

"Reset," the AD shouted, and everyone began shifting back toward the squad car, a human wave moving along with the repositioning of the camera.

Conrad leaned over to Ivy. "It all makes sense once it's edited together—TV sense, that is, not real-life sense."

"You mean real street cops don't wear uniforms that look like they're sprayed on?" Ivy whispered.

Touché, Conrad mouthed in response.

"Action!"

The cops came bustling down the apartment stoop with a scruffy-looking young guy in handcuffs sandwiched between them.

"I don't know what you're talking about," Scruffy Guy said. "I've been home all day. Ask my kid, he'll tell you."

Hudson, convincingly distraught, rushed down the stairs after them as a small crowd of extras playing neighbors and bystanders gathered near the stoop to gawk. Nakia opened the door of the squad car, while Ceci shoved the guy's head down and slammed him into the back seat.

Hudson ran down to the sidewalk beside the car, stifling tears and yelling, "WHERE ARE YOU TAKING MY DAD?"

"Cut! Nicely done, people," Dexter said. He flashed a smile and a thumbs-up to Hudson.

"Scruffy Guy and Son of Scruffy Guy are released," the AD shouted, pointing Hudson toward Conrad and Ivy across the street. "And we're moving on."

"Did I do good?" Hudson said, as he hurried over.

"Not just good. Fabulous." Conrad high-fived him. "And in only one take!"

"It was my idea to cry. Did you like it?"

"By far the best crying I've ever seen," Conrad said to him, as Ivy looked on smiling.

"What if I take you to In-N-Out Burger to celebrate before we head home?" Ivy said to Hudson. She turned to Conrad, "If it's okay with you, that is."

Conrad didn't answer. His face was drained of color, and he was clenching his fist tightly against his chest.

"Conrad?" Ivy said. "Are you all right?"

Conrad gasped for air, his face glistening with sweat.

"Conrad, talk to me!" Ivy shouted.

Mak heard Ivy's cry from across the street and came running. She was already dialing 911 when Conrad crumpled like a cast-off tissue. Ivy caught him awkwardly, and they landed in a tangled heap on the sidewalk.

Within moments, an ambulance—a real one—pulled up and parked on the street next to the squad car and Conrad was strapped onto a gurney by a paramedic while another placed an oxygen mask over his face. Despite the intensity of the moment, Ivy couldn't help but think how odd it was to see the real ambulance alongside the fake cop car. She wondered fleetingly if the actors ever confused their actual lives with their characters' lives.

"I'll go with him," Mak said, but Ivy stepped in.

"No, let me go with him, if you don't mind. Can you see that Hudson gets home?"

Mak paused for a moment, as if considering who should accompany Conrad, then nodded. The paramedics slid the gurney into the ambulance as Hudson ran around to the open door.

He began to cry as he shouted, "Where are you taking him?" Once again, Ivy had the eerie sense that life was imitating art as Hudson reiterated his line from the TV show almost verbatim.

"To the hospital, honey. Mak's going to get you home to Fernanda, and I'll call you as soon as I can. I promise," she said. Ivy scuttled onto the bench in the back of the ambulance and they roared off down the street, lights and sirens blasting, looking for all the world like a scene from *Pulaski & Jones*.

"How's he doing?" Ivy asked the paramedic as he hovered over Conrad, monitoring his vitals and hooking up a main line and covering his face with an oxygen mask.

"I've seen worse," he told her.

"Can he hear me?"

"I doubt it. He's out."

Ivy looked at his ashen face, one arm hanging limp off the side of the gurney.

"Hang on, Conrad," she murmured. "Please."

Conrad opened his eyes. "Ivy?" he asked in a woozy tone, his eyes flickering shut again.

"What happened? Is he all right?"

"He's going in and out of consciousness," the medic said. "But we're less than three minutes away, ma'am."

The paramedic handed Ivy a bandage, then nodded to a scrape on her forearm where she had grazed the sidewalk. She hadn't even noticed the blood trickling down her wrist.

Three minutes suddenly seemed like a very long time. Ivy took Conrad's hand and gazed into his deathly pale face.

"Come on, Conrad. Stay with me."

His eyes fluttered open again.

"I have a box," he said, his voice thin and breathy through the mask.

"What?

"At the Bowl. Hollywood Bowl."

"Maybe you shouldn't try to talk."

"And tickets. *Rigoletto*. Next month."

"That's good. Try to rest now," she urged.

"Go . . . with . . . me."

"Where?"

"The Bowl."

"Sure, just be quiet."

"So you'll go?

"If it will get you to stop talking."

"Deal," Conrad said with a loopy grin before he passed out again.

37

The rain came down in a steady mist, softly at first, then with increasing intensity. Ivy didn't care. She liked the feel of her bare feet sinking into the dirt path, the squish of mud as the earth began to liquefy and wedge between her toes.

She wondered why it was so cold, much too cold for Malibu, then realized she was in Yosemite, walking through a sodden meadow, mountains in the distance, wild flowers springing to life on either side of the path as she passed. The sun appeared above a peak and a beam of pure light unfurled across the meadow, stretching from sky to earth.

Ivy began to follow the light, picking up her pace until she was sprinting across the valley. The path ended abruptly at the bottom of a hill, and she began to climb. She saw a figure far above her and began to move faster, though it was difficult to gain purchase on the rough terrain.

She could tell it was a man. He was too far away to identify for certain, but she thought she recognized his solid bulk and shaggy hair sneaking down his collar. She tried to run to him, but the mud was getting deeper with every step. The man turned, and even at a distance, she recognized his bright-blue eyes. *Will.*

He turned back to the hillside and continued his climb, then stopped and turned around again and gave her a little wave. *Hello? Goodbye?* She couldn't tell.

He smiled reassuringly, blue eyes blazing in the sunlight. But these were different blue eyes. *Conrad?* She was confused. Was Will Conrad or was Conrad Will? She tried to extricate herself from the mud, but the more she strained, the more it slurped at her feet and ankles and knees until she could no longer move.

Suddenly, she heard a roar, deep and throaty like an explosion echoing through the mountains, then saw that the hillside had turned into a giant slide. She knew she had to warn the man, who she now understood was both Will and Conrad, that he was in danger of tumbling down the slide to his death. She screamed but no sound emerged.

38

*M*ak led Conrad through the back entrance of the cavernous Sound Stage 29, once the home of *Solid Gold* and *The Arsenio Hall Show*. The light was dim, so she made a show of stepping gingerly over the lengths of cable taped to the floor behind the flats that contained the interior sets for *Pulaski & Jones*.

"Why is it so dark?" Conrad asked crossly.

"You'll see."

As they came around to the front of the police precinct set, the lights went from low to full bright with a loud mechanical clack. The entire cast and crew of *Pulaski & Jones*, from stars to gaffers to grips, cheered as Mak led a begrudging Conrad center stage.

"Is this your doing?" he asked sotto voce.

"You think I could talk them out it?" Mak whispered, as two production assistants wheeled in a cart draped with a black cloth. "Everyone saw you keel over, boss. Take it as a compliment."

Television people, always up for a good time, Conrad thought, trying to stifle his annoyance. Though a part of him was grateful for what he knew was coming, celebrating his return from a two-week medical leave was hardly something he wanted to highlight. Nonetheless, he smiled gamely as Ceci and Nakia, dressed in cop wardrobe and massive hair, emerged from the crowd. With a theatrical flourish, the two stars moved in to do the honors, lifting the cover off the table as everyone cheered.

"Surprise!"

"Welcome back!"

Conrad smiled, doing his best to enjoy the hubbub as he gazed at what appeared to be a giant heart of chunky pink goo surrounded by asparagus and zucchini spears.

"It's a salmon spread cake," Ceci warbled in her Wisconsin accent, clapping her hands together and bouncing up and down like a little girl at a birthday party.

"Heart healthy, plenty of Omega-threes," added Nakia, giving Conrad a peck on the cheek. The team crowded in, slapping and clapping and welcoming their boss back to the trenches.

"Thank you all so much. It was very thoughtful of you. I can only imagine what you might have done if I'd been out another week," he said, dipping an asparagus spear into the salmon and pretending to take a bite with an *mmmm* of approval. He was squeamish, mentally and physically, on his first day back, but knew he needed to play along. Morale and whatnot.

Two more PAs rolled out another table, this one topped with bagels, juice, and coffee. Other than a Best Series Emmy, nothing could bond a television crew better than food. As everyone dug in, Conrad turned to address the group.

"I have been told that I have a heart of gold . . . once. And I've been told that I have a heart of ice—many times. My doctor says I have a heart of excess calcium. But I can guarantee you one hundred percent that this is the very first time I've ever had a heart of salmon."

The group laughed, then continued to munch and mingle until Mak called for the stage to be cleared and readied for the shoot in fifteen minutes. Everyone moved into high gear, removing carts, touching up hair, setting props in place.

"And . . . action."

Conrad watched the monitor as a former pop star, once known as DidiK, strode onstage. He'd never been a fan of her music, but he'd always found her craggy face, magenta hair, and balls-out energy exciting. It hadn't taken the network much convincing to allow Conrad to cast her as police chief, considering the potential publicity coup she could bring to the show.

"Get Pulaski and Jones in here," she bellowed in character. A rookie cop jumped up from his desk and hurried into the squad hallway, waiting behind a flat for a couple of beats. The stage manager cued the young cop, who returned onstage with the two stars sauntering in behind him.

"Hey, Cap," Pulaski said.

"What's up, Chief?" Jones added.

"That guy you pulled over on the D-dub last night, what's the story there?" the captain asked.

"Just another drunk scumbag we caught on a bar close. Why?"

"O'Malley's working a rape and thinks he fits the physical. He still in lockup?"

"That he is. I'd be happy to deliver him to O'Malley personally," Pulaski said in a mock Irish brogue.

"O'Malley will owe you big time, girl," Jones said to the captain as they ambled out of her office, high-fiving each other for bringing in a big fish. Conrad grimaced at the corny high-five, but since Dexter had decided to make it a signature gesture and it more or less worked, he let it go.

"That's *Captain*. Don't let me hear you say 'girl' again, girl," the captain growled after them. Conrad watched the monitor as the camera moved in tight on the singer's distinctively hawklike profile.

"I've got to admit," Dexter whispered to him, "that was a brilliant casting move."

"Everybody loves a comeback. Especially Hollywood."

39

*I*vy parked the Prius on a rain-slicked Santa Monica side street. Dodging the unexpected downpour, she and Mak darted to the overhang in front of a vintage duplex-turned-gallery. The sign outside read PHILLIPA GRAY ARTSPACE.

"This is nuts," Mak said, attempting to smooth her rain-frizzed hair. "Remind me why I'm here again."

"You're here supporting me supporting Conrad supporting JP," Ivy answered as she ran up the sidewalk and pushed open the front door. They queued up behind a group of casual chic LA Westsiders in the front hallway to check in and get a gallery handout. Above them on the exposed brick wall was a huge poster announcing the show—"Repoussé and Chasing: The Art and Craft of Metalwork"—along with a striking detail of a piece of metal curled like the top of an Ionic column.

"Wow," Mak said, gazing at the poster. "Have you seen his stuff?"

"I've seen a few pieces. That night I took Hudson to his place when Conrad was in the hospital the first time."

"Right, your dinner date."

"Hardly," Ivy replied rolling her eyes.

"Is Conrad coming?"

Ivy nodded. "Since he got a clean bill of health from his cardiologist he can pretty much do whatever he wants now."

"Well, well, lucky you."

Ivy rolled her eyes at Mak's innuendo.

"And what's happening with the two of you?"

"We have officially decided to slow things down—partly because of his health, but also because of, well, a million reasons."

"First sensible thing you two have done," Mak said, giving Ivy a look of approval.

"Welcome," said a handsome man wearing a bolo tie. "Here's a program with details and pricing for each piece. Enjoy!"

"Thanks," Ivy said as she signed the guest book.

"Let's go get us drunk," Mak stage-whispered. "I don't think I can do art without booze." They headed into the main gallery space, which was stark white and dissected into two main rooms by a movable air wall. The front half featured a display of black-and-white photographs of architectural images that contrasted industrial materials with elegant details from furniture, doorways, and buildings.

Mak spotted a bar on the side wall, grabbed a couple of plastic cups of white wine, and handed one to Ivy.

"To old friends," they said in unison, clinking their cups. Ivy frowned, noting the sea of one-use plastics on the bar top.

"Ooh, I love the contrast in these," Mak said, examining the photos.

They took a lap around the front gallery as the crowd began to grow and circulate through the space.

"Let's go find JP's work," Ivy suggested.

Ivy and Mak rounded the corner into the back half of the gallery and gasped in unison. Several of JP's metalwork pieces hung on the whitewashed walls, others sat atop stark white pedestals with pin spots highlighting them for dramatic effect. Strips of lacy aluminum fluttered birdlike from the ceiling in Calder-style mobiles. As they came closer, they could see images from nature in the pieces. Flowers, leaves, insects, all intricately detailed in different metals.

"Oh. My. God," Mak exclaimed.

"I know. They're beautiful, aren't they?"

"And so is he."

Ivy followed Mak's gaze to where JP, in dark jeans and a worn leather jacket, was standing beside a mounted sculpture chatting with a circle of people.

"You've seen him before, Mak."

"Not like that, I haven't. He's so hot."

Ivy and Mak moved to the edge of the circle, and JP grinned and threw them a little wave as he continued his conversation with the group, a sleek middle-aged woman with oversize glasses and a pixie haircut—apparently Ms. Gray herself—standing proprietarily alongside.

"JP is one of the few artists in the country equally skilled at using ancient and modern metalworking techniques," Phillipa explained. "He combines blacksmithing, truly a lost art, with woodworking, metal manipulation, and rapid prototyping. By weaving together various metals and processes, he creates these beautiful designs that, despite their heft, look as though they're swaying in a gentle breeze."

The crowd nodded appreciatively.

"I love the juxtaposition of man-made and natural elements. Shaping a hunk of steel into a grape vine or a piece of rebar into a hawk gives me such a kick," JP said.

Ivy realized that the sculpture they were looking at was the piece she'd seen hanging over JP's couch just a few months ago. Now, as she examined the wall card, she learned that it was a rusted metal rendering of the LA skyline centered around downtown's Grand Park, Southern California's aspirational answer to Central Park.

A fiftyish fellow with a prodigious man-bun stepped forward and whispered into Phillipa's ear. After a brief back-and-forth, she leaned forward and placed a red dot at the base of the piece.

"Sold!" The crowd cheered as Phillipa gave JP a happy hug.

"Congratulations!" Ivy said, after the crowd dispersed and she and Mak could work their way forward to greet JP.

"We brought you good luck," Mak said.

"Then stick around. I'll take all the luck I can get," he replied, giving Mak a warm smile.

"I'm going to say hello to Fernanda," Ivy said, spotting her with Hudson across the room.

"I think I'll hang here and let JP show me his sketches," Mak said.

Ivy grinned and headed to other side of the increasingly crowded room, where Fernanda was holding Hudson's hand. She was glowing with pride at her nephew's achievement, and Hudson—in shorts, button-down shirt, and bow tie—was hopping up and down.

"Ivy, did you see that? JP sold his couch art," Hudson said gleefully.

"His what?" Ivy asked.

"His couch art. JP says people in LA like to buy art that goes the long way to put over their couch."

"He is very talented, my nephew," Fernanda said proudly. "His first sale tonight."

"Not exactly," Conrad said, appearing alongside them. He winked at Fernanda, gave Ivy a kiss on the cheek, and ruffled Hudson's hair.

"No?" Fernanda raised an inquisitive eyebrow.

"There's one more room. Take a look on the back patio."

"I want to go!" Hudson cheered, as he dragged Fernanda by the hand.

"May I buy you a glass of free wine?" Conrad asked Ivy.

"Absolutely."

He took Ivy by the elbow and gently steered her toward the bar.

"How are you feeling?" she asked.

"Happy to be alive," Conrad said, handing her a glass.

"Cheers to that."

"I'm glad I could come," Conrad said. "JP is very talented and, from what I hear, quite a good chef."

"Funny. I've heard that too," Ivy shot back at him.

"Of course, you haven't tried my cooking yet," Conrad said with a flirtatious grin, as he escorted her to the next room. "What do you think of the show?"

"I love JP's work," she said, "though I don't know much about art. Much to my parent's chagrin. They were always trying to get me to work in their gallery. But I'm a total left-brain nerd. I don't have a creative bone in my body."

"Are you kidding? You're a visionary. How else could you have invented your product? Besides, there's really nothing to know about art. Either a piece moves you or it doesn't. It's like wine, which people also turn into an exercise in elitism."

"Well, don't tell my parents. That's their favorite part."

Conrad chuckled and said, "Let's go check out the pièce de résistance."

They reached the little back garden where JP was again holding court. Ivy saw the final piece and instinctively reached out and clutched Conrad's hand.

"It's breathtaking," she said.

There, on the brick patio surrounded by ferns and flowering plants, was the fountain that Ivy had seen in an early stage in JP's basement. Only now it stood four feet high and the metal strips that had once been a rusted tangle were woven together into braid-like vines that opened into a basin of broad leaves detailed with stems and veins. At the top was an open flower of shimmering silver.

"It's aluminum," JP was explaining to the appreciative crowd that had clustered around the fountain. "I wanted the flower to contrast with the rust of the base."

"Mr. Suarez's inspiration was the Floralis Genérica in Buenos Aires, one of the most beautiful sculptures in the world," added Phillipa.

"And my personal fave," JP added.

"Look," Hudson yelled excitedly, pointing at the pool underneath the fountain. "There's a red dot in the water!"

"Yes, the fountain has been purchased by an anonymous patron," Phillipa told the crowd. "But we are happy to take a few orders on custom commissions for what JP is calling 'La Fuente de las Flores.'"

Several of the onlookers closed in on JP and Phillipa.

"That's so exciting for him. I hope he made a bundle on that fountain," Ivy said.

"I hope he doesn't quit on me. I need him back on the job. I have a big project waiting for him," Conrad responded.

"You didn't—"

"What?"

"Buy that fountain."

Conrad smiled as he said, "Not the job I.was referring to, but I guess you'll know if you see it in the garden someday."

Summer

40

*S*ettling onto her floor cushion at Healing Haven, Ivy scanned the circle, nodding at all the familiar faces as Toby kicked off the discussion, her once-mysterious accent—which Ivy had long since learned was Hungarian—now a welcome sound.

"Major holidays can be difficult, of course, but at least everyone shares those dates, and there is often the distraction of religious ceremonies, family dinners, and other traditions to help ease the pain of loss, if only for a little while."

Ivy felt the tears starting to build. She'd missed the last meeting and wanted to be with the group to acknowledge a milestone she'd dreaded.

"On the other hand, because birthdays and anniversaries are specific to the person, they can be particularly painful. On those days, we are often intensely aware that we can't share the moment, that we'll never be able to share the celebrations or even the set-backs with our loved ones again. We have two such occasions to memorialize today."

Ivy took a deep breath, readying herself to plunge in. But Calvin spoke up first.

"Last Tuesday was Madison's second birthday," he said, his eyes misting up. "I know Megan would have done it much better. All that little-girl sugar-and-spice stuff. But I bought some pink cup-cakes, put two little candles on one of them, and invited her grand-parents over to watch her blow them out. And I made the wish."

Group members nodded and smiled. *Good for you.*

"You did it," Toby said, glowing with her usual positivity. "You'll always love Megan, but you're also moving on with your life. For Madison. For you."

Calvin nodded his head, the tears running freely down his cheeks.

"Ivy?" Toby asked expectantly after an appropriate pause.

"Um, right," Ivy said, heads turning toward her.

"Last week was the one-year anniversary. Of Will's . . . accident . . . death."

The group murmured condolences, low and throaty like a saxophone on a distant balcony.

Ivy stifled a sob before she could continue.

"He loved this Emily Dickinson poem that he taught in his freshman poetry class. 'Because I could not stop for Death, He kindly stopped for me.' I can't get it out of my head. It's been making me crazy."

Ivy paused, glancing at Penny, who'd lost her teenage son to an overdose. At Ray, whose wife had died after a prolonged battle with Alzheimer's. And Cathy, whose sexy, funny husband died of cancer.

"There's nothing kind about death," Cathy said, "unless you happen to keel over on the dance floor from an aneurysm that takes you out so fast you don't even have time to finish your box step." She snapped her fingers, as if to say, *That's how fast it can happen*.

"Maybe that's it," Ivy said, a look of realization on her face like she'd just solved the problem of quantum gravity. "It's like there's a part of me that doesn't want to change, even though everything has changed, and another part of me that is conscious that there might still be so much more waiting for me. And all this time, I've felt guilty for thinking about the *more* part. But maybe I'm wrong. Does that make any sense at all?"

Ivy looked around the room, expecting to see faces filled with outrage at her foolhardy hopes for the future. But there they all were, smiling and nodding and looking at her with nothing but understanding.

41

A stiff summer breeze off the ocean whipped Ivy's hair around her face as she stood in the garden beside the raised wooden beds that JP had built. After her talk at UCLA and her visits to the Village Preschool, word had begun to spread about the brainy gal in Malibu with the organic gardening business, and Ivy had decided to use her newfound notoriety to test her product with interested amateurs.

She gazed at the sun trying to break through the marine layer, then smiled as Hudson, carrying a wicker basket, led a small but curious group into the garden. "Welcome. Thank you all for coming," Ivy called to the fifty or so people standing nearby: environmentalists, horticulture enthusiasts, neighbors, Malibu Garden Club members, and even a few of the moms from the Village Preschool in their designer leggings and platform Nikes. "I brought all the stuff for your talk, Ivy," Hudson said as he carefully placed the basket full of paper bags at Ivy's feet.

"Excellent," she said, smiling warmly at the crowd. "For anyone who doesn't already know me, I'm Ivy Bauer, resident gardener. Of course, you've already met my assistant, Hudson, or as he's known locally, the Hudster." Hudson grinned and gave a little wave to the group.

"I certainly don't have to tell all of you that California is in the midst of a drought. In fact, scientists are suggesting that we are well into a megadrought that could last as long as another fifty years . . . or indefinitely. But there's a lot we can do, which is what I want to talk about today."

Ivy stepped up on the ledge of the wooden bed and motioned for the others to gather closer around. Hudson sat on the edge near Ivy as the adults began to form a semicircle around them. Ivy watched in satisfaction, thinking that for such a linear person, she seemed to have a lot of circles and semicircles in her life lately. The grief group, Hudson's circle time, and now a circle of friends and fellow gardeners.

"Healthy soil is a lot like a sponge that soaks up water. It's a fine balance between saturation and drainage. Some of the water goes directly to feed plants and trees, but it also goes deep into aquifers, that is, the empty spaces between rocks and sediment that holds water underground and feeds streams and rivers. If we cut down trees and plow the grasslands, there's nothing left to hold the rainwater, and it compacts the soil, which causes flooding and, eventually, strips the land of its topsoil."

Ivy heard a distant banging, and noticed that some of the visitors were looking around to locate the noise.

"Anyway, that's the basic premise. Now for the fun part," she said, drawing their attention back toward her. "Hudson, may I have the large bag, please?"

Hudson jumped up and pulled the bag out of the basket, handing it to Ivy. "Should I give everyone their bag?"

"Not just yet, but you can take the jar and the little packet out of my bag."

"Happy to assist," Hudson replied with a little flourish. Ivy smiled, recognizing the phrase Conrad often said when he helped Fernanda in the kitchen.

Hudson handed Ivy the packet, then held up a clear glass Mason jar. "It's re-useful. Right, Ivy?"

"That's right, it's reusable. Just one way we can all help the environment." Ivy opened the wide-mouth jar and showed the crowd that it was filled with water. The onlookers watched closely as she poured the white powder into the jar and then gave it a good shake.

"This is something I've been working on for the past few years," she said, continuing to shake the jar gently as she spoke. "It's a nontoxic water retention gel called HydraHold. It absorbs more than one hundred times its weight in water. Take a look."

She stopped shaking the jar, unscrewed the wide-mouth top, and slowly turned the jar upside down just like she had in the UCLA class. At first, nothing happened. She smiled, enjoying a bit of showmanship, so unlike her early teaching days, which had been agony.

"Hudson?" He stepped up and put his palms together to form a cup as Ivy gave the jar a little tap on the bottom. After a moment, the wobbly gel slid into his hands. Hudson grinned at the goop like it was the best Christmas present he'd ever gotten.

"Wow! What just happened there?" asked one of the moms.

"Did it absorb all that water?" A short guy with a khaki sunhat leaned close to Hudson and gave the gel a tentative poke.

"That's exactly what it did. And when you place the gel at the roots of your beds when you plant, the plants will find the water there, thus reducing the need for irrigation."

"Check it out," Hudson said, extending his gelled hands to the group.

A ripple ran through the crowd of adults as though they were a group of kindergartners waiting for a blob of fresh Play-Doh. Ivy laughed as people came forward and she and Hudson plopped the gel into their hands.

Ivy shared the HydraHold origin story about her early test with diapers, much to the group's delight. After a few minutes of touching, smelling, and in one case, tasting the gel, Hudson circulated through the crowd, handing out recycled paper towels.

"Combustible," he told the group, as he collected the used towels. "No, wait. Com-pos-table. That means they can turn into plant food. Right, Ivy?"

"Absolutely. Now here's the big question . . ." Ivy had their attention. "Who wants to try HydraHold in your garden?" Hands shot up, heads nodded, everyone was in except for one middle-aged woman in a striped poncho who was shaking her head doubtfully.

"I've always wanted to garden, but I swear I have a black thumb. I can't keep a houseplant alive," she said. "Are you sure you want to include me?"

"Definitely. No gardener left behind," Ivy replied with a grin. "Okay, so here's what we're going to do. Each of you will get a bag with the gel and two packets of radish seeds, along with written instructions."

"You have to follow the instructions," Hudson admonished.

"Radishes are really easy to grow. All you do is use the Hydra-Hold, per the instructions, on one plot, and leave it alone. And you'll water on the other plot as we have outlined. If you want, you can plant the seeds in containers and start your own container garden. The best part is, your crop will be ready for consumption in about a month. Hudson, will you do the honors?"

Hudson proudly handed out the paper bags with the seeds as people crowded around to thank Ivy.

"I'm so gratified that you all came out today to learn about the environment, *your* environment. I'll be checking back with you in a week or so in case you have any questions. And please, tell your friends so they can come to my next talk. Hudson, will you escort our guests to their cars?"

"Please stay on the path, everyone. I'll show you our butterfly garden on the way out!" Hudson said, excited to be leading the way. The group set off with Hudson in front, a reverse Pied Piper with a knowing child leading a group of willing grown-ups.

Ivy picked up the basket and headed to the main vegetable patch, where Hudson's pole beans were growing up the sides of the tepee. As she turned a leaf over to inspect for insects, she heard the banging resume from somewhere nearby. She ventured toward the sound, now discernable as hammering, until she came to a little clearing near a stand of liquidambar trees.

A short distance away, she saw JP framing a wooden structure that appeared to be about the size of a two-car garage. As she got closer, she saw that he was dancing as he worked, swaying his hips and swinging his arms to some unheard music pumping through his earbuds.

Ivy stopped to watch. *This is what joy looks like*, she thought. A line from a birthday poem Will had written for her along with a self-deprecating "those who can't write, teach," popped into her brain unbidden.

Joyous expressions / earth's efflorescence / my garden sprite.

"JP!" she yelled.

No answer.

Louder. "Juan Pedro!!" Ivy yelled, remembering what he'd told her was his actual name.

He turned around and grinned, white teeth flashing against

his olive skin, reminding Ivy just how handsome he was. JP yanked the buds out of his ears and stuck them in his pocket.

"Yo, Ive. How you been?"

"Great, I just gave another talk to a local group. A lot more people this time."

She stepped over the wooden frame and into the center of the would-be foundation. "What are you making? I didn't know there were any plans for outbuildings."

"Conrad seems pretty pumped about this. It's an outdoor office and greenhouse. He said you and I could geek out on the passive design elements."

"Passive design?" Ivy asked, confused.

"You know, natural lighting and air cooling . . ."

"I know what passive design is. I just didn't know that Conrad did."

JP grinned. "Fair point. I guess you're rubbing off on him. Anyway, the passive design stuff and the blueprints are on the desk in his study. If you want to go grab them, we can walk it through. But we better get started, it looks like it's about to rain."

"Sounds good. Be back in a jiff."

She turned toward the path, and JP said, "Hey, if this is supposed to be a surprise for you, don't tell Conrad I told you."

"Our secret," Ivy replied, drawing a big X over her chest.

"Bring cookies!" JP yelled after her, popping the buds back in his ears and picking up his hammer and his groove.

Ivy headed toward the house, inhaling the salt scent of ocean brine mixed with the pungent smell of freshly turned earth. She felt the warmth of the morning sun on her face and realized she was smiling. Really, truly smiling. After all this time, she was happy. And not just in this moment. A feeling of contentment had somehow wedged its way into her body and found a home.

"Fernanda?" Ivy called as she entered the house. The housekeeper was nowhere to be seen, though there was evidence of her having recently been in the kitchen in the form of oatmeal cookies left to cool. Ivy grabbed a cookie and headed toward Conrad's study.

It was strange to be in the study without him, she thought. She'd hardly set foot in this room since he'd first hired her. She looked around the lavish space, with all its accoutrements of success, and her eyes lighted on the black-and-white photos of Conrad, Hudson, and Dawn.

She moved to Conrad's desk, ping-ponging between a newfound sense of belonging and a feeling that she was an intruder who might get caught trespassing at any moment. Shaking off the thought, she turned her attention to the leather binder on Conrad's desk. *Conrad's brain*, Fernanda called it, as he could never seem to function without it close by.

Ivy unzipped it and saw a brochure and plans for a greenhouse tucked inside. Smiling, she picked up the plans and sat down in Conrad's desk chair to look through them. As she did, she noticed what looked like screenplay pages underneath. She glanced at the first page, curious to read one of Conrad's scripts in progress and stopped in horror when she saw the character description for . . .

DR. BEACHUM
(hot soil scientist in her early thirties)

42

INTERIOR: RESEARCH GROW LAB

Jones and Pulaski interview Dr. Beachum.

DR. BEACHUM
(hot soil scientist in her early thirties)

I understand you have some questions
about pesticides used in agriculture.

PULASKI
That's correct, Doctor.

JONES
Hypothetically speaking, could you
kill someone by putting . . .
(looks at notes)

organophospates in their oatmeal?

DR. BEACHUM

I never deal in hypotheticals, officers.
I'm a scientist, a total left-brain
nerd.
I deal in facts and figures.

PULASKI

But if you had to speculate . . . ?

DR. BEACHUM

In high enough quantities, sure.

JONES

Thanks, Doc. That's all we needed.
                    (to Pulaski)

Let's bounce, partner.

43

"ure, *Pulaski and Jones* is a procedural drama," Conrad said to the reporter sitting across from him in his office at the studio. "But that doesn't absolve us from trying to inject a level of originality into a well-established genre. Fortunately, I have a few ideas up my sleeve." Unlike his study at home, his production office was strictly utilitarian. Standard-issue gray metal file cabinets, a pressed-wood desk, and a small round table with four chairs. The less he spent on the production office, the more he had to spend on the production, where it really mattered. The only concession to decor, or perhaps to vanity, were the framed title cards for all six of his previous shows hanging on the wall—*Directed by, Written by, Produced by Conrad Reed*—lined up in matching black frames.

The reporter hadn't failed to notice them when Conrad escorted her into his office. Now, she was scribbling away in a reporter's notebook, her iPhone on the table between them recording the conversation.

"What would you say is the most important thing *you've* added to the genre?" she asked.

"Ultimately, that's for the audience to judge, Ms. Baker. But our goal has been to create compelling characters with some degree of verisimilitude," he said, glancing outside as it began to pour.

Conrad winced inwardly as the reporter wrote *verisimilitude* on her pad and underlined it. As if producing yet another cop show wasn't bad enough, having to promote it to an endless horde of reporters, radio hosts, and podcasters was even worse. *Part of the job, Connie, enjoy it*, he could almost hear Dawn's warning voice in his ear.

"Then we put the characters in challenging situations, most of which they solve in forty-two minutes—that's minus the eight minutes of commercials, of course. We just try to stay out their way," he continued with calculated humility.

She smiled. Few people could resist Conrad's charm.

"Why do you think the show has taken off so quickly? As you say yourself, it's a pretty straightforward procedural," she said.

"Because I let the writers own their ideas."

"What do you mean by that?" she asked, sniffing a good sidebar for her story.

"I abhor the writers' room," Conrad said with a thoughtful frown. "Not the writers, mind you. They're the stars of the whole operation. But traditional writers' rooms often operate with a stifling kind of collaboration, where everyone is trying to finish each other's sentences, one-up their ideas. It flattens the imagination. Even in a cheesy construct, uh, scratch that, would you make that 'traditional construct' please? I don't want to bite the hand that feeds sixty-four people. Anyway, even in a traditional network series construct, my goal is to let our writers run with ideas they're passionate about without the entire team kibitzing them to death."

Someone knocked on the office door, then the skinny production assistant Zeke cracked it open slightly and poked his head through.

"Sorry to interrupt. You have a call from Ivy, something about a script. It sounded kind of urgent."

"Thanks, Zeke. Tell her I'll call her back right after we're done here."

"Roger that," Zeke responded, closing the door behind him.

Conrad turned back to the reporter with a warm smile. "Where were we?"

"You were about to tell me about the pairing of the female leads. It was a pretty gutsy move using total unknowns," she said.

"Sure, Beth. May I call you Beth, Ms. Baker?"

She nodded.

"That is the question, isn't it? But since this is a roundup piece about network dramas in general, let's save that for another time and another story. I'll give you the entire chronology on how we developed our two lead characters."

"I'd like that," she said, barely able to contain her excitement at getting a second shot at Conrad Reed.

"And now, Beth, I must get back to work. Be careful on the road, this storm's gonna be a bitch."

· · · · ·

*B*ack in the conference room, Conrad took his seat at the head of the long oval table. Like his office, this room, though much larger, was equally austere. Production office basic, just as he liked it. No goofy basketball hoops or distracting pinball machines; leave those to the sitcom nerds. His team was meant to focus on the work. He had no sympathy for creative histrionics, missed deadlines, or unwarranted all-nighters. He ran his show like a business where people worked reasonable hours, were managed and measured, and got the job done.

"Where are we?" Conrad asked the group of eleven writers seated around the table, a multiracial mix of men and women. Some older and seasoned with an arm's list of credits on IMDb, some in their twenties or early thirties, a few right out of the writers diversity programs that had, thankfully, become de rigueur for the studios. Cheap labor, sure, because they were total rookies, but also a lot of talent. Conrad always felt good about being able to give a few gifted kids a shot in a tough business.

"We're up next," said a writer, referring to herself and her partner. "Working title: Confidence. Here's the setup: a confidential informant tries to pull a con on P and J."

"And the CI is hot."

"Extremely hot."

"We get it," Conrad said. "Continue."

"When the girls realize the CI is conning them, they turn the con on him."

"We want to have some fun with this one, let the ladies show their comedic chops. See what it's like for seasoned cops to fall for a pretty face, just like anyone else."

Conrad cringed inwardly for a second, thinking of how Mak had been duped, then dismissed the thought. "I like it. But I want this to sparkle. I mean dialogue that is crisp and smart and, dare I say, witty. I doubt if you've ever seen *Moonlighting*—"

"You mean *Moonlight*, the movie that won Best Picture?"

"No, *Moonlighting* the TV show. As in early Bruce Willis and Cybill Shepherd. That sparkled. Or go back to Capra, Cukor, Sturges, and learn something about comedy writing."

Conrad got up and wrote CONFIDENCE on the whiteboard. Despite the reproach, the pair grinned at Conrad's green light.

"Now I've got a pitch," Conrad said. The room stilled.

"Here goes. The ladies are called in to work crowd control

when a fellow cop, a white guy, is arraigned for shooting an un-armed Black teenager in Inglewood after a traffic stop. The ladies know the cop, and although they think he's generally a decent guy, they are divided about his culpability. Thoughts?"

The writers remained silent for a long moment. Conrad could see their minds spinning on the idea, well aware that this wasn't their usual type of story.

Finally, one writer broke the ice. "Are you sure we want to do a ripped-from-the-headlines story? Not our usual space."

"Yeah, our show is entertainment, not enlightenment."

"Can't we do both?" Conrad asked.

"The network's going to hate it."

"I think we should go for it. It's the least we can do for all the people of color—disproportionate I might add—who have been harassed by the police."

"I agree. Let's do it," added another.

"It'd be a game changer," said the Black writer, Jocelyn.

"Are you saying that because the idea has merit or because you're a suck-up?" Conrad asked pointedly.

"Can't it be both?" Jocelyn quipped, as the others chuckled.

"Show of hands. Should we do it?"

All but two hands went up.

Conrad nodded. "Let's see if the suits have any gonads. Any-one got a working title?"

"Routine Traffic Stop," Jocelyn shot back.

Heads nodded all around, and Conrad stood up and wrote RTS in all caps on the whiteboard.

"I'd like you to work on this, Jocelyn," Conrad said to her.

"Go, Joss," one of the writers shouted, clapping her on the back.

"Are you profiling me?" she asked mischievously.

"No, I'm exploiting you. And don't you forget it," Conrad joked. "Okay, folks. Story outlines by Wednesday, new pitch ideas by Friday. Hey, and if anyone here knows anything about pesticides, I have a story idea I want to run by you."

A few of the writers looked at Conrad curiously, though they'd heard odd ideas before.

Zeke, the production assistant knocked loudly and entered, with Mak a few feet behind.

"Sorry to interrupt," Zeke said to Conrad. "But you asked me to give you a heads-up if the storm got worse. They just issued a flash flood warning and possible evacuation in burn areas, so it's getting pretty hairy out there."

"Thanks, Zeke. All right, everyone, that's a wrap for the day. I want you to get home in one piece before every idiot in California forgets how to drive," Conrad told the group.

The writers began to drift out of the room, chattering among themselves. Conrad saw that Mak was hanging behind as he shut his laptop and stuffed it into his computer bag.

"Mak, have you seen my leather binder? I can't find it anywhere."

"Boss, can we chat in your office?" It wasn't a question.

Hearing the intensity in Mak's tone, Conrad looked up and saw more distress etched on her face than he'd ever seen, despite dozens of tense moments they'd shared. "What is it?"

"Office, boss. Now, please."

She led him down the corridor and into his office, shutting the door behind them and slumping against it.

"He's here," Mak said.

"Who's here?" Conrad asked.

His jaw tightened when he realized who she meant. "Sal? How did he manage to get onto the lot?"

"Like anyone else, I'm sure. Gave security a little smile and they waved him right through."

"Where is he now?"

"He's in my office. Zeke is standing guard."

"Bring him in here," he said. "On second thought, have Zeke bring him in. You clear out. Now."

Mak opened the office door, then turned back to face Conrad. "Boss, you know how sorry I—"

"It's not your fault, Mak. Never was. Now go home."

She nodded somberly and left the room.

Conrad was seated behind his desk when Zeke led Sal into the room.

"Want me to stay, Mr. R.?" the PA asked.

Conrad shook his head and Zeke exited, throwing a suspicious glance back at Sal before he left. Conrad noticed that Sal had a padded mailer tucked under his arm. It was just an envelope, but it seemed somehow ominous, like it could come to life and spring at him at any moment.

Conrad waited a long beat, letting Sal squirm, until he finally spoke. "I know all about you. Petty thief, part-time paparazzo, just out of jail for passing bad checks. Lucky for you our prisons are so crowded."

Sal remained silent, but the corner of his lip curled up in a nasty half smile.

"I thought we were finished," Conrad snarled.

"Well, see . . . I wanted to give you another shot. You know, let you see these photos before I go public. You might decide to change your mind and, you know, take 'em off the market."

"You really think you're going to embarrass me with naked photos of my wife? She was one of the most beautiful women on the planet."

Sal made a thin, strangled-sounding laugh. "No, man. They're not naked photos. They're crash photos. Some doozies I took at the scene and a few more from my buddy at the morgue, just for good measure. You and I may know what really happened. But *TMZ* and the *National Enquirer* don't. Be pretty bad if these went viral—the Jayne Mansfield myth all over again."

Conrad leaned forward against his desk, as though his body were suddenly heavy. "I don't believe you. No one would ever run that kind of photo."

"You really want to take that chance? The internet isn't all that picky, pal," Sal said.

With a bravado Conrad hadn't seen until now, Sal tossed the envelope onto his desk. "See for yourself. Could be a big story. A shame for such a pretty girl. And think how awful it would be for the kid when he finds out how his mom actually died. Whoa, the look on his face. Now that'd be a photo all right."

Conrad lunged at Sal, but before he could grab him, Sal was out the door. Shaking, Conrad collapsed back into his chair. He sat and stared at the envelope for a long moment, then ripped it open and with terrified fingers slid out a batch of 8 x 10 photographs.

He gasped. What he'd heard described to him by Billy and all those police officers after Dawn's accident had little relationship to what he now saw in the starkly crisp images before him. His precious, beautiful, radiant Dawn. Her head nearly severed by the shattered windshield, face and body covered in blood, thick and viscous as the chocolate syrup Hitchcock used for the shower scene in *Psycho*. But production blood and television crash scenes were no match for this. This was real life, or rather, death. Hideous, violent, heartbreaking death.

Heaving with sobs, Conrad slowly ripped the photos in half,

then fourths, then eighths, and on and on until his office floor was littered with tiny pieces of celluloid. He stared at them, knowing full well that Sal would still have the negatives and that this wasn't over. Then he leaned over and vomited into the trash can, his retching nearly drowned out by the rain on the production office roof.

44

*I*vy stood at the front window of the cottage, forehead against the glass as she watched the rain pouring down in metal-gray sheets. She was dry eyed, but her face was swollen and stained from the tears she'd shed since reading Conrad's script pages.

She had her phone in one hand, a half-finished glass of red wine, not her first, in the other. "I shouldn't have trusted him, Charlotte."

"That's a little harsh."

"Come on, a hot soil scientist in her early thirties? It was like he was making a mockery of what I do, of who I am."

"I read those pages you sent. Granted, not a particularly clever scene, but I didn't get the impression he was mocking you."

"Even if he wasn't, it made it so clear that he doesn't see the importance of my work . . . or me, for that matter. I am not someone who wants to be a part of his crazy Hollywood machine. I hate Hollywood."

"Have you stopped to look at it from his point of view?" Charlotte asked.

"What do you mean?"

"Well, when Randy and I were first dating, he would bring

me these bouquets of sunflowers and lavender. At first I was insulted, because those were exactly the flowers I grew in my garden. I felt like he was making some kind of statement about my incompetence as a horticulturist. I finally blew up at him one day, and he looked at me and said, 'I bring you those flowers because I know they're your favorites.' Boy, did that shut me up."

"So you're suggesting that this scene is a tribute to me? Like his suggestion that I give up my lab and rush down to Southern California so I can be with him? He's so presumptuous, so self-centered."

"I'm suggesting you discuss it with him. All of it. Find out what he's thinking. Not what you think he's thinking."

"After everything I've worked so hard for, I can't just change my entire life for a man. Especially one who doesn't even know who I am."

"Promise me that you'll at least speak with him," Charlotte urged.

"I called his office and said it was important, but he was in an interview. They told me he'd call me right back, but he never did. I guess what's important to me isn't necessarily important to him."

· · · · ·

*F*resh basil, pine nuts, and olive oil were strewn across the kitchen island, rich and inviting as a Cezanne still life despite the storm raging outside. Fernanda and Hudson stood side by side, Hudson perched happily on his little kitchen stepstool. Fernanda watched as he lifted the top of the food processor and stuck a spoon inside to test a bit of their in-progress pesto. Rory circled a couple of times and then lazily dropped onto her bed in the corner, lifting her head for a moment as the intense smell of garlic wafted past.

"I think it's too thick," Hudson said, giving Fernanda a taste.

"So you know what to do."

"A little more oil?"

"That's right. But use a spoon so you don't pour too much."

Hudson carefully measured out a tablespoon of olive oil and poured it into the processor. He looked at Fernanda for permission and, when she nodded, put the top on and pressed the pulse button. Just then, the front doorbell rang.

"Ah, that's probably FedEx with Conrad's new office lamp," she said, patting Hudson's hand. "I can't believe they made it up here in all this rain. Be right back, *precioso*."

• • • • •

*I*t was late afternoon, but nearly dark as Conrad drove as fast as he dared toward Malibu. He'd tried Fernanda from the car, but the call didn't go through. Not so unusual—cell reception could be spotty in the hills, especially in a storm as bad as this one. He had gotten through to Billy, who promised to call his friend at LAPD now that Sal had actually attempted to extort money from Conrad.

Conrad couldn't believe he'd ripped all those photos to shreds. If he'd learned anything from producing cop shows, it was that you never destroyed evidence. He tried to banish the sickening images from his mind, but it was impossible, of course. Seeing those horrifying photographs of the real thing was much more painful than any TV violence he would ever inflict on the viewing audience. *My Dawn . . .*

Grim faced and exhausted, he pulled the Mercedes into the

garage and entered through the kitchen, ready to pour himself a stiff drink when Fernanda rushed to him in panic.

"Is he in the garage? Did you see him?"

"See who? What's the matter?" Conrad asked, dropping his computer bag and jacket on the counter.

"Hudson. We were cooking. I went to answer the doorbell, and when I came back, he was gone," she said, almost in tears.

"How long ago?"

"Five minutes maybe. I was about to call you, but I was sure he was here somewhere."

Conrad's face went white. "Sal," he said, thinking how easily he could have made it to Malibu before Conrad did, distracting Fernanda and getting Hudson alone somehow.

Conrad raced toward the front hallway. Taking the stairs two at a time, he yelled over his shoulder, "I'll look upstairs, you look down."

Within minutes, they'd covered the entire house, checking all of Hudson's favorite hideouts: the media room, the wine cellar, under the big desk in Conrad's study. There was no sign of him anywhere. Even if was playing a joke on them, Hudson would have come out of hiding when he heard the grown-ups' frantic calls.

"I'll text Ivy. You call 911," Conrad said.

Hudson missing. Have you seen him?

OMG. Haven't seen since am.

Sal at studio today. Fearing the worst.

A moment later, Ivy entered through the kitchen door. She ran her hand through her hair, shook out her windbreaker, and stomped her wet tennis shoes on the mat.

"The police are on the way. There are trees down from the storm so it will take them an hour or more," Fernanda said, hanging up the kitchen phone.

"We can't wait that long," Conrad responded.

"Where's Rory?" Ivy asked abruptly, glancing at the vacant dog bed. Conrad and Fernanda realized they hadn't seen her when they searched the house.

"Maybe she's is in the garage," Fernanda suggested.

"His whistle," Ivy said, looking at the doorknob on the kitchen closet.

"What?" Conrad asked.

"Hudson's whistle is gone. He always takes it on the trail."

"Oh my God," Conrad said, grabbing a flashlight from a kitchen drawer.

"I'm going with you," Ivy said.

"No, I'll go alone." Conrad looked outside at the sky, bruised and angry. "Someone needs to wait for the police."

"Fernanda will be here," Ivy protested.

Conrad looked at her, conflicted.

"I know those trails better than you do," she insisted.

Silently, he got another flashlight, grabbed his jacket, and they headed into the storm.

· · · · ·

*F*ueled by fear and adrenaline, Conrad and Ivy took off at a run toward the trailhead above the house. Ivy thought about Conrad's weakened heart but didn't slow her pace. The foothill path, usually so serene, with only the sounds of birdsong and rustling leaves to break the stillness, groaned like some prehistoric beast as the wind and rain bore down on it.

Their flashlights illuminating the trail, Ivy and Conrad skid-ded along, scanning the edges of the path for signs of Hudson or Rory, yelling their names against the wind. Dodging ankle-deep puddles and downed branches, they finally reached the quarter-mile marker. Ivy glanced over at Conrad. He was breathing hard, his chest heaving with the exertion. Ivy stopped to catch her breath, hoping Conrad would follow suit.

"Are you all right? Do you need to head back?" Conrad yelled above the storm.

"No, let's keep going," she replied, jerking away and starting to run. She knew it was useless to tell him to slow down. They pushed on, each step more arduous as the mud turned to wet ce-ment beneath their sneakered feet, offering little traction.

"Hudson!" Conrad yelled over and over, cupping his hands around his mouth for amplification, but his cries barely regis-tered above the ferocity of the wind.

Ivy slipped, grabbing a low-hanging tree limb for support. Conrad reached for her, but she pulled back, regaining her bal-ance without his help.

When they came to the Y intersection in the trail, Conrad turned to the left, taking a route they'd hiked before.

Right.

Ivy looked around, sure she'd heard a voice, but that was im-possible.

Right, she heard again, this time more insistently.

Ivy stopped dead, staring at the fork in the path.

"Conrad!" she called out. "This way. I know where he is."

They headed toward the uphill path on the right. Rocks and vegetation began to lose their hold on the earth, fragile from the prior year's fires, and tumbled onto the path in front of them. Ivy slipped again and Conrad grabbed for her, insistent on taking her hand this time. They trudged on, leaning against each other for support until Conrad stopped and shone his flashlight ahead on the path, its beam piercing through the darkness.

The climbing cave.

"There," Ivy shouted. They could barely make it out in the darkness, but there it was, a hundred yards ahead on the trail, the little cave perched on a rock ledge that Hudson liked to explore. One small foot in a red high-top sneaker poked out of the opening.

Ivy looked around to assess the storm and caught a glimpse of something moving on the downhill path below them. She gasped, and Conrad followed her gaze to see a man struggling along the trail, grabbing for anything that could keep him upright in the strong wind.

"Sal!" Conrad said. He doubled his pace toward Hudson, grabbing a stick for support and taking Ivy's hand. They stumbled along in the muck, sliding more than climbing, until they reached the cave mouth. The cave was more of an indentation in the rocky outcropping than an actual cave, but it was big enough for a kid and a dog to climb inside.

"Hudson!" Conrad yelled, crawling up the slick rocks toward the cave. "Are you all right?"

As they shone their flashlights inside, they could see Hudson huddled inside the cave with Rory squeezed in beside him. Hudson was trembling with fear, clutching Rory's fur for dear life.

Conrad climbed up to the cave opening, leaned in, and swept Hudson into his arms.

"You had me so worried. I thought I'd lost you."

"Are you mad at me?" Hudson managed to squeak out.

"Mad? I've never been so happy in my life!" Conrad told him.

Ivy watched, relieved beyond words but aware she had no

place in this family reunion. Conrad began to pull Hudson gently out of the cave, making space for Rory to crawl forward.

"That man . . . came to the back door . . . Rory got out . . . she was so scared . . ."

"It's okay, honey. Don't try to talk now."

Ivy heard a terrifying snap, and she and Conrad looked up the hillside, where an enormous oak tree was beginning to give way, its roots losing their purchase with a horrific rumble.

"Conrad, we need to go," Ivy yelled.

"Should we try to ride it out here?" Conrad asked her. "Maybe we can all squeeze in."

Glancing up, Ivy saw a saturated stretch of canyon above the path and realized that the earth was beginning to liquefy. She wasn't sure if Conrad saw what she did, but she knew it wouldn't hold for long.

"No. We need to go. Now!"

Conrad heard the urgency in her voice and looked up to see the oak start to shudder and pitch over. He handed Hudson to Ivy and reached back for Rory, who was so crazed with fear she was moving further inside.

"You take Hudson. Rory will be hard to handle," Conrad said to Ivy.

Ivy told Hudson to jump up piggy-back style while Conrad struggled to grip Rory underneath her belly, but finally got her in his arms. Ivy ripped off her scarf and handed it to Conrad to put over Rory's face in hopes it might calm her down. Ivy was every bit as terrified as Rory. She knew what the combination of earth and rain could do to a hillside, especially one that had experienced fires in the recent past, as this one had. With water rapidly collecting in the ground, the surge of water-soaked rock, earth, and debris could consume an entire village, let alone a hillside, in mere minutes. This entire trail might not even exist by morning.

They slogged their way back along the footpath, as the earth turned to mud under their feet. Sal was on the trail just below them, desperately grabbing at a low-hanging tree branch. His hand slipped off the rain-slick branch and he lost his footing, tumbling further down the slope.

Ivy grasped Conrad's arm, barely getting out of the way as the giant oak finally broke loose with a crash and careened down the hillside, branches splintering in every direction. She yelled for Hudson to close his eyes and hold on so he couldn't see what she and Conrad were witnessing—Sal being swept down the hillside in a tsunami-like wave, buried underneath a mountain of mud and debris.

Hudson kept his face pressed tightly against Ivy's shoulder, but she could still hear the little boy's frightened cries despite the deafening roar. She almost lost her balance as the earth shifted beneath her and a sinkhole opened up in the pathway, but Conrad steadied her and they pressed on.

As she ran, Ivy thought that this was what losing Will had been like. She'd never been able to define it before, but this was it. The cataclysmic sense of being off-balance, the loss of control, the world as you knew it giving way beneath your feet. Well, she'd been through that once and wasn't going to let it happen a second time. In a burst of speed, Ivy bolted down the trail, avoiding downed trees and branches, which seemed to rain from the sky.

Finally, they made it to the trailhead and onto the paved path toward the house. The sky was dark and heavy, but they could just discern the light outside the kitchen door. Almost there.

On firmer ground now, Conrad and Ivy flew past the flooded tennis court and the overflowing pool, water splashing up from their footsteps. Passing the gardens, Ivy knew they'd be ruined by wind or water or both, but that didn't matter right now. Getting home. That was all that mattered.

45

Safe inside, Conrad kneeled on the floor beside Hudson and stripped off his muddy pants, T-shirt, and high-tops. Hudson held his body stiff, convulsed with sobs as Conrad wrapped a towel around him and pulled him into a tight embrace.

Ivy felt numb, incapable of moving another step as she collapsed against the kitchen door, not caring that she was smearing mud on everything she touched. Fernanda handed her a giant beach towel, and Ivy saw that, prepared as always, Fernanda had placed stacks of towels, blankets, and first-aid supplies across the island.

"It's okay now, honey. It's okay," Conrad repeated until Hudson's sobs subsided into gulping hiccups. Ivy was surprised to feel a stab of regret that she'd never feel Conrad's arms around her again. That she would miss Malibu after she left. And that she was already feeling the loss of not having Hudson in her life. She wished she could cry with the abandon of child. That she could banish the grief and disillusion of the past year in an ocean of tears.

"The police will be here soon," Fernanda said. "The storm flooded PCH and they got stuck behind a jackknifed truck." She sank to her knees and began wiping down a mud-caked Rory, who dropped into her bed almost immediately. "I also called your agent."

Conrad looked at her in surprise.

"I know he has the private investigator."

Conrad nodded. "Good thinking. Thank you."

"I need to get Hudson into a hot bath."

"Just a sec," Conrad said, giving Hudson a soothing smile as he dried his hair. "Can you tell me what happened, sweetie?"

Fernanda frowned and shook her head. *Too much too soon.*

Hudson took a big sniff and said, "A man came to the back door."

"I was answering the front door," Fernanda explained, her eyes shining with tears. "I am so sorry."

Conrad put his hand on Fernanda's shoulder, as if to say, *It's not your fault*, then waited patiently until Hudson was ready to continue.

"He wanted pictures."

"What pictures, honey?" Conrad asked, trying to keep his voice even despite the tightening of his jaw.

"Of me. And mommy. That big one."

Conrad glanced over at Ivy as he realized Hudson was talking about the portrait of Dawn in the cottage. Ivy grimaced, but said nothing.

"Then there was a big boom and Rory ran out."

"And you went after her?"

Hudson nodded.

"That was so brave of you. Did the man chase you?"

Hudson dissolved into tears once again. "Am I in trouble?"

"No, *hijo*. You are not in trouble," Fernanda said, squatting down beside him and sweeping him into her arms.

The doorbell rang, and Hudson, having just begun to calm down, started to shake violently once again.

"Bath time, *precioso*," Fernanda said, leading him gently up the stairs.

· · · · ·

*I*vy was still trying to process all that had just happened as two rain-soaked detectives followed Conrad back into the kitchen. She grabbed a blanket and joined him at the kitchen table across from the detectives, a younger guy and a slightly older woman.

Conrad walked them through their ordeal on the hillside—finding Hudson, seeing Sal, the mudslide. Ivy sat by silently, her head bowed low as if the weight of it was too much for her to bear.

The detectives listened intently, asking questions and taking notes.

When Conrad was finished, the female detective shut her notebook and said, "Here's what we know so far. His name is . . . was . . . Salvatore Francis Horner. Small-time operator—check fraud, drug deals, occasionally worked as a legit photographer. But your friend's PI filled us in on Sal's latest line of work, which we are in the process of confirming. He'd started selling crash-scene photos on the dark web."

"Crash-scene photos?" Ivy repeated, confused.

"Yeah, it's a thing," the male detective said. "Part of our new digital world. Sleazebags like Horner auction off photos and video footage of accidents, the grislier the better. These sicko buyers are like wacked-out art collectors who bid for the stuff. When it's a celebrity accident, they think they've hit the jackpot."

"Your PI—good investigator by the way—went online to engage

Horner's collector and discovered he was a total nut job who wanted crash photos from your wife's accident. Apparently, he was obsessed with her."

Ivy saw Conrad's face go white underneath the streaks of mud. He stood up, grabbed a bottle and snifters from the cupboard, and set them on the table.

"Brandy?" he asked the detectives, and they both shook their heads no. Conrad poured two glasses and slid one in front of Ivy.

"It's not so unusual for these guys to become fixated on a particular star and then start asking for more specific things."

Conrad took a sip.

"Like what?" he asked after a long pause.

"He also wanted photos of your stepson, even the dog. Weird, right? Oh, and he wanted a portrait, I guess it's pretty famous, of your deceased wife."

"It's in the cottage out back. Where Ivy lives." Conrad closed his eyes for a minute, then gulped down the rest of his brandy.

"We've got some uniforms already on the hillside, and a search and rescue team, more of a recovery team, based on what you're saying, on the way," the older detective said. "We're just glad you all made it back safely. I've seen a lot of natural disasters working in LA County the past fifteen years, but I've never seen anything like that mudslide."

"Precipitation volatility," Ivy mumbled.

They all turned to look at her, she'd said little so far. When Ivy realized they were waiting for her to continue, she took a small sip of brandy and winced at the taste. "It's the cycle of extremely dry summers followed by extremely wet winters, the volatility of the rainfall amounts. It creates very unstable ground. That's what caused the mudslide."

"We wouldn't be here if Ivy hadn't realized what was happening and gotten us out of there in time," Conrad said. He reached for her hand, but she pulled it away and picked up her brandy instead. If she was leaving Malibu soon, she couldn't bear to prolong any sort of affection.

"That's California for you," the male cop remarked.

"We've got to get back to the station," the other detective said as the two stood to leave. "The other guys have this, though there's not much they can do until after the storm."

"Thank you," Conrad said, extending his hand.

"We're happy to help out, Mr. Reed. Thanks to you, my kid actually thinks what I do for a living is pretty cool."

While Conrad escorted the detectives to the front door, Ivy slipped out and headed back to the cottage. She went into the kitchen, adrenaline and exhaustion hitting her hard. She grabbed for the nearly empty bottle of wine that was still on the counter. Then, thinking better of it, poured herself a big glass of water.

Suddenly her legs buckled beneath her. She clutched at the counter, then slid, her back against the wall, until she was sitting on the kitchen floor with her knees tucked up under her chin. Too tired to cry and too lost to think, she sat on the cold lino-leum in a dazed heap. After a while, she considered getting up, shedding her filth-covered clothes, and climbing into a warm shower, but the sheer contemplation of the act wore her out.

Ivy's thoughts drifted bitterly back to her grief group. Toby's false optimism and the group's approval of her getting her life back on track. As if her life could ever improve, as if she would ever heal. Pain just begat more pain. Loss more loss. She leaned her head against the wall, and her eyes landed on the binder with the script pages that she'd grabbed from Conrad's study—the script pages that sent her into this downward spiral in the first place.

What else is in that binder? Do I even know Conrad?

After staring at the binder as if it might come to life and speak to her, curiosity trumped fatigue. Ivy set her water glass on the kitchen floor, pulled herself to her feet, and headed for the coffee table. She reached for the binder, her hands shaky as she ran her forefinger along the initials on the front cover. She shivered, realizing she was still wearing her wet clothes, but knowing that wasn't the reason for the chill.

Ivy grasped the zipper pull and slowly worked it open along three sides of the binder, not sure she wanted to see any more of its contents, but irresistibly drawn nonetheless. She paused for a moment, wondering if she should care that she was brazenly trespassing into Conrad's private world. No, she was too tired to care about anything, anyone, anymore.

She spread the binder open on the table to reveal a lined yellow pad with page after page of handwritten notes. At first she wasn't sure what she was seeing, but as she flipped through the notepad, Conrad's jumbled cursive came into focus.

Show notes. Reminders to the staff. Memos to the network. A crazy mishmash of his creative brain. Something she would never understand, just as he couldn't seem to fathom her need for facts and figures, for logic and certainty.

Ivy started to zip up the binder, then noticed that there was a pocket on the left-hand side. She loosened the flap and saw what looked like a legal form of some kind. Unable to curb her curiosity, she pulled out the document and read the title: Petition for Second-Parent Adoption.

Conrad was planning to adopt Hudson!

46

*I*vy wasn't entirely sure how she got there, but within minutes of reading the adoption petition, she was standing outside Conrad's closed bedroom door. She remembered dropping her shoes, socks, and blanket on the kitchen mat so she wouldn't track mud through the house, but she had no recollection of climbing the stairs or walking down the hallway toward the double doors of the main bedroom.

She began to lose her nerve when, suddenly, the door opened, and she and Conrad were inches apart, face-to-face on the threshold. He was freshly showered, wearing a silky gray bathrobe, comb marks visible in his wet hair. Ivy could smell something musky, shampoo or cologne, and thought the scent might make her pass out.

She glanced down, thinking how ludicrous she must look— her eyes pink and watery, her mud-covered clothes clinging to her skin, and her sludge-stiffened hair sticking up like a bird's crest. They locked eyes, neither ready to break the silence, until Conrad reached out and pulled her into his arms.

"I'm filthy."

"You're perfect."

They stood together in a tight embrace, mud from Ivy's denim shirt trickling onto Conrad's robe. He swept her up into his arms and carried her inside, shutting the bedroom door quietly behind them.

"You disappeared. I was worried about you."

"I need to talk to you," Ivy started.

Conrad shushed her with a kiss, then laid her on the bed and began stripping off her muddy garments one at a time, oblivious to the sludge spilling onto his thousand-thread-count sheets. He went into the bathroom and returned with a wet towel and began to rub the muck from her skin. She lay still as he gently washed her body, then she reached for him, ignoring the mud. He returned the embrace and shed his robe as the kiss became more intense. In an instant, they were on each other, touching, teasing, exploring with the intensity of pent-up emotion in the aftermath of danger.

"You are so, so beautiful," Conrad whispered.

Ivy nodded frantically, not trusting herself to speak. Conrad's hands were on her breasts, his lips on her neck. She had thought about, dreamt about, making love with Will so many times in the past year. But no matter how intensely she'd conjured the image, it was always ephemeral, with Will drifting away like a wisp of cloud in the wind.

But here was Conrad, so real, with his taut biceps and sandy chest hair and pounding heart. So solid and strong on top of her. She felt him harden against her belly as she sank back onto the silky sheets beneath her. Conrad entered her and she moaned. The feeling of being filled was so magnificent. She had the sensation of something familiar and yet completely new. *Like riding a bicycle.* The thought popped into her head, and with it, Will. But she refused to accept the image, refused to see Will on his bike as she had a thousand times since his death, shutting it out as she shifted even closer to Conrad.

Sensing her longing, Conrad pulled her legs over his shoulders and pushed even further inside her, his thrusts like waves rising in rhythm against a breakwater, each crash more powerful than the last. Ivy clung to him, feeling a light sheen of sweat on his skin as he held off his climax. She couldn't wait any longer. She came with a massive vibration that started where their bodies joined, then spread like wildfire across her skin.

Seconds later, Conrad climaxed with such volcanic release that it rattled the enormous wooden headboard above them. Instinctively, he reached out to steady it so as not to wake Hudson and Fernanda. He held Ivy with one hand and the headboard with the other.

"Note to self: tighten bolts," Conrad said as they looked into each other's eyes, bright with the afterglow of lovemaking, then began laughing like two college kids caught red-handed in their dorm room.

Spent and satisfied, they lay together listening to the rain, its pitter sound soothing now rather than treacherous, as it had been just hours before. After a while, Conrad jumped up and went into the bathroom. Ivy sighed and buried her face in his pillow, ingesting the heady fragrance. A moment later, she heard the water running.

"Come, love," Conrad called from the bathroom. Reluctantly, she got out of bed and glanced around the semidarkness, realizing with a thrill that she'd never been in his room before. She headed into the bathroom and saw that Conrad had filled the huge freestanding tub with bubbles.

"First this," he said gently, opening the shower door and handing her a loofah. She stood under the warm water, letting the mud run into the drain, Conrad stepping in with her to rinse off. A few minutes later, Conrad held out his hand to help Ivy into the tub. She sighed with contentment as she sank into the warm water.

"May I join you?"

"Please," she replied. Conrad slid into the opposite end of the tub, and Ivy wrapped her legs over his. They sat neck-deep in the creamy froth, unable to take their eyes off each other.

"I'm so sorry about—" she said.

"Shhhh. Later. Turn around," Conrad said, settling Ivy in the crook of his legs, her back against his chest. He grabbed a bottle of shampoo and began to gently wash the rest of the grit from her hair. She sighed with pleasure when he leaned her head back and ran the warm water over her head to rinse away the suds.

"I want to look at you," Conrad said finally, turning her back around to face him. "I can't believe you're here. I was so afraid I'd lose you out on that hillside. And I came so close to losing Hudson. I don't know what I'd do without the two of you." He shook his head, banishing the thought.

"I'm so sorry, Conrad. I was afraid—"

"I'm not sure what you're apologizing for," Conrad said. "But it doesn't matter. You're here now."

"Please, I need to talk this through with you." She took a deep breath and fiddled with the spigot, adding hot water to the tub while she collected her thoughts. "I was so afraid things were moving too quickly, that it was wrong to forget my husband—"

Conrad started to protest, but she put a soapy finger over his mouth.

"Let me finish," she said and Conrad nodded.

"I was planning to leave. I'd built this story in my head, for my own protection from getting hurt, I guess."

"That I had pushed you, that I expected you to drop everything you've worked for—"

"Something like that, but worse. That you only cared about yourself. But it didn't add up."

"And you do love your metrics," Conrad said, pushing a curl off Ivy's forehead and looping it around her ear.

"Especially after I saw . . ."

"Saw what?"

"The adoption papers," Ivy said. "I picked up your notebook by accident."

"Ah, one mystery solved," Conrad said, then shook his head as a sudden realization hit him full force. "Wait a minute. So you saw that awful scene I wrote with the hot scientist character?"

"Yes."

"And that was the final straw. That's what proved to you I was a selfish jerk."

"Something like that. Until I saw the adoption petition, and I knew it was an act of pure love. So unselfish it's unmeasurable."

Conrad smiled. "Even for someone who loves metrics."

"And I realized how I had misjudged you, how I had let me own fears get in the way. I could have ruined everything."

Ivy looked Conrad in the eye, a tear running down her cheek.

"No, you couldn't. We would have worked it out. I'm sure of it."

"Me, too," Ivy said.

"And just so you know," Conrad added, "I would have run that scene past you. Except that it was so awful, it was never going to see the light of day."

· · · · ·

A beam of morning sunlight slanted through the wooden shutters, waking Ivy. She had a moment of peace before the daily jolt of awareness struck her as it had for the past year. *I'm alone. I'm a widow*. Then, waking fully, she glanced around and realized she was lying on fresh sheets on Conrad's bed. She shut her eyes again, submerged in a sea of emotions. *The search for Hudson, the horrendous mudslide, Sal. And her night with Conrad.*

After the wave subsided, Ivy smiled and reached for the rumpled pillow beside her, sinking her face into the down as she had the night before, smelling the lingering fragrance. Rising, she pulled a clean robe out of Conrad's closet fingering the delicate fabric, so different from her terry-cloth one back in the cottage. She put it on, moved to the window, and opened the shutters, happy to see the sun shining down, guileless, as if there'd never been a storm.

Ivy turned to look at the room, comforted to see that it was understated, more soothing than lavish, with muted tones and uncomplicated furniture, a flagstone fireplace dominating one wall. She was staring at the painting above the mantel when Conrad entered, balancing a breakfast tray and *The New York Times*.

"Your hockey picture," she said, demurely tying the robe tighter around her waist as though he hadn't seen her naked body already.

"My what?" asked Conrad, amused.

"Your hockey picture. Hudson told me you had a famous hockey picture. I never realized what he meant."

"Ah, right," Conrad said, smiling. "My *Hockney* swimming pool painting. It cost me an arm and a leg, but I love it."

"I do, too," Ivy agreed, thinking how strange it was to be carrying on a normal conversation after the events of the past day.

"That was one of the first things that struck me about you. That you were a swimmer. You always looked so elegant in the water."

Ivy laughed self-consciously "Really? Funny, after everything that's happened, it feels like years since I've been in the pool."

Conrad spread coffee and muffins on the table in front of the window, as Ivy eyed the linen napkins and vase of flowers warily.

"Fernanda did this?" she asked, knowing their secret was out.

"She did."

"There's something I need to tell you," Ivy said.

"Tell away," Conrad said, as he stopped pouring coffee and looked up at her.

"I'm going to buy out Alexandra. I want to own my company outright."

"Good for you," Conrad said, then thought for a moment. "You have that kind of money? No offense. I just mean . . . first an academic, then a gardener."

"I have a savings account and Will's life insurance. And I'd like to sell my house. Charlotte and Randy have offered to buy it."

"And stay in Malibu?"

"And stay in Malibu."

Conrad took her hand. "As long as you're staying, why don't you move in with us?"

Ivy drew back, uncertainty clouding her face.

"What is it, love? Whatever it is, we'll work it out."

"What would Hudson think?"

"He'll be thrilled," Conrad replied. "Why wouldn't he be?"

47

*I*vy sat in in an angular Lucite chair outside Alexandra's office. It was three days after the storm and, in her navy pantsuit and neat bun, she looked put together if a little nervous. She'd told the young assistant, who could have been a male model on the side, that, no, she didn't have an appointment but would wait as long as necessary to see Alex. He'd apparently taken her at her word, because she'd been waiting nearly an hour, checking her notes and twisting a piece of hair around her little finger.

"Yes, she's still here," the assistant said into his headset, then turned to Ivy. "You can go in now."

As she pushed the door open, Ivy had the strange sensation that she was playing out a scene from one of Conrad's drama series—meek inventor confronts corrupt CEO—and said a silent prayer that Conrad's coaching would kick in. "Think Academy Award performance," Conrad had told her.

"Sit," Alexandra said.

Ivy sat down awkwardly in a chair shaped like a giant hand across from Alexandra's desk, crossing her feet primly at the ankles in hopes it would stop her legs from shaking. She glanced at her talking points and plunged in.

"I'd . . . I'd like to buy you out of the company."

"And why would I want to let you do that?"

Ivy took a deep breath. "Because you're in breach . . . that is, of the contract, and I can prove it."

"Give me a break, Ivy," Alexandra laughed. "You don't know what the hell you're talking about."

"I do, actually," Ivy said, glancing down at her talking points. "And I can buy you out and you can walk away with a somewhat tarnished reputation. Or I can sue you. And you'll lose."

"You're bluffing. You never did understand the first thing about business."

"See for yourself," Ivy said, taking a massive bound report out of her bag and setting it onto Alexandra's Danish Modern desk.

Alexandra let out a condescending snort.

"Oh, wait," Ivy continued, anger giving her a boost of confidence. "I forgot, you're not a scientist. You probably won't understand any of this. Maybe I can get a lab intern to write a summary or a PowerPoint deck for you."

"You ungrateful bitch. You'd never be this close to market-ready if it weren't for me."

"Or I can get the UC Davis Co-op team to debrief you. Because they've got all the data from the synthetic chemical version that your shadow team created after you stole my formula."

Ivy was grateful Conrad had taken her through a rehearsal— an entire role-play of how this conversation might go—before she got on the plane. After a patent attorney buddy of Conrad's had gone through all forty-seven pages of her contract, they'd discovered that Alexandra had no right to change any aspect of the HydraHold formula without Ivy's express written consent. Which she didn't have and never would.

"It's really simple," Ivy continued, emboldened by knowing she had the upper hand. "Buyout or lawsuit? Because, sadly, your flagrant breach of contract is not going to play well in front of a judge or jury. You know, humble female academic versus slick Silicon Valley investor."

Alexandra's bravado was beginning fade, but she shot back with one final snarl. "You may be book smart, but you're definitely not street smart. This is not over, my dear. Not by a long shot."

"On that point, we agree. You'll be hearing from my attorney soon to finalize the sale. At a deep discount, of course."

48

*C*onrad steered the Mercedes into a parking spot outside a warehouse-like building in Playa Vista, LA's latest tech and entertainment hub. Shading his eyes as he got out of the car, he glanced up at the searingly blue sky. Still cleansed of soot and smog even three days after the rainstorm, the whole of the Los Angeles basin was visible, though the locals never failed to express surprise whenever the low-rise sweep of the city and the mountains beyond were on full display.

As he walked into the lobby for the television meeting Billy had scheduled for him, pitch packets in hand, Conrad couldn't help but think that he, too, felt cleared of the storm clouds that had hung over him recently. He felt purged of old habits, old stories, and ready for a resurgence.

Conrad stopped when he spotted the name on the door. CoolerTV was a new streaming service that had quickly built a reputation for content that actually lived up to its name by sparking watercooler conversations—or their social media equivalent—not for their shock value, but for great storytelling. He was bringing in the police anthology series that the network had turned down, with an outline for the first three seasons and a list of casting suggestions that he was certain would resonate with this group.

Suddenly, a random memory popped into Conrad's head. It was the best lesson he'd learned from the only writing class he'd taken when he first came to LA. The instructor had asked her students, all eager aspiring writers: *What's the story that only you can tell? And how do you capture the specificity that is true to you within the universality that is true for everyone?*

Just as Conrad was about to push open the door, an entirely new idea materialized, a gift from out of the ether. *Is Dawn whispering to me? No,* he thought, *it's Ivy.*

With a little smile on his face, he dumped his pitch packets into the nearest trash can and marched into the CoolerTV office.

· · · · ·

*B*ack in Malibu after her quick San Francisco trip, Ivy and Mak trudged through what was left of the garden, Ivy carrying her full arsenal of gardening tools. The afternoon sun was just beginning to set as they dodged puddles and potholes as they surveyed the damage. It was bad, with branches down and flower beds obliterated, but it could have been much worse. At least the trees and structures were still standing.

"When were you going to tell me about the sex? Was it amazing? Is that why you're moving in?" Mak asked.

Ivy said nothing, but couldn't disguise a telltale ear-to-ear grin.

"Well, it's about time. You two have been sniffing around each other long enough."

"Oh, so now you approve?"

"I'm just glad to see you getting laid."

Ivy shot her a glance.

"Like I said, I'm just happy to see you happy again."

"Thank you," Ivy said, then nodded toward the house, where Hudson and Rory were coming out the back door. "There's just one thing . . . it's Hudson. Ever since Conrad told him I'd be moving into the house, he's been giving me the cold shoulder."

"It's not you, hon. He's been traumatized. It'll take him some time to feel safe again."

"I hope you're right."

"I'm always right. You'll see."

Hudson and Rory were up ahead, romping through the mud. When they spotted the two women, Rory lunged ahead to greet them, tail wagging and tags jingling. But Hudson hung back.

"Hey, Hudson," Mak yelled as she stooped to pet Rory. "Come check out the garden with us. We're inspecting the damage, and we could really use your help."

Ivy smiled at her friend, grateful for the intervention.

Hudson glared warily, but started down the path toward them, stopping a few yards short.

"That was some storm," Mak called.

Hudson shrugged his shoulders.

"I heard you had to hide in a cave."

He shrugged again.

"It must have been scary. Until Ivy and Conrad found you."

"Hudson was so brave," Ivy said to Mak. "He was trying to rescue Rory—"

"But I didn't. You guys did," he snapped at her, running past them into the garden.

"See?" Ivy mouthed to Mak so Hudson wouldn't hear her.

"Give him time. He's been through a lot."

They continued on the walkway, past the washed-out Shakespeare garden that Ivy had started planting with herbs just months before. She sighed, checking out the watery beds where thyme and basil and lemon balm had just begun to flourish but now looked like strands of green mush melting into the ground.

"Let's go in here," Ivy said, turning off on a little side path.

Inside the clearing, Hudson's pole bean tepee stood at a drunken, sideways tilt, stripped of most of its vines, the leaves hanging limp around the bottom of the structure. Ivy found a dry spot and set down her gardening kit. She extracted shears and twine, as Mak settled herself on a bench to watch.

"Hey, I thought you were helping," Ivy protested, as she began cutting lengths of twine.

"My back is a little sore. I don't think I'd be much good to you," Mak said, nodding to where Hudson was hovering on the outskirts of the clearing.

"Well, this is a two-person job. I need someone to help me sink these poles and get the vines tied back on."

"All this was from the storm?" Mak asked, as Hudson edged into view a few yards from his tepee.

Ivy stood it upright. It was still a little off-kilter, but at least it was vertical. "It was," Ivy responded, pretending not to notice Hudson lurking on the periphery. "But you know what? It'll be even better now. All that rain is going to make the vines grow super-fast."

"You mean sometimes when things seem bad they can actually be good?" Mak asked, playing along.

"Happens in nature all the time. Like wildfires having a positive effect on a forest."

"Come on," Mak scoffed. "Is that true?"

"Fires can burn down trees that are sick," Hudson said, sidling closer.

"You're kidding," Mak said.

"He's right, Mak," Ivy said. "Hudson, grab that vine for me. I want to tie it back onto the pole so we can get it climbing up the tepee again."

Gingerly, Hudson reached for the creeper. Suddenly, his face collapsed into a mask of misery, and he threw the vine on the ground. "No," he replied crossing his arms over his chest. "I'm not doing it."

"Come on, Hudson. If you don't do it, I'll have to," Mak coaxed.

"No," he said more emphatically. "I won't help you."

"Why not, honey? What's wrong?" Ivy asked, crestfallen.

"I don't even want that stupid tepee," he shouted.

"I thought you loved it," Ivy said.

"I don't care if the whole thing falls down."

"But you were so excited when we built it. Don't you want to help me fix it?"

"Okay. I'll fix it." Angrily, Hudson grabbed a piece of vine and ripped it out of the ground with unexpected ferocity.

"Hudson!" Ivy cried out.

He kicked at the tepee, then shoved as hard as he could until the whole thing toppled onto the ground in a muddled heap.

"There. It's fixed!"

"Hudson, honey, let's talk," Ivy said, stricken, as Hudson stalked off down the pathway. She started to go after him, then hesitated. What made her think she could help? Why would she have any maternal instincts? She wasn't a mother. Natural selection had made sure of that.

"I'll go," Mak said, jumping to her feet.

Ivy nodded, watching Mak disappear down the walk. Her face flushed, Ivy stared down at the vine in her hand, wondering why its leaves were shaking so furiously.

49

*Y*ou want to keep this?" Conrad asked, popping a wilted straw hat onto his head.

"Yes," Ivy smirked, grabbing the hat off Conrad's head and stashing it in a cardboard box safely out of his reach. He smiled and stacked a storage bin on top of the pile while Ivy returned to sifting through running shoes and leggings.

They worked on in silence as music played softly in the background, an amber glow settling over the cottage as sunlight began to give way to dusk. Ivy would have found the hush companionable but for the nagging concern that Conrad's quiet might be an indication that he was also worrying that Hudson had yet to accept the fact that they were now a couple. *Am I going to be an outsider, an intruder, forever?*

"You sure you don't want to keep the cottage for extra office space? Or as an escape from me?" Conrad asked.

Ivy shook her head.

"I have an escape. Or I will as soon as JP finishes the greenhouse-slash-office-slash-lab. I've been thinking, if I can get Alexandra out of the business—and that's still a big if—I'd like to create a training program, maybe even a nonprofit foundation so I can teach people how to use HydraHold. If we get enough users, we could actually shift farming practices and make systemic change."

"So you'd be teaching after all," Conrad mused.

Ivy smiled, thinking how different this kind of teaching would be from academics.

"And I could produce your training videos," he added, "but only if you want me to. I do not want to be a buttinsky."

"I could certainly consider it," Ivy said, smiling. "Hey, I almost forgot to ask. How'd your pitch go today?" She gave herself a mental pat on the back for letting the Hollywood phrase roll off her tongue so naturally.

Conrad shook his head and frowned. "I tossed it. Dumped the entire thing. I just couldn't do it."

"What? I thought you were dying to pitch those Cooler guys. You said they had the best storytelling taste of anyone in the business." *Another win for knowing my Hollywood lingo.*

"I was going to pitch them on the anthology series about LA cops. Remember, it was too edgy for the networks?" Conrad said, air-quoting *edgy* with a hint of disdain. "But I made a last-minute decision and went in a completely different direction."

Ivy caught the beginning of a grin on Conrad's face.

"What?" she asked.

"This idea just hit me as I was about to walk into the room. It must have been rattling around in my brain, because it came out of my mouth almost fully baked."

"Tell me!"

"I pitched them on a romantic comedy."

Ivy gave him a look of surprise. "Wow!"

"I know. A far cry from cop shows. It's a love story, a sort of unexpected romance between opposites—a cardiac surgeon and a winemaker."

"An oenologist?"

"Yes, a vintner, maker of wines, grower of grapes. Not a hot soil scientist in sight."

Conrad held out his little finger, offering a pinky swear and Ivy laughed.

"Title?" she asked, once again inwardly applauding herself for remembering what was important about television shows.

"*Hearts and Vines*. What do you think?

"Very clever," Ivy said, giving him a quick kiss.

"But there's a twist!"

"Of course there is."

"Every season the two lead characters take on each other's roles."

She gave him a confused look.

"So in season one, the winemaker is the guy and the cardiac surgeon is the woman. And then in season two, the woman is the winemaker and the guy is the surgeon. Everything else stays the same—their house, their kids, their dog—except for their jobs, but we see the impact of their work on their relationship."

"You mean how their careers affect their love story?"

"Something like that. I haven't figured it all out yet."

"What did the CoolerTV guys say?"

"They loved it. The novelty, the opportunity for comedy, the commentary on gender roles."

"I would definitely watch that show," Ivy said.

"No higher praise has ever been spoken," Conrad said, leaning in for a much longer kiss.

When they separated, Conrad glanced up at the portrait above the fireplace and Ivy followed his gaze to Dawn's face. The waterfall of blond hair, the mischievous green eyes, the wary intelligence.

"What should we do with Dawn?" Conrad asked.

"Leave her," Ivy said. "She loves it out here."

A few minutes later, they were headed up the walkway with a dollyload of boxes, when Ivy spotted Hudson with Rory at the far end of the garden.

"I'll be with you in a bit," she said, dropping her cartons on the patio.

She walked toward Hudson, who sat cross-legged on the grass near the edge of the property, gazing at the sun setting over the coast. He turned when he saw Ivy approach and gave a wary little frown, but didn't object as she settled on the grass a few feet away.

Ivy sat quietly for a few minutes, listening to the beehive hum of the traffic far below as she watched Hudson stare into the distance. The sun, orange as an egg yolk from the free-range chickens at the Santa Monica organic market, was dipping below the horizon.

"Something on your mind?" she asked gently, trying to dispel the tension.

"No," Hudson said defiantly.

"You watching the sunset?"

"No."

"What are you doing?"

Hudson glowered, then leaned toward her and said matter-of-factly, "I was talking to my mom."

Ivy nodded as though that was exactly what she expected him to say.

"Conrad does it," Hudson justified.

"You're right. He does." She waited patiently, hoping Hudson might thaw a bit.

Finally, she said, "Could you ask her something for me?"

Hudson eyed her suspiciously and then gave a little *whatever* kind of shrug. He faced front again, closed his eyes, and scrunched his face into a tight little ball of concentrated effort. After a moment, he opened his eyes and said, "She says you should ask her yourself."

"Okay, I will."

Mirroring Hudson, she closed her eyes and scrunched her face. "Dawn," she started, "we never had the chance to meet, but I know I would have liked you an awful lot. And I know I could never ever replace you, but I'm wondering if it would be all right if I loved Conrad and Hudson too."

Hudson listened intently and then began to shake his head in horror. "No," he said. "You can't!"

Ivy opened her eyes. "Why not, sweetheart? What's wrong?"

Hudson curled his arms tightly around his knees, rocked back and forth, and began to make a low keening sound that made Ivy ache.

"What is it? Tell me," she said urgently.

"You can't," Hudson said. "You can't love us. If you love us, you could die."

"What do you mean, honey?"

"My mom," Hudson sobbed, barely able to form his mouth around the words. "Mommy loved us both. Conrad and me. And she died in a crash."

Ivy felt her heart rip open, thoughts of Will and Dawn coming at her with gale force. She grabbed Hudson, unconcerned whether he would protest, scooped him into her arms, and pulled him onto her lap as though he were a toddler.

"No, Hudson. You don't have to worry about that."

"How . . . how do you know?" he asked. Ivy held him close, stricken that this little body could hold so much anguish.

"You know I'm a scientist, right?"

Hudson nodded.

"And I deal with numbers, facts, that kind of thing, right?"

He nodded again.

"Well, the odds of my dying a premature death . . . that is, dying anytime soon . . . are less than two percent. Which means it's very, very, very unlikely," she said, wiping his eyes with her fingertip and turning him around to look at her.

"Two percent?"

"That's right," Ivy reassured him. "Which means that I'll be around to love you and Conrad for a long, long time."

"It does?"

"It does," Ivy answered. "If you don't believe me, just ask your mom."

Hudson closed his eyes, then opened them and looked back at Ivy solemnly. "You ask her too."

"Okay, we'll both ask her," Ivy said.

They closed their eyes, sitting together until the last sliver of sun sank below the horizon.

After a moment, Hudson opened his eyes, looked over at Ivy, and smiled.

"She says you're right."

50

I t was the kind of glorious blue-sky summer day seen in movies set in Southern California. Fernanda opened the kitchen door and waved to Ivy, who was trimming the hedges near the house.

"Ivy," she yelled. "A woman is here for you."

"Did she say who she was?" Ivy asked, wiping her hands on her jean shorts.

"No, just that she needed to see you."

Ivy walked around to the front door, where a young woman, innocuous enough in her slacks and print blouse, stood holding a large envelope.

"Ivy Bauer?" the woman asked.

Ivy nodded.

"You've been served."

· · · · ·

A few hours later, Conrad sat behind the desk in his study while Ivy paced back and forth on the Aubusson rug, angrily waving the Summons and Complaint she'd received.

"Dereliction of duty," she fumed. "Alexandra claims that I

willfully abandoned my lab and moved to LA County for an extended period of time, thereby putting our joint business effort at risk."

"Do you have anything in writing where she agrees to your leave of absence?"

"NO! It never even occurred to me I'd need anything. It was all verbal. And she was more than happy to grant me the time off."

"Yes, to get her hands on your formula," Conrad said as Ivy paced. "She is one ruthless shark."

"What if she takes the company from me? After all I—we— went through to figure out how to restore the organic formula and get her out of the business."

"Slow down, sweetheart, you don't even have to answer the complaint for thirty days."

"And then what?"

"I actually think I might have an idea. I just need to go for a little drive."

"Great. Because I am fresh out of ideas," Ivy said, collapsing into a chair. "Do you want me to come with you?"

"No, this is more of a solo mission. But first I want to be one hundred percent sure that you want my help. Because, as you know, I have a tendency to butt in occasionally."

"Yes, I am one hundred percent sure I want your help."

Conrad wrapped Ivy in a warm embrace.

"Thanks for asking, though," she added with a smile.

· · · · ·

Conrad and Billy sat at the bar at Spago on North Canon Drive in Beverly Hills, two martinis, a salmon pizza, and a tower of Kumamoto oysters in front of them.

"I get the picture," Billy said, downing half of his martini in a single swig.

"So you think it could work?"

"It's certainly worth a try. I have a buddy who's been a producer over there for close to twenty years. And after that Theranos debacle, where Elizabeth Holmes faked the data to get investors on board, this is a great follow-up story. Only this time, it's an investor faking a formula to get other investors on board. They'll eat it up."

"I've got to hand it to you, Billy. You still have the connections," Conrad said, genuinely impressed.

"That's my job," the agent said. "And you can buy the next round."

· · · · ·

A few days later, Ivy sat on the couch in the cottage, cell phone in one hand, remote control in the other.

"I'm sorry I can't be there to watch it with you," Conrad said in Ivy's ear.

"Don't worry about it. I know you have a night shoot," she responded. "I can't thank you enough for everything you've done."

"Don't thank me yet. We still need to see how this works out."

Ivy turned up the volume on the little television set when she heard the familiar *tick, tick, tick.* "It's coming on," she said. "I'll talk to you later."

After they hung up, Ivy fixed her gaze on the TV in the corner of the living room. She was spellbound as a good-looking reporter in a dark-blue suit gave a quick overview of the piece to follow. After the commercial break, she saw a long shot of Alexandra clicking her way down a San Francisco sidewalk in her stilettos, heading for the front door of her office building. Just as she approached the door, the reporter who'd introduced the segment stepped up alongside her, casually blocking her entry.

"Ms. Varsha," he called out, moving in close to her. "Bill Yuhn from *60 Minutes* here. I'd like to ask you a few questions about HydraHold, the water-retention product created to irrigate drought-stricken areas. I understand you're suing the inventor."

Ivy was sure she saw Alexandra's face turn white under her carefully applied makeup as she tried to back away. Then, seeing there was no escape from the reporter and his crew, she took a deep breath, visibly composed herself, and turned her body full-on to the camera with a big smile plastered across her face.

"How can I help you?" she said, brushing her bangs off her forehead.

"As I understand it, the inventor—PhD candidate Ivy Bauer—created an organic formula to help increase crop yield to combat global warming. Yet while she was on bereavement leave, having lost her husband, you decided to sue her for abandoning the business. Right?"

"Well, she wasn't supposed to be gone so long."

"Her team confirmed that they were in constant communication, isn't that correct?"

"Well, yes. But she moved to Malibu and—"

"And still managed to produce and test an organic formula that would be a boon to farmers as our planet heats up."

"Yes, but she should have—"

"When we talked to agricultural experts at UC Davis, they had some pretty impressive statistics about her product. So, did you have a problem with her work? Or was it that you wanted her out so you could start adding synthetic chemicals to the formula? Which might have had some positive short-term results, but could ultimately put enough toxins into the ground and water table to cause cancer, birth defects, and genetic mutations. Correct?"

"Yes. No," Alexandra replied, getting more flustered with each rapid-fire question.

"No, you didn't have a problem with her work? Or yes, the toxic chemicals you favored would cause massive destructive to human and plant life?"

Ready to explode, Alexandra shouted, "No. I am not suing her. In fact, I have sold the company outright to Ms. Bauer. You should go talk to her and leave me alone."

Alexandra shoved her way past the reporter, pushed open the front door, and charged into the building, the reporter and *60 Minutes* crew following right on her heels.

Ivy whooped out loud at her victory, then reached for her cell phone to call Conrad.

51

*I*vy was beaming as the late afternoon sun shone on the garden, riotous with red poppies and blue salvia and bright orange fuchsia. Native grasses, now fully grown, lined the pathway and swayed with the breeze. She and Conrad headed down the walkway toward the little pergola carrying a giant summer salad and a platter of grilled vegetables, which they placed in the center of a wooden table set for a party.

"Look!" Ivy cried out as they neared the outdoor seating area. "Who made these gorgeous garden signs?"

A wooden sign reading DAWN'S SHAKESPEARE GARDEN led into the area planted with vibrant rows of green and gray herbs, now adorned with beautifully carved handpainted signs, a child's writing for the plant name and an old-fashioned cursive script for the descriptions:

LAVENDER *for love*

ROSEMARY *for remembrance*

IVY *for faithfulness*

JP's Feunte de las Flores held the place of honor in the center of Dawn's garden, its auspicious gurgle providing the soundtrack for bees and butterflies as they skimmed along the path.

A moment later, they heard a happy whoop as Hudson came flying out toward them with Rory at his heels. "Did you see? JP and I made them as a surprise for you and my mom. Do you like them?"

"I don't like them. I *love* them, especially because you made them," Ivy said, grabbing Hudson in a big hug, deeply touched that he had included her in this tribute to his mom.

"Are we starting the party now? Kenny's not here yet," Hudson said.

"No, we'll wait for everyone. But I'm glad you're here first," Conrad said, as all three settled on the rattan sofa. "I have something important to ask you."

"What?" Hudson asked.

Conrad leaned in close to Hudson, and Ivy couldn't help but smile, despite Conrad's serious tone.

"I wanted to ask if it would be okay if I adopted you."

"Yeah!" Hudson yelled, then added thoughtfully. "What's adopted mean?"

"It means I wouldn't be your stepdad anymore."

Hudson frowned. "You wouldn't?"

"No, I'd be your *dad*. Your real dad. That is, if you'll have me—"

Before the words were out of Conrad's mouth, Hudson jumped up and wrapped his arms around Conrad's neck. Ivy could see the tears begin to stream down his cheeks as he wordlessly nodded his head up and down.

"Is that a yes?" Conrad asked.

"Yes!" Hudson shouted, then leaned over to pull Ivy into the hug. Ivy took Conrad's hand in his and the three stayed together in a joyful little tangle until Hudson broke free. He jumped to the ground and grabbed Rory around the middle.

"Rory, we're getting adopted!"

As if adding its own congratulations, upbeat jazz began to play on the outdoor speakers as Fernanda, Mak, and JP came down the path from the main house carrying yet more trays of food. Ivy's parents, Elaine and Howard, followed along with the silverware. A boy in glasses about Hudson's age brought up the rear.

"Kenny, guess what?" Hudson yelled to his erstwhile nemesis. "Rory and I are getting adopted."

"Cool!" Kenny yelled back.

As the sun began to set in California Technicolor, dinner was served. Ivy looked around the table, her face flushed with contentment, at the family gathered there. Blood relatives and fast friends. Scrappy and sentimental. Loved and loving. As she clinked her glass against Conrad's, she heard the soft whisper of a poem underneath the ping of crystal on crystal.

"*Spirit convalescing, déjà vu a blessing, love not truly gone.*"

Will. It had to be. And then she realized the poem she heard was her own.

Acknowledgments

Although I've written nonfiction books, writing a novel has always been my ultimate dream. I certainly didn't do it by myself, so there are many people I need to thank for helping me make this dream come true.

I'm still pinching myself at my great good fortune for having found a home at Penguin Random House and Pamela Dorman Books. I am so grateful to Pamela Dorman and Marie Michels for their talent and creativity, not to mention their patience in guiding a newbie novelist. I also want to thank all the other PRH folks that I don't even know yet who are supporting our efforts to get this book into the world.

It is a joy partnering with Alice Martell, who loved my book from the start even though it wasn't "her usual kind of thing." Thank you for taking a chance on me. I appreciate your advice, humor, and championship. And to Beth Howard, who introduced me to Alice and also read early versions of my book.

I could never have finished this book if not for my writing group: heartfelt thanks to Kevin Mitchell Jones for his amazing talent and grasp of plot; and to Claire Whitcomb for her wonderful notes only on my manuscript but also on gardening and the environment. I hope the three of us can continue our coast-to-coast writing bubble forever.

To all the readers and cheerleaders who were kind enough to give me encouragement and/or feedback at various stages of messiness: Belinda Phillips, Alyssa Phillips, Sharon Williams, Shela Dean, Carolyn Akel, Charlotte Robinson, Rand Hoffman, Karen Olan, Mitch Becker, Connie St. John, Sandie Alison, Theresa Howard, and Brielle Hutchinson.

To the Rogue Valley Book Club, especially Nancy Kline, I am so grateful that you cheered me on for months and were the very first book club to put me on your reading list. You are the best!

To all the farmers, gardeners and educators who took the time to answer my many questions, including the teachers from Oregon State University's horticulture program; and Beth Hoffman and her book *Bet the Farm*.

To my tech team, Kimberly Wadsworth and Kristen O'Connell, thank you for your creativity and skill—and for making me smarter about how to reach readers who might like a good read about a scientist and a TV producer.

To my sons, Zack, who critiqued multiple drafts and gifted me with the penultimate line of this book from one of his gorgeous poems, and Harrison, who always keeps me laughing at the absurdity of the world. To my extended family, Rachel Stern, Jacob Stern, and Aditi Maliwal-Stern and precious Maia, I am so fortunate you are in my life.

And finally, to my loving, brilliant, and ever-patient husband, David Stern, who read numerous drafts, all while making us fabulous meals and answering my wine questions. You are the one who nearly got away but, thankfully, didn't. For that, I will be eternally grateful.